hope larson
chiggers

lettered by
jason azzopardi

ATHENEUM BOOKS FOR YOUNG READERS
New York   London   Toronto   Sydney   New Delhi

ATHENEUM BOOKS FOR YOUNG READERS ∗ Simon & Schuster Children's Publishing Division ∗ 1230 Avenue of the Americas, New York, NY 10020 ∗ Copyright © 2008 by Hope Larson ∗ All rights reserved, including the right of reproduction in whole or in part in any form. ∗ Atheneum Books for Young Readers is a registered trademark of Simon & Schuster, Inc. ∗ Also available in an Atheneum Books for Young Readers hardcover edition. ∗ Designed by Sonia Chaghatzbanian ∗ The text of this book was handlettered. ∗ Manufactured in the United States of America ∗ First Aladdin Paperbacks edition June 2008 ∗10 9 8 7 6 5 4   ∗

Library of Congress Cataloging-in-Publication Data
Larson, Hope.
   Chiggers / Hope Larson.
      p. cm.
   "Ginee Seo books."
   Summary: When Abby returns to the same summer camp she always goes to, she is dismayed to find that her old friends have changed, and the only person who wants to be her friend is the strange new girl, Shasta.
   ISBN-13: 978-1-4169-3584-1 (hc.)
   ISBN-13: 978-1-4169-3587-2 (pbk.)
   1. Graphic novels. [1. Graphic novels. 2. Camps—Fiction. 3. Popularity—Fiction. 4. Friendship—Fiction.] I. Title.
   PZ7.7.L37Ch 2008
   741.5'973—dc22
   0415 MTN   2008009557

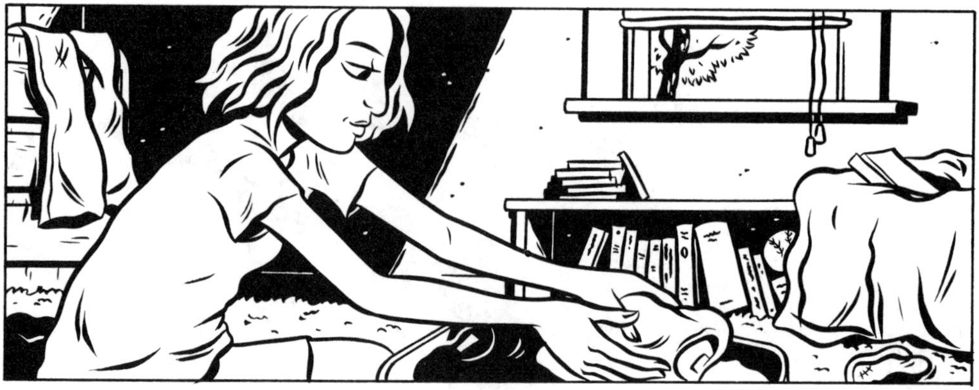

for Marcella

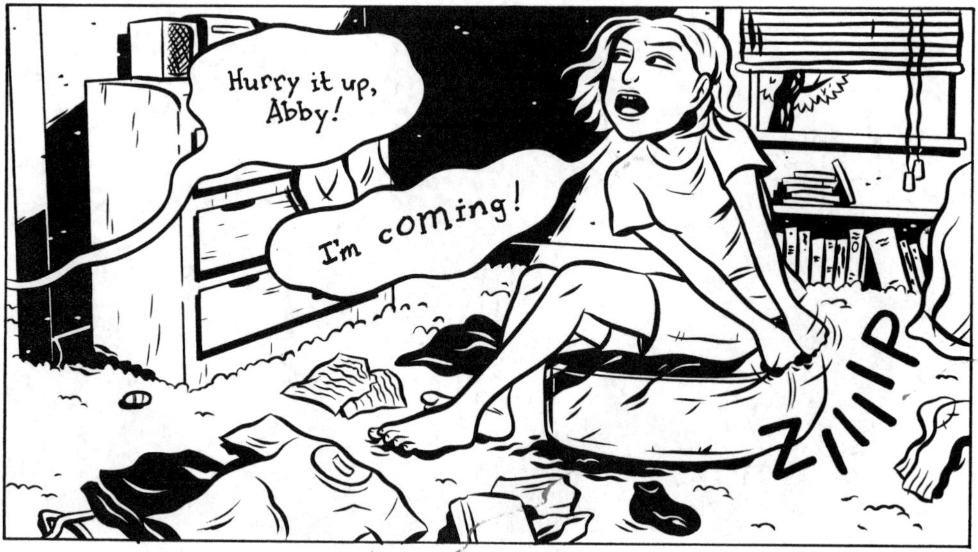
Hurry it up, Abby!
I'm coming!
ZIIIIP

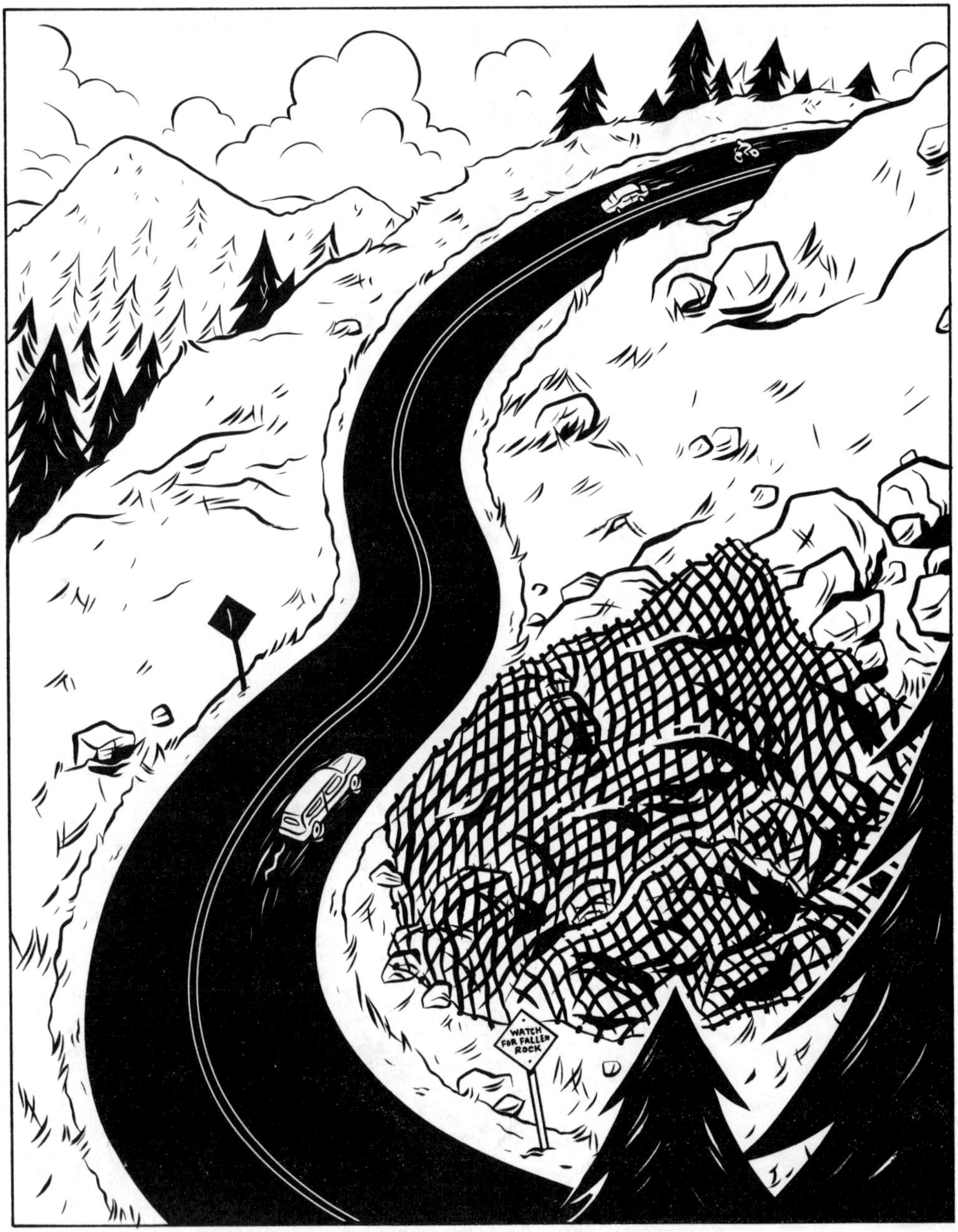
WATCH FOR FALLEN ROCK

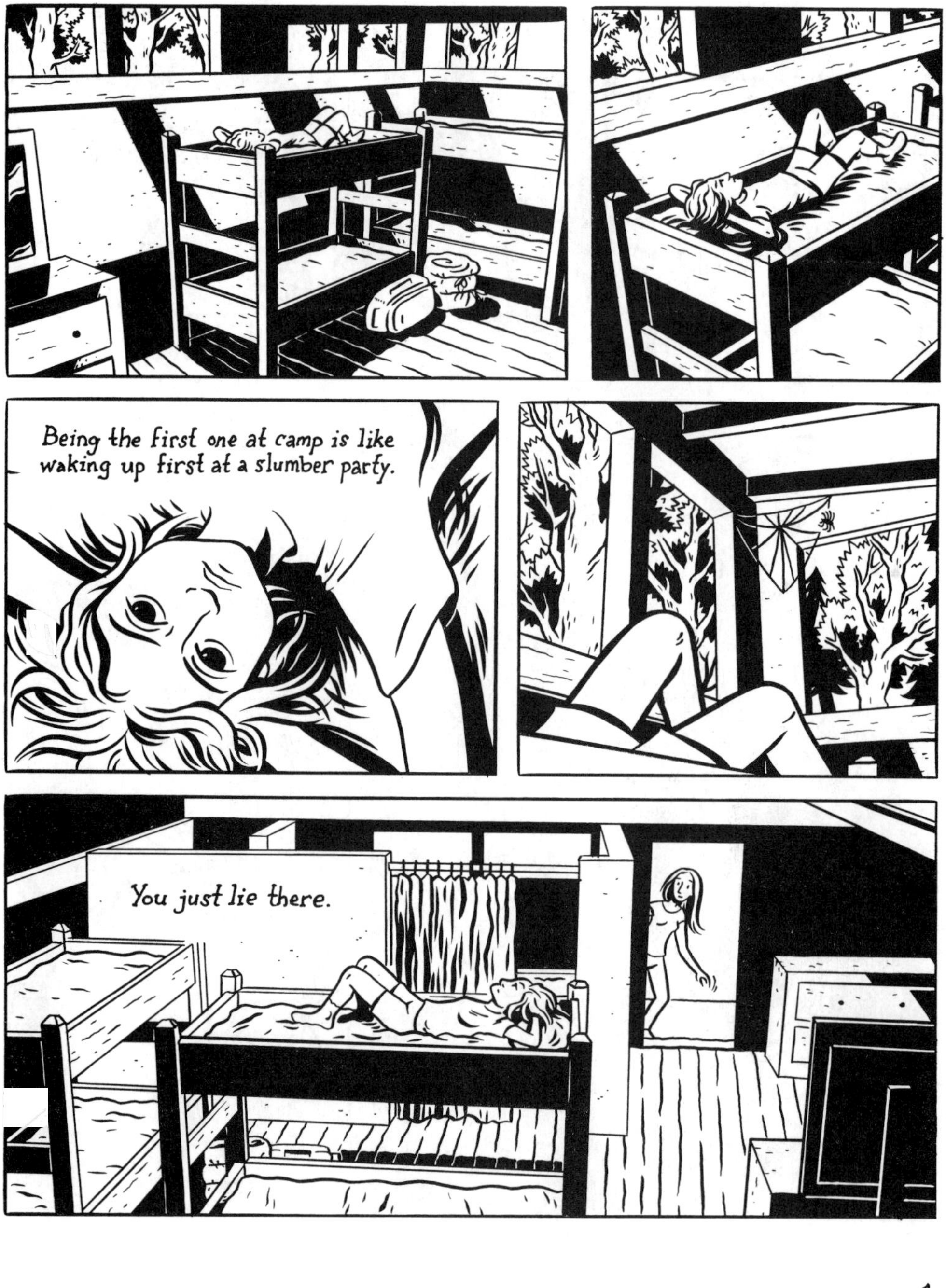
Being the first one at camp is like waking up first at a slumber party.
You just lie there.

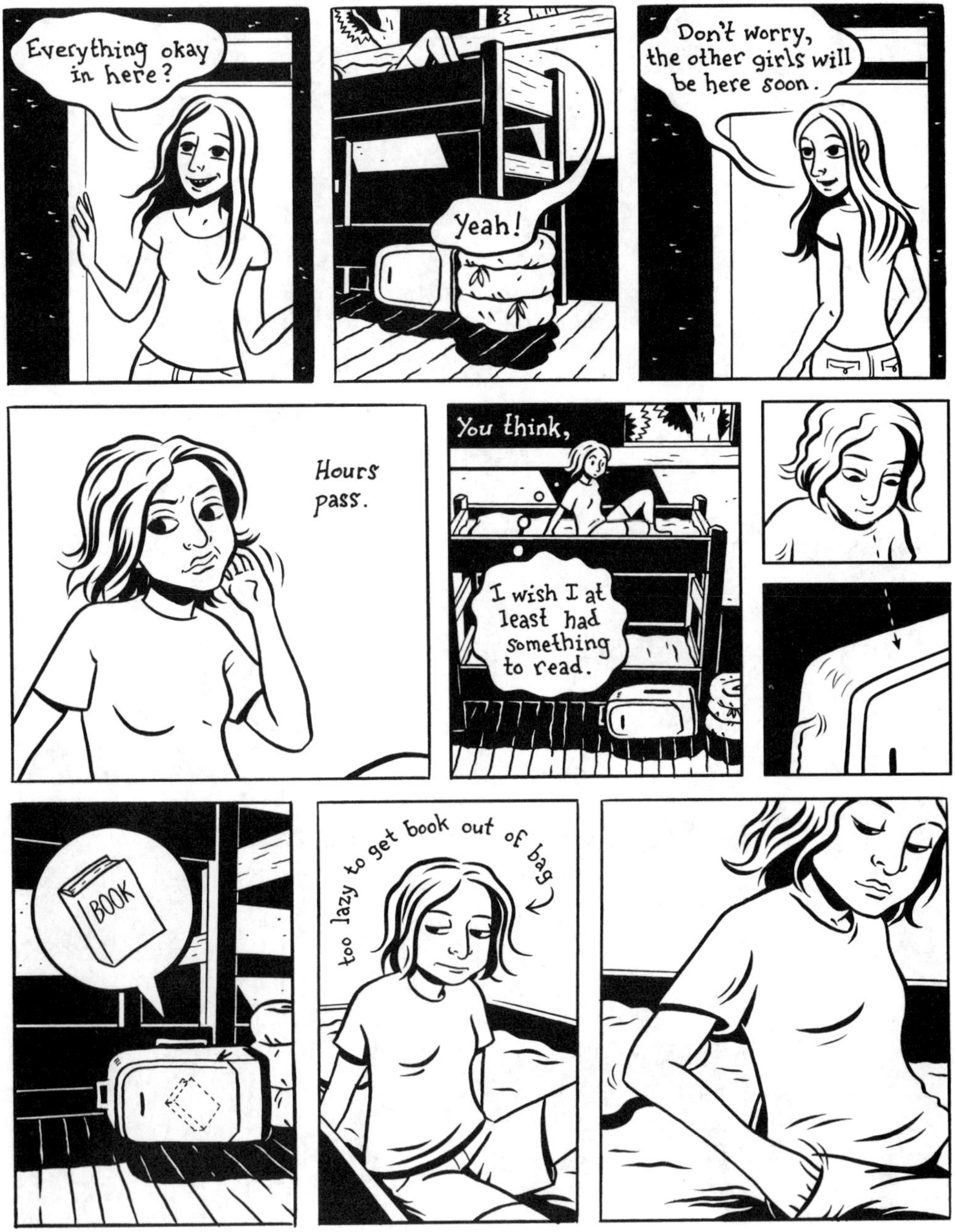
Everything okay in here?
Yeah!
Don't worry, the other girls will be here soon.
Hours pass.
You think,
I wish I at least had something to read.
BOOK
too lazy to get book out of bag

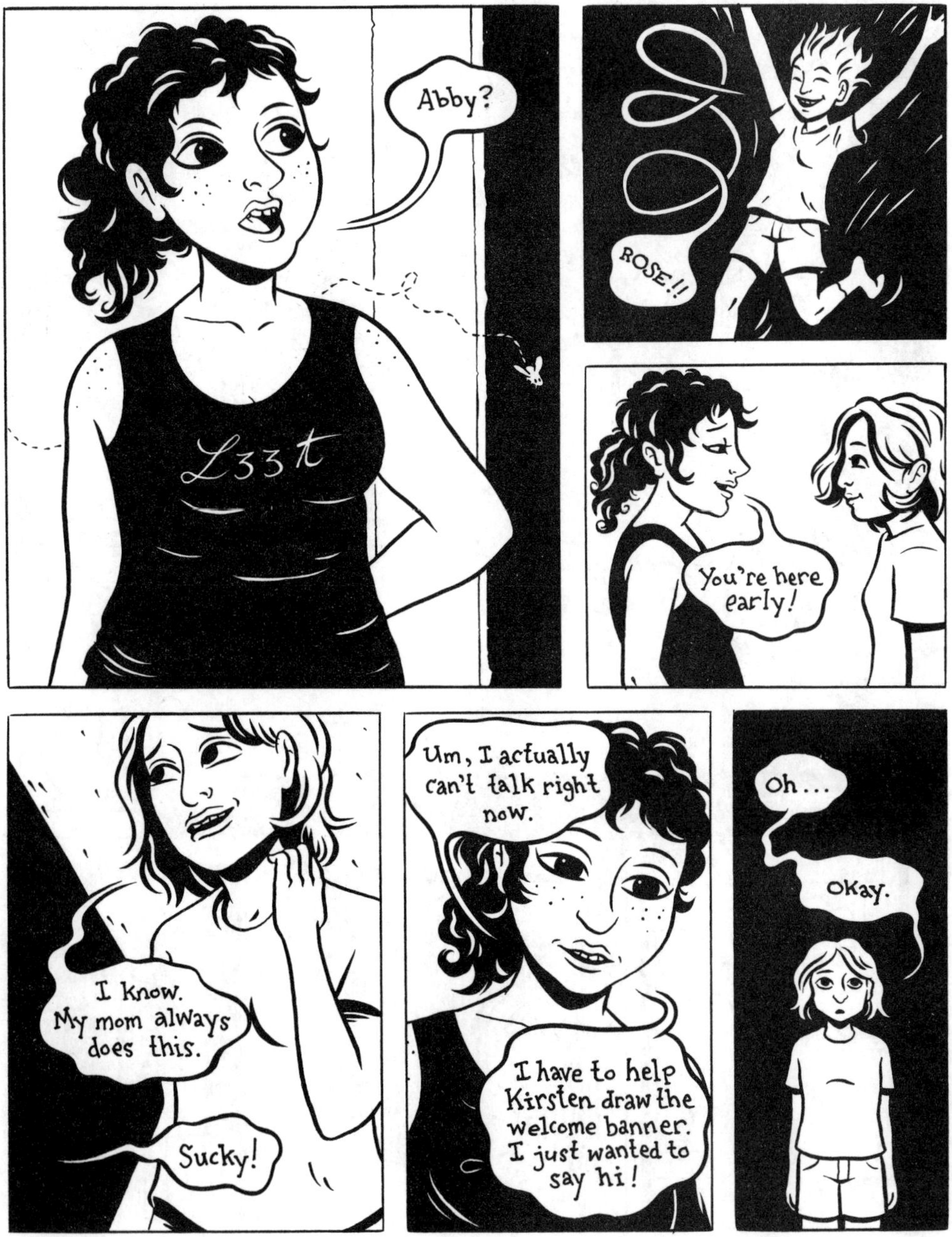
Abby?
L33t
ROSE!!
You're here early!
I know. My mom always does this.
Sucky!
Um, I actually can't talk right now.
I have to help Kirsten draw the welcome banner. I just wanted to say hi!
Oh...
Okay.

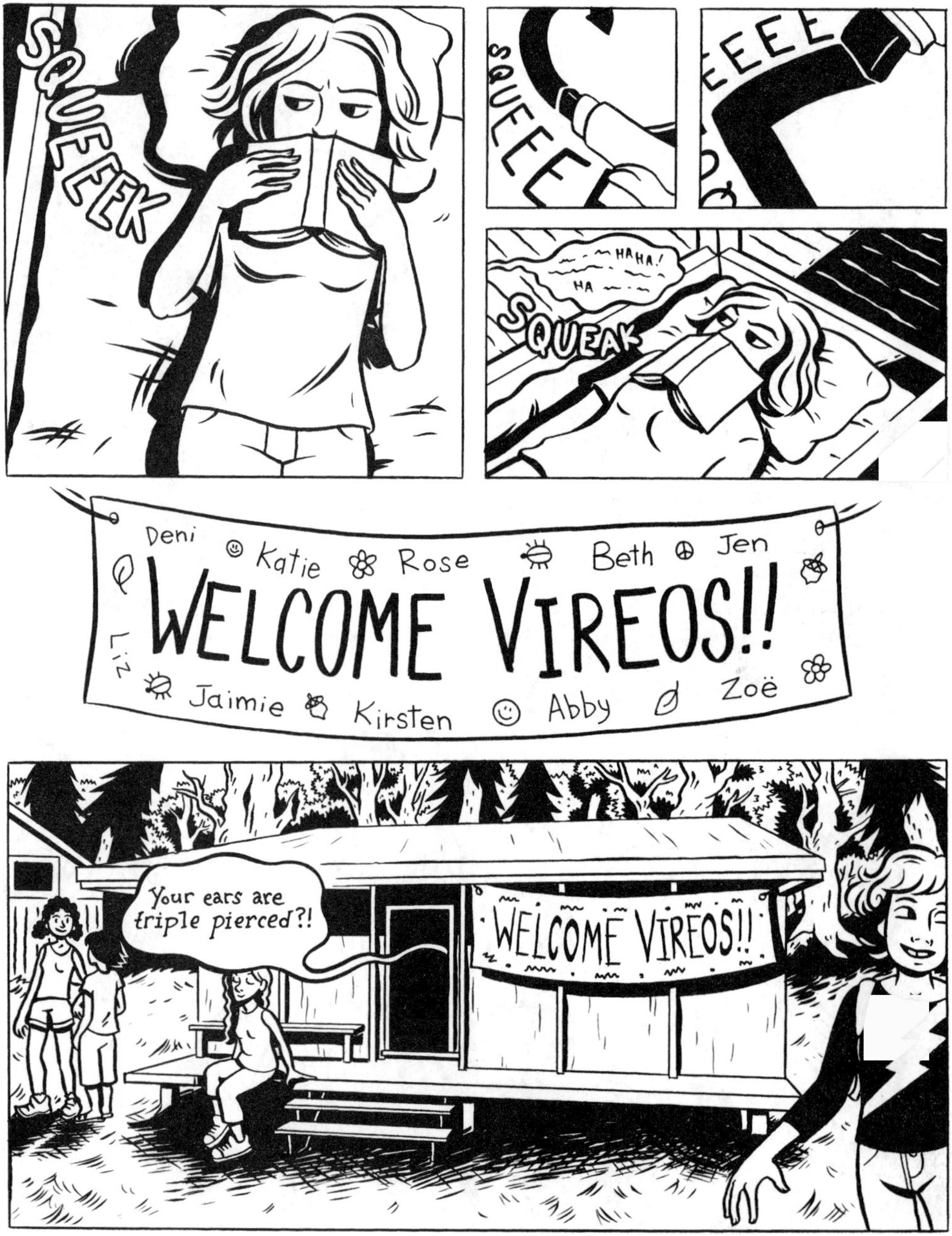
SQUEEEK
SQUEEEE
EEEE
HAHA!
HA
SQUEAK
Deni Katie Rose Beth Jen
WELCOME VIREOS!!
Liz Jaimie Kirsten Abby Zoë
Your ears are triple pierced?!
WELCOME VIREOS!!

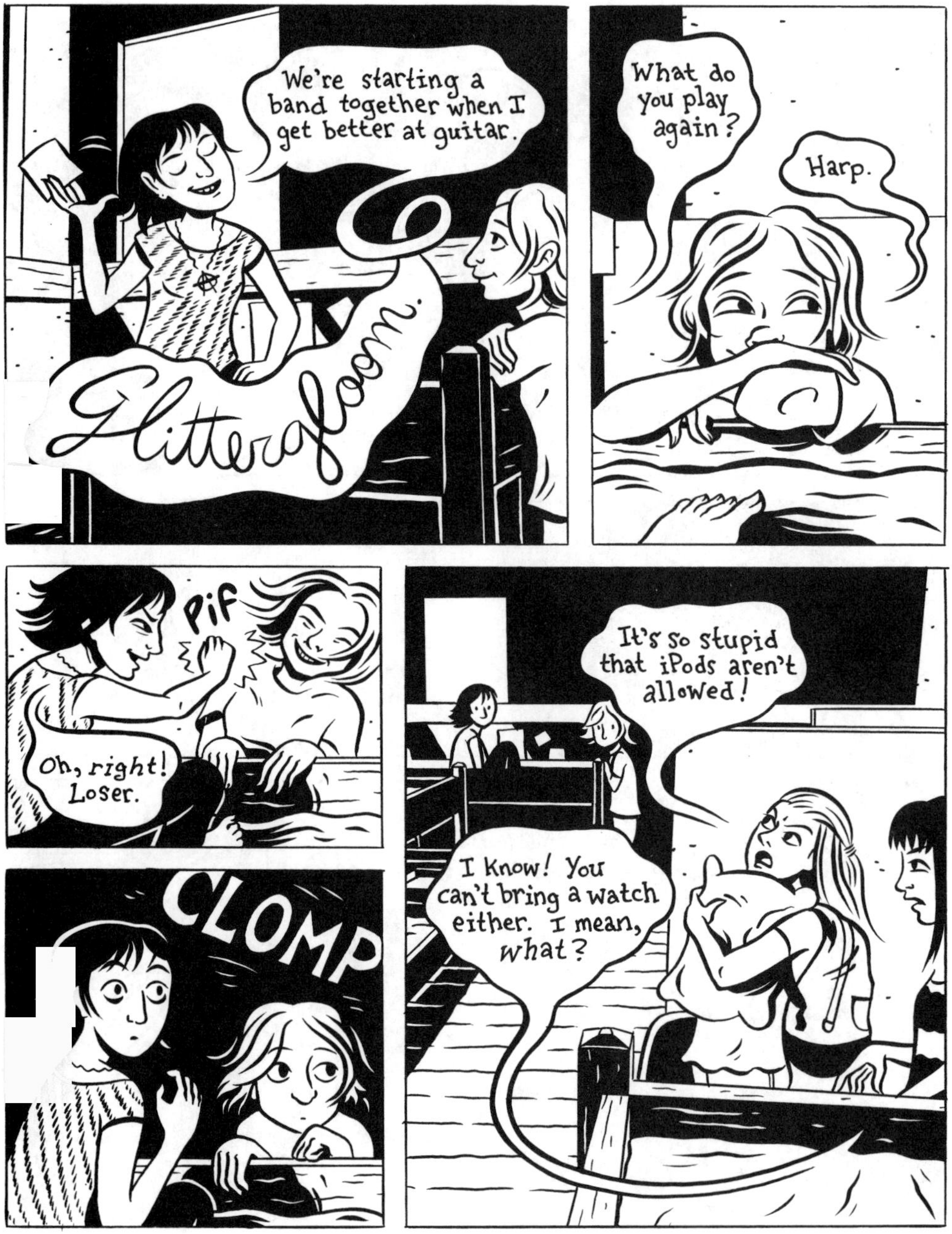
We're starting a band together when I get better at guitar.
Glitterfoam.
What do you play again?
Harp.
PIF
Oh, right! Loser.
CLOMP
It's so stupid that iPods aren't allowed!
I know! You can't bring a watch either. I mean, *what*?

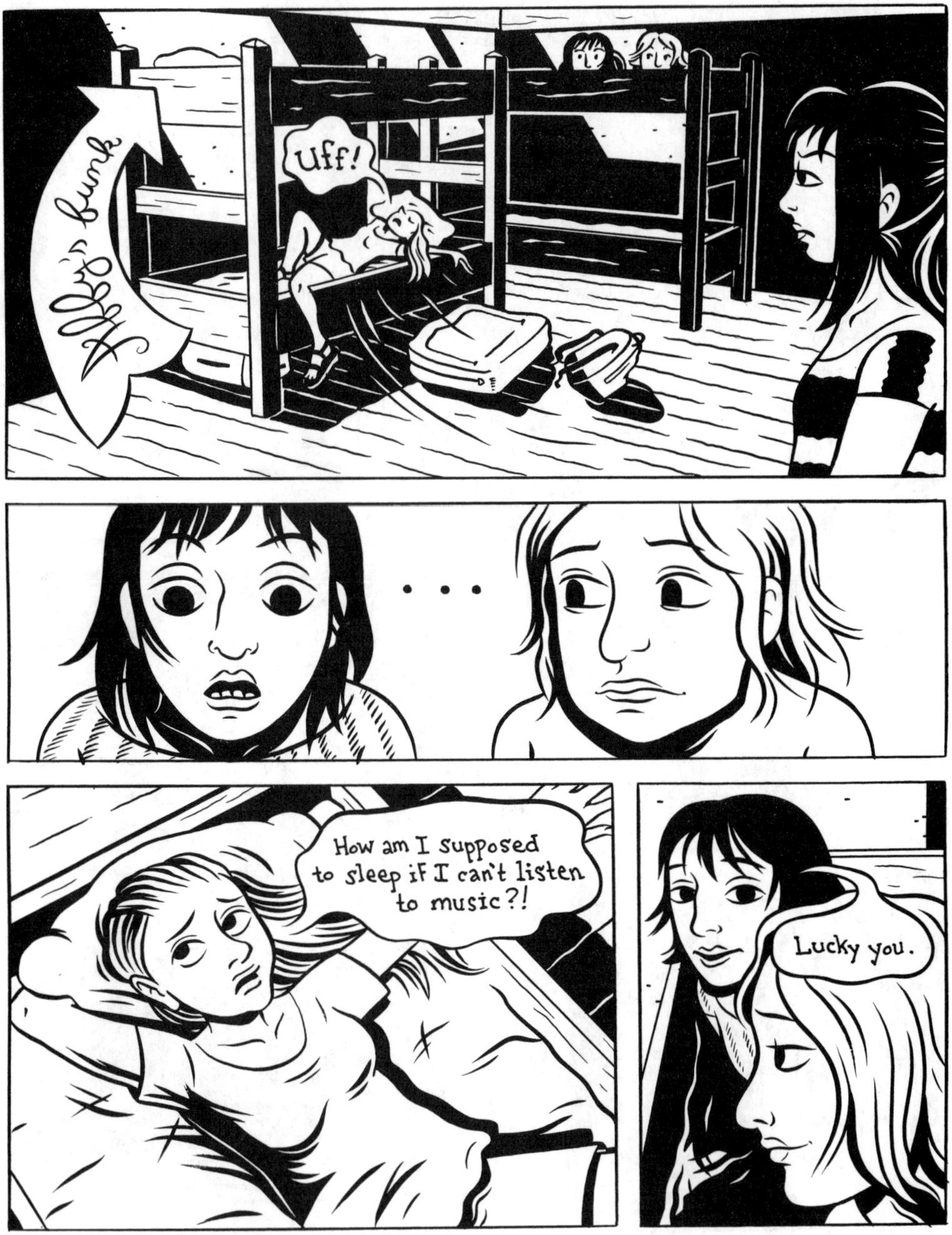
Abby's bunk
Uff!
. . .
How am I supposed to sleep if I can't listen to music?!
Lucky you.

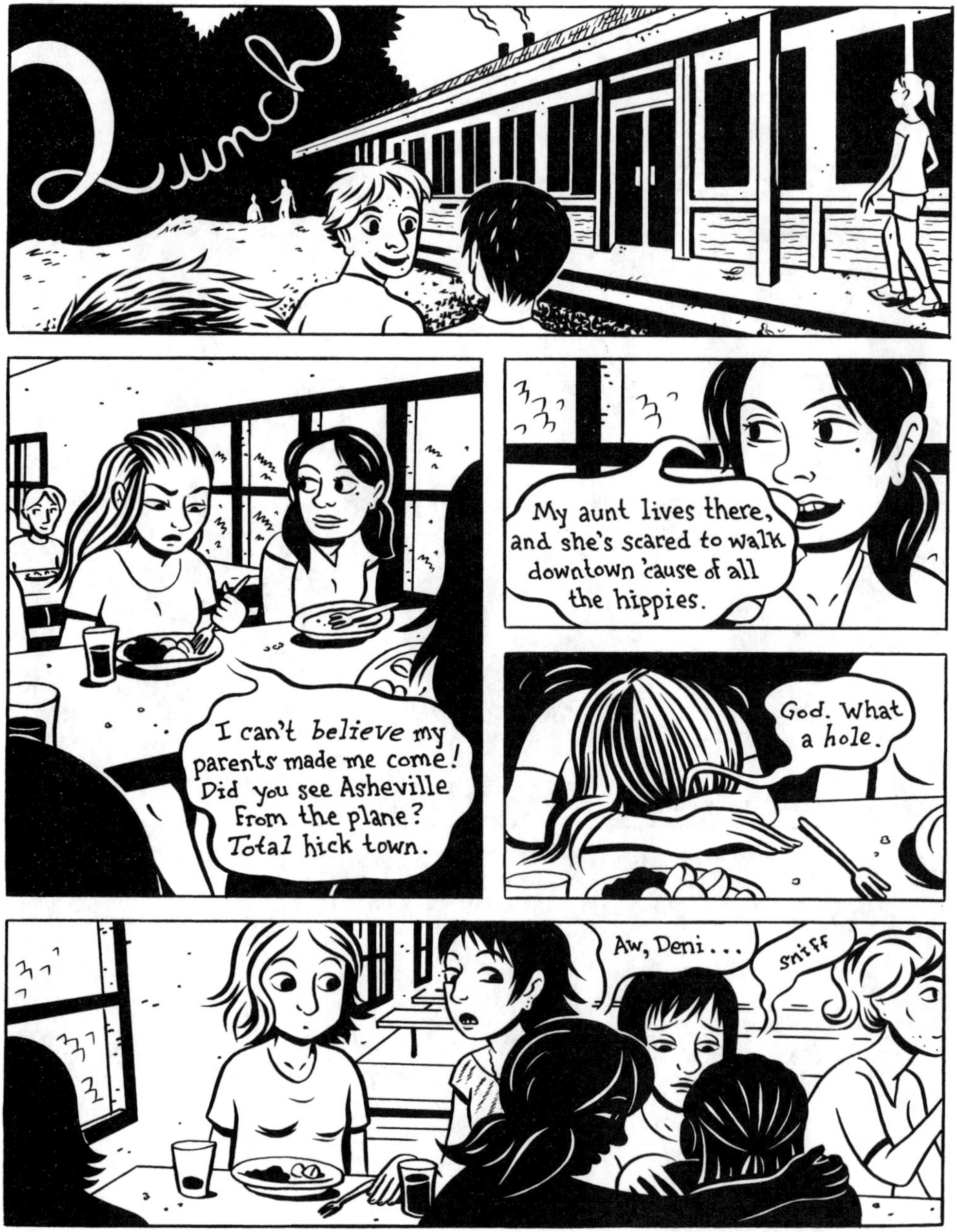
Lunch
I can't *believe* my parents made me come! Did you see Asheville from the plane? *Total* hick town.
My aunt lives there, and she's scared to walk downtown 'cause of all the hippies.
God. What a *hole*.
Aw, Deni . . .
sniff

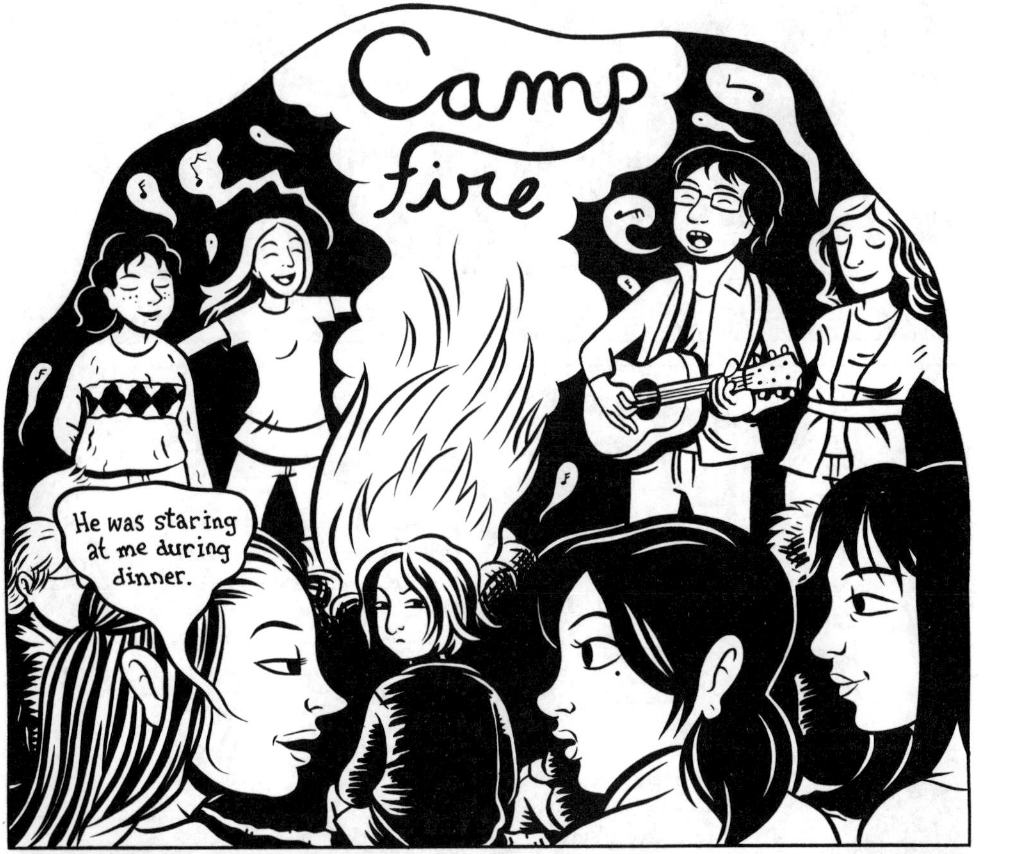
Camp fire
He was staring at me during dinner.

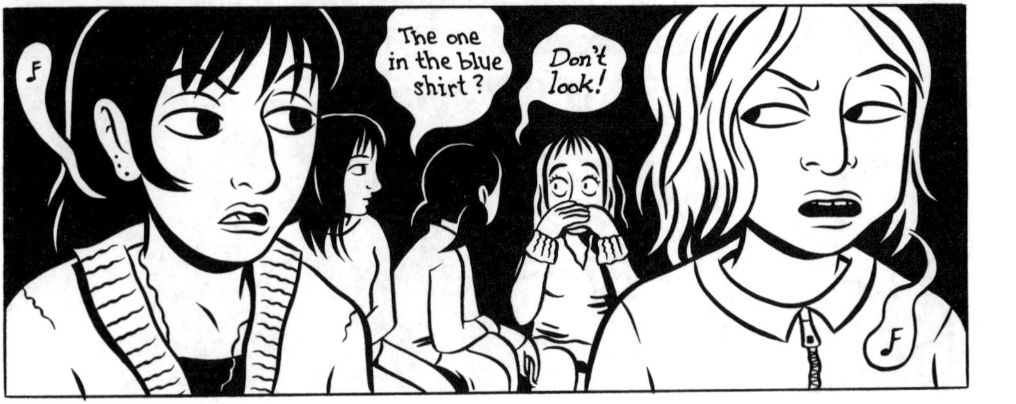
The one in the blue shirt?
Don't look!

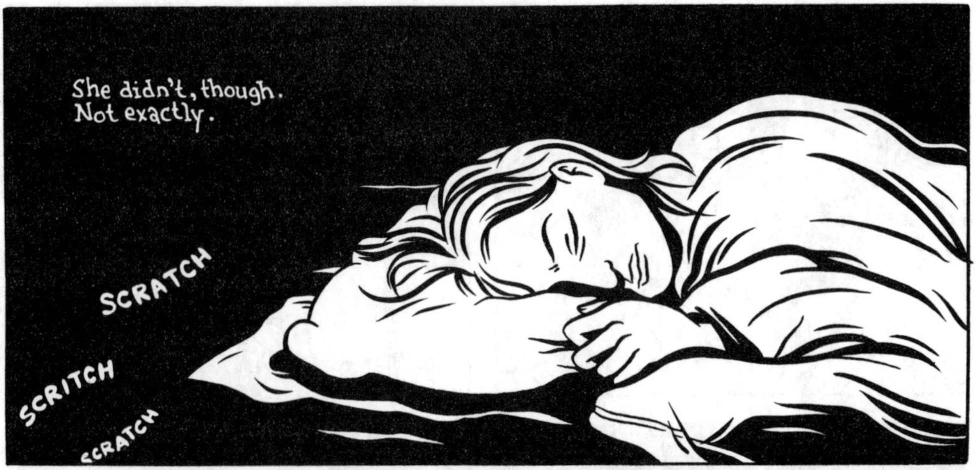
She didn't, though.
Not exactly.
SCRATCH
SCRITCH
SCRATCH

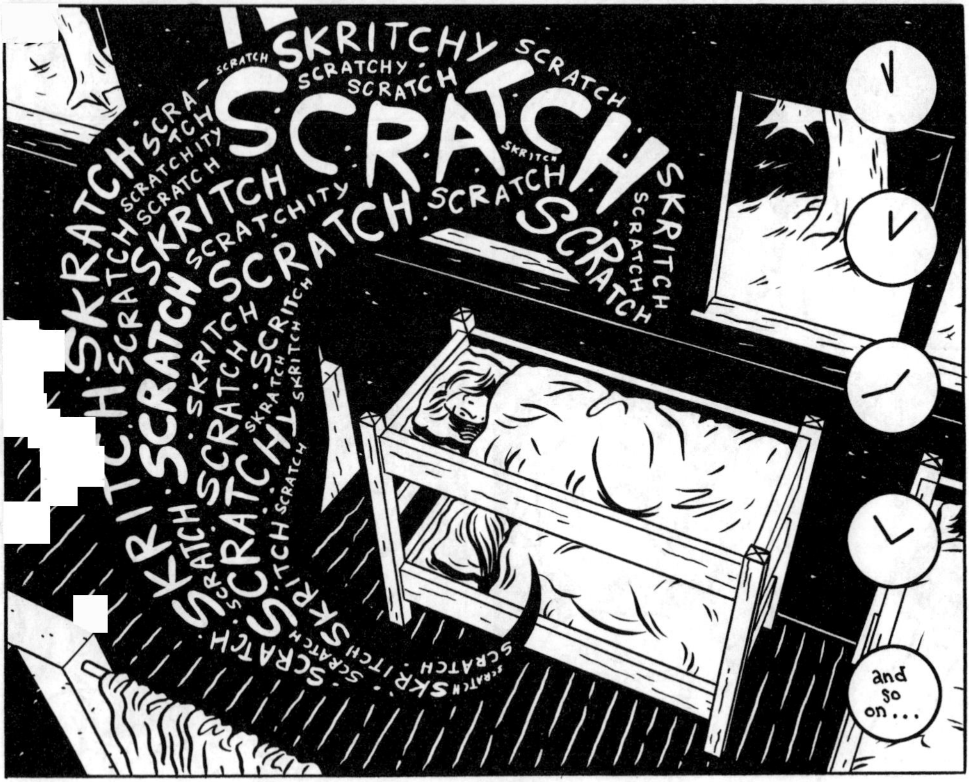
SKRITCHY
SCRATCH
SCRATCHY
SCRATCH
SCRATCH
SCRATCH
SKRITCH
SCRATCHITY
SCRATCH
SKRITCH
SCRATCHITY
SCRATCH
SCRATCH
SKRITCH
SCRATCH
and so on...

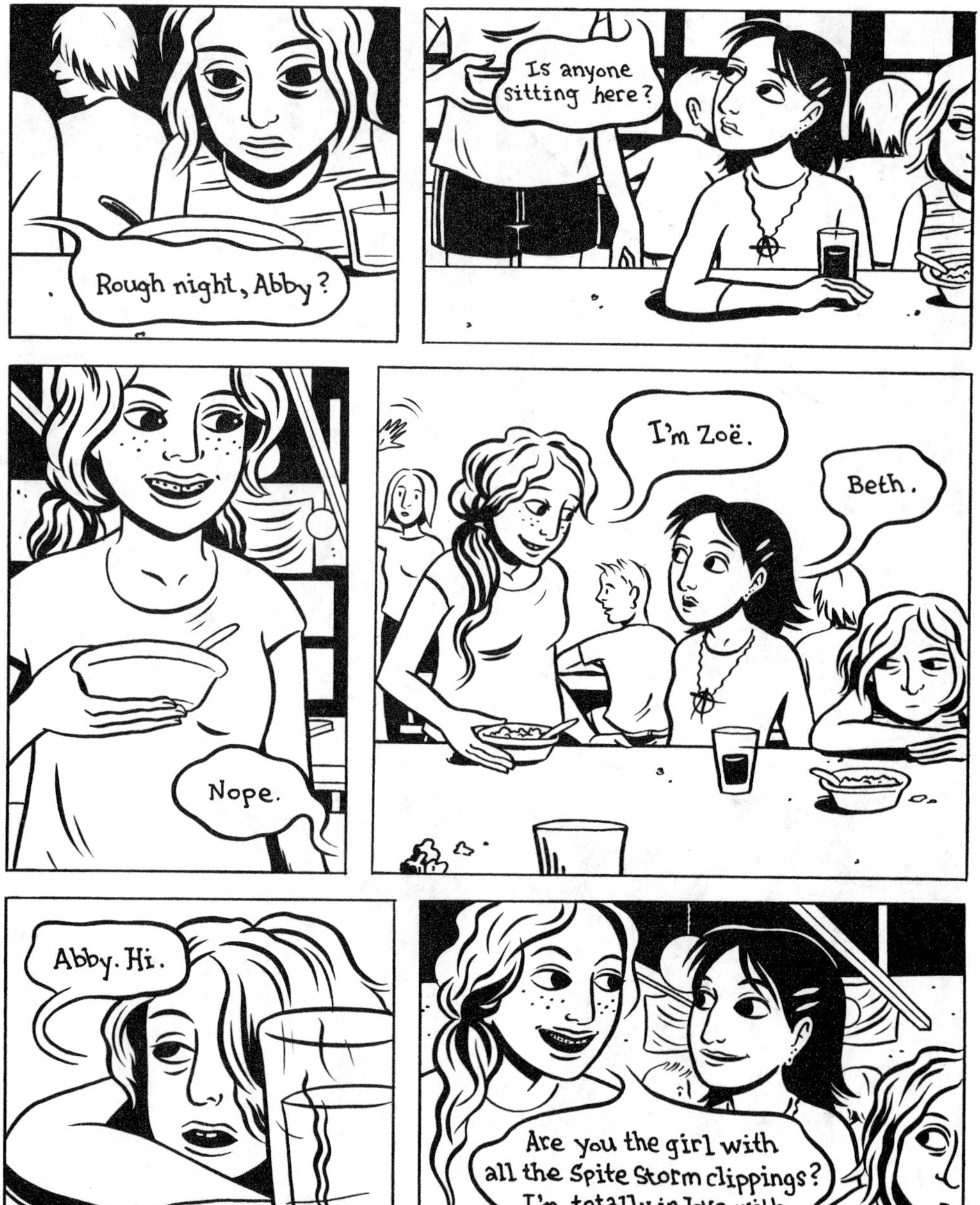
Rough night, Abby?
Is anyone sitting here?
Nope.
I'm Zoë.
Beth.
Abby. Hi.
Are you the girl with all the Spite Storm clippings? I'm totally in love with Ricky Vee.

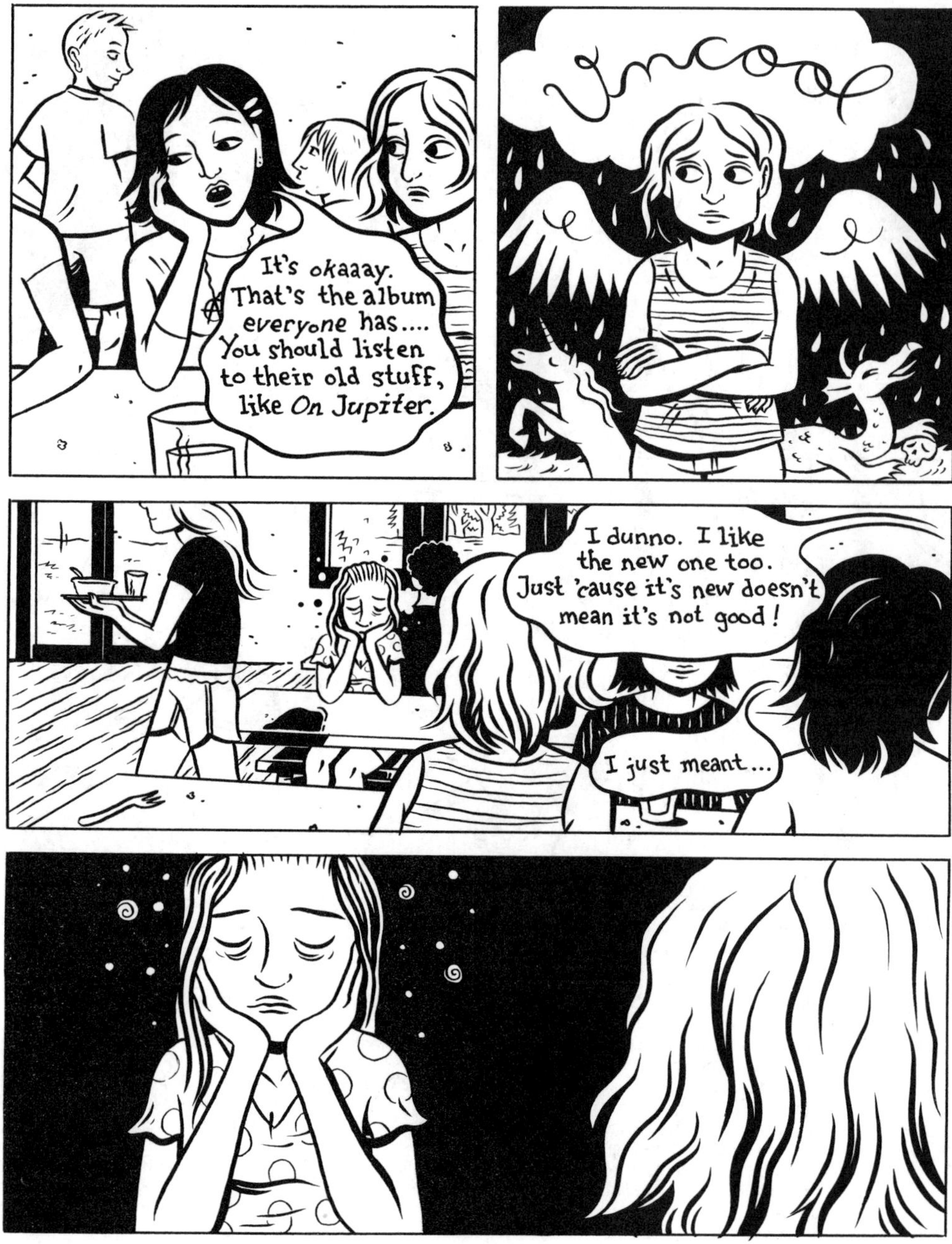
It's *okaaay.* That's the album *everyone* has.... You should listen to their old stuff, like *On Jupiter.*
Uncool
I dunno. I like the new one too. Just 'cause it's new doesn't mean it's not good!
I just meant...

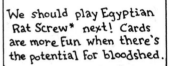

*Egyptian Rat Screw

You will need: A deck of cards with jokers removed, a sturdy table (or the floor), and two or more players.

Objective: The winner of ERS is the player who succeeds in taking all the cards.

The deal: Players sit in a circle. The dealer shuffles the deck several times and deals it evenly among all players who pick up their stacks of cards without looking at them.

Play: The first player, seated to the left of the dealer, takes the card from the top of her deck and plays it without checking to see what it is. Play continues clockwise, each participant playing one card until a face card (ace, king, queen, or jack) is played. In this case, the next player has a set number of chances to beat the face card: four chances for an ace, three for a king, two for a queen, and one for a jack.

   - If she manages to play a face card, play passes to her left and the next player must try to beat it.

   - If she doesn't, the player to her right takes the whole stack of cards and adds it to the bottom of her own.

If at any time two of the same card are played–if, for example, a 2 is played on top of a 2, or a jack is played on top of a jack–all players slap the cards, and the player who slaps first takes the stack. If you lost all your cards or weren't an original player, you can try to "slap in" on doubles. Be careful not to slap when there AREN'T doubles on the stack, though! If you do, you must pay the penalty: take the next card in your hand and place it, face up, on the bottom of the stack in play.

Deni!
whisper whisper
giggle

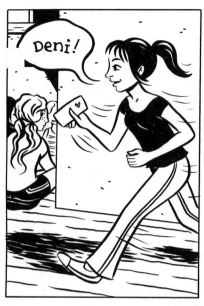

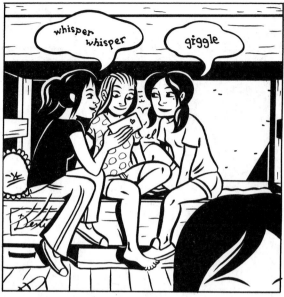

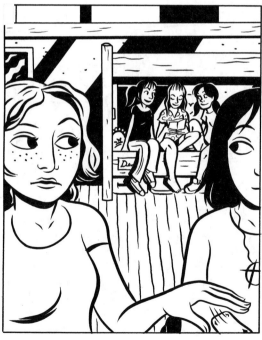

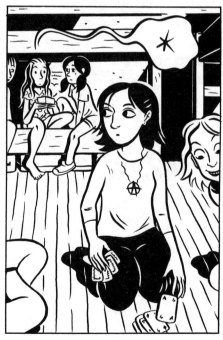

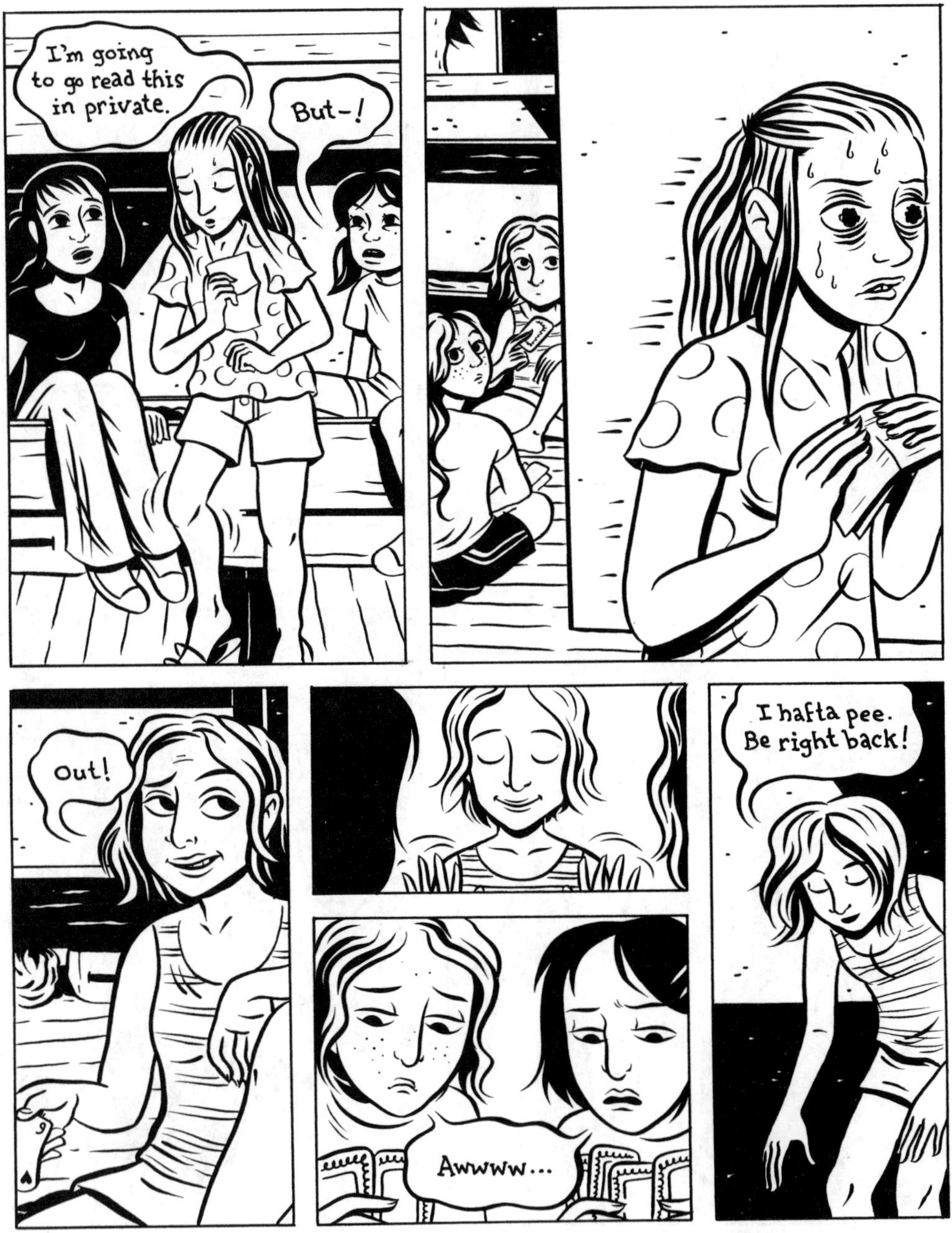
I'm going to go read this in private.
But-!
Out!
I hafta pee. Be right back!
Awwww...

rustle

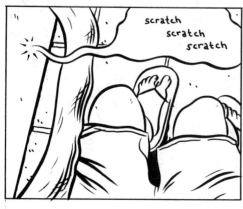

scratch
scratch
scratch

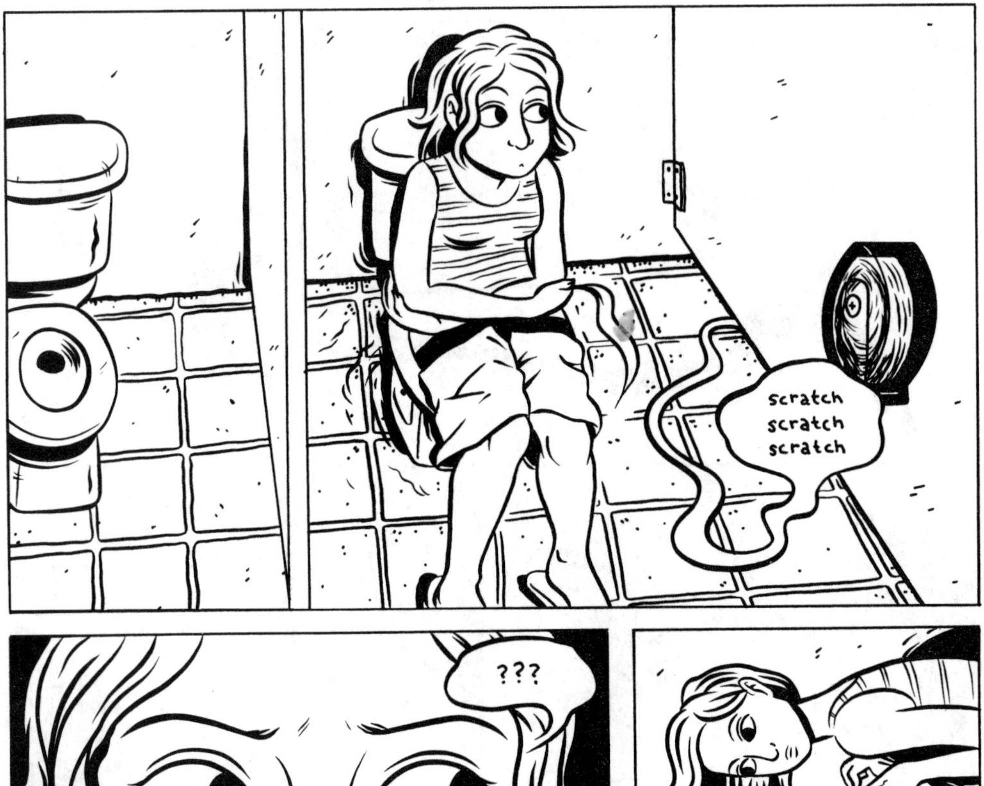
scratch
scratch
scratch
???
scratchy
Deni?

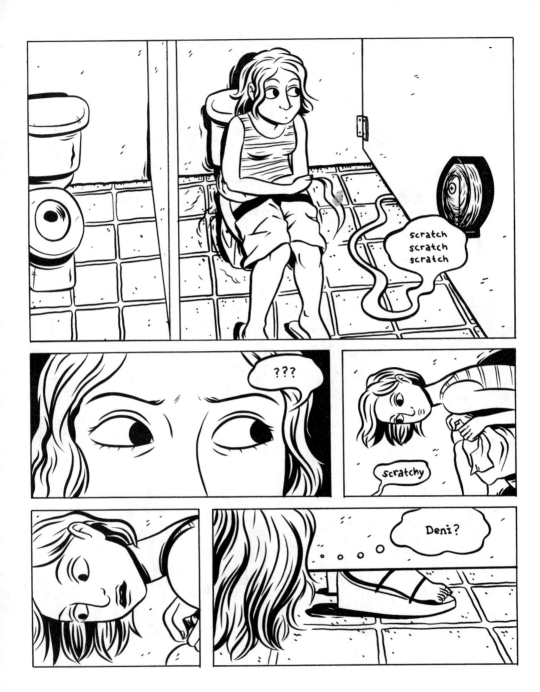

What's up?
Uh... Nothing.
What's taking her?

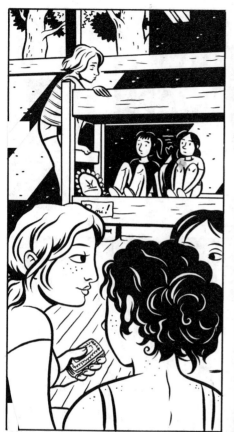

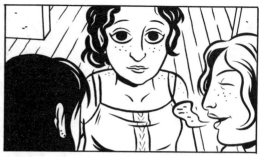

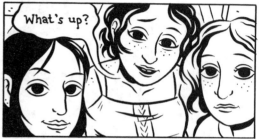

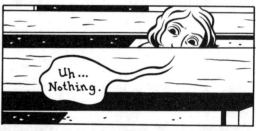

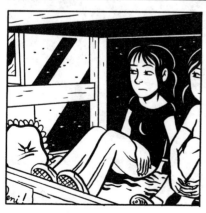

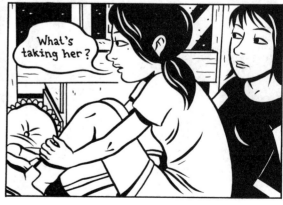

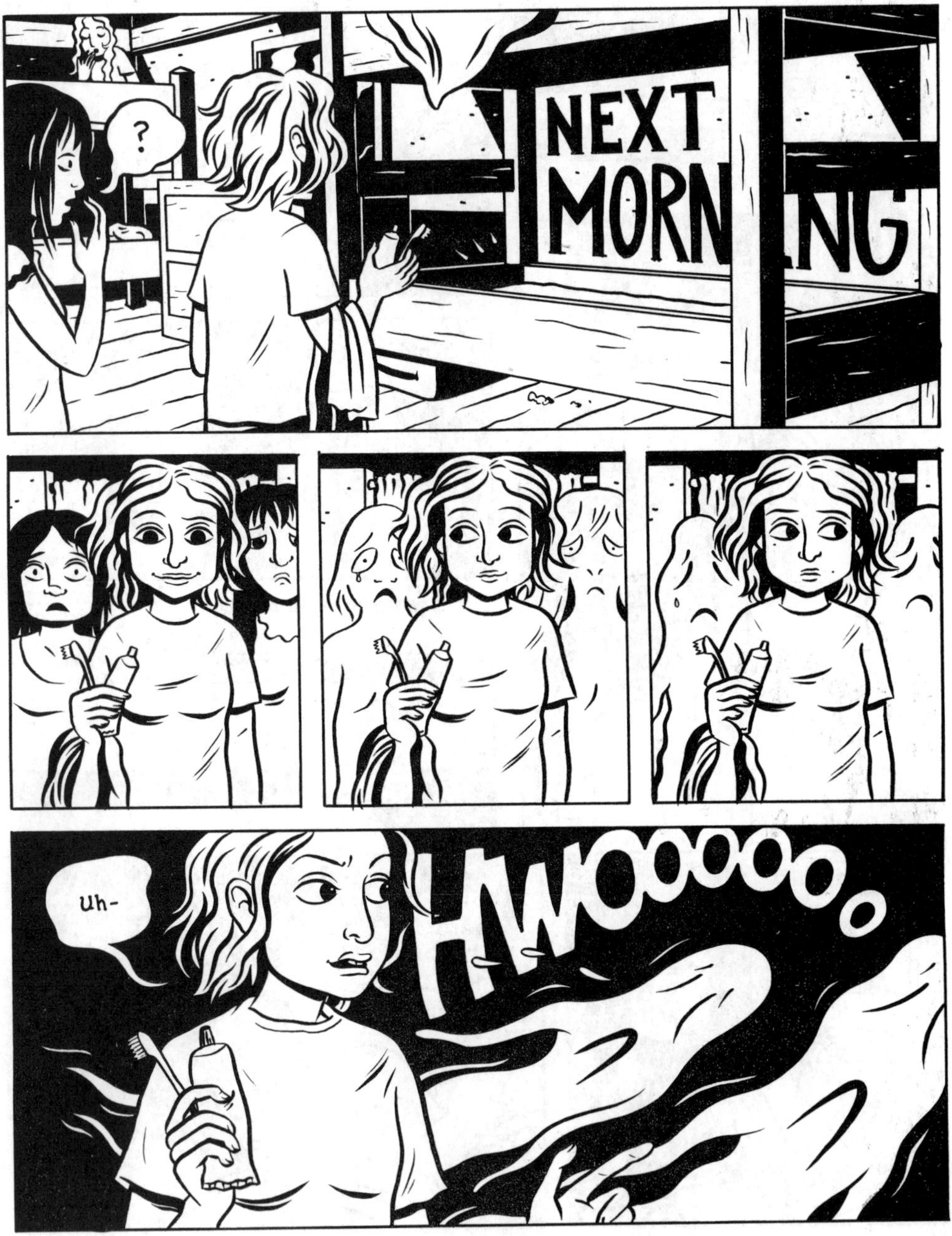
NEXT MORNING
?
Uh-
HWOOOOOo

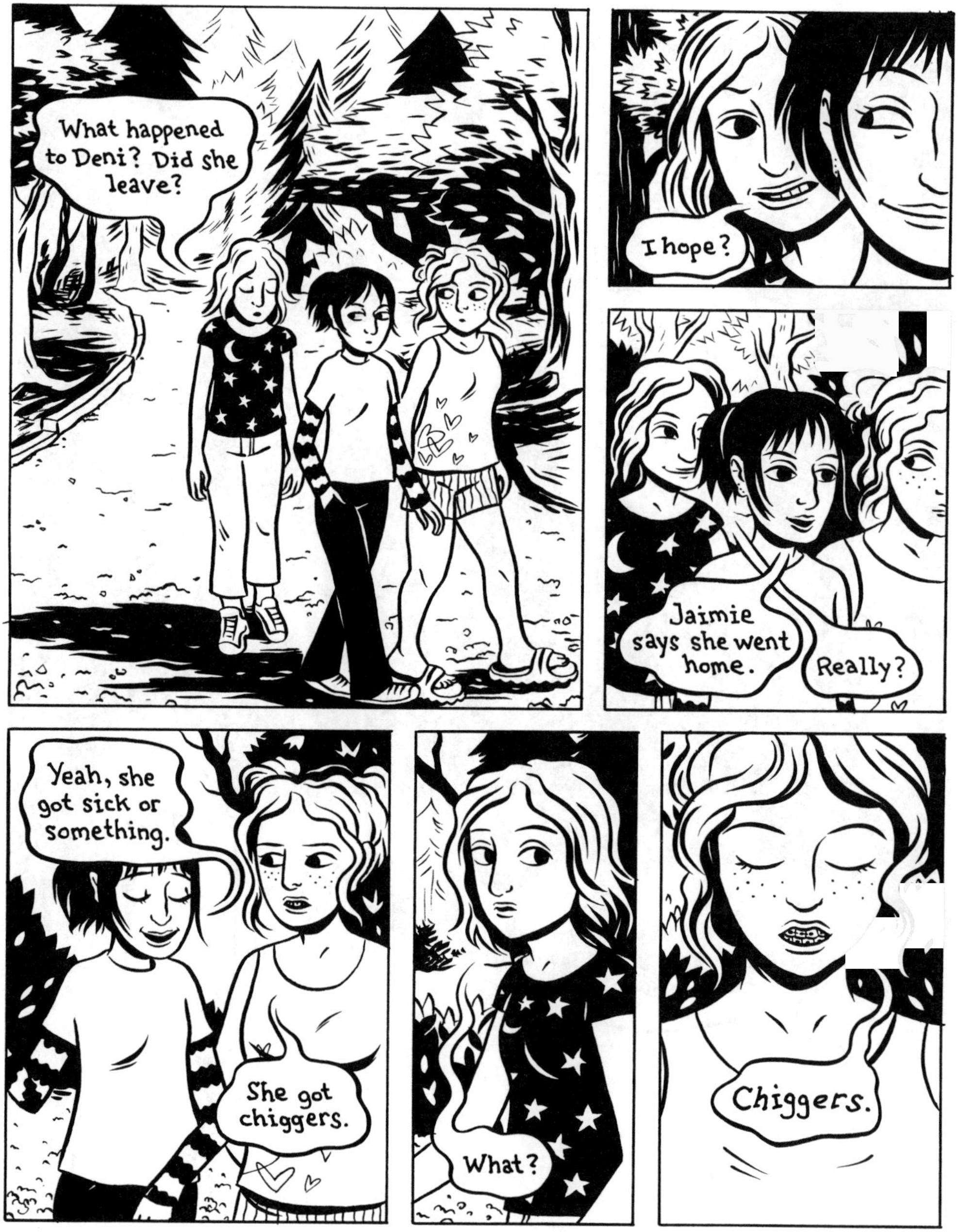
What happened to Deni? Did she leave?
I hope?
Jaimie says she went home.
Really?
Yeah, she got sick or something.
She got chiggers.
What?
Chiggers.

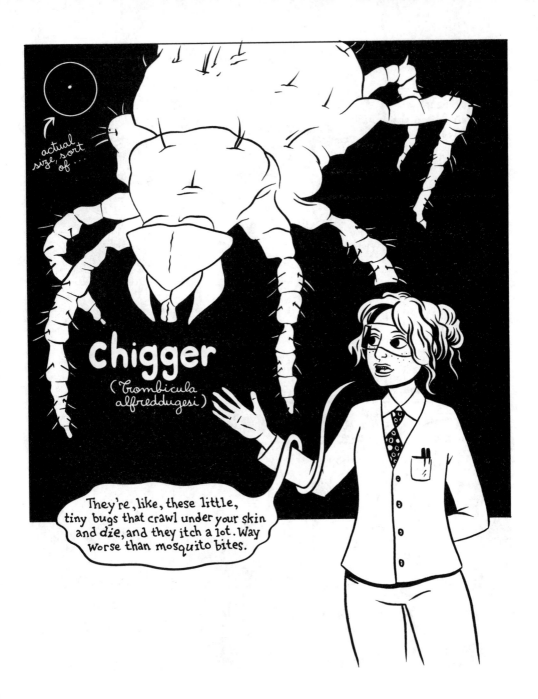

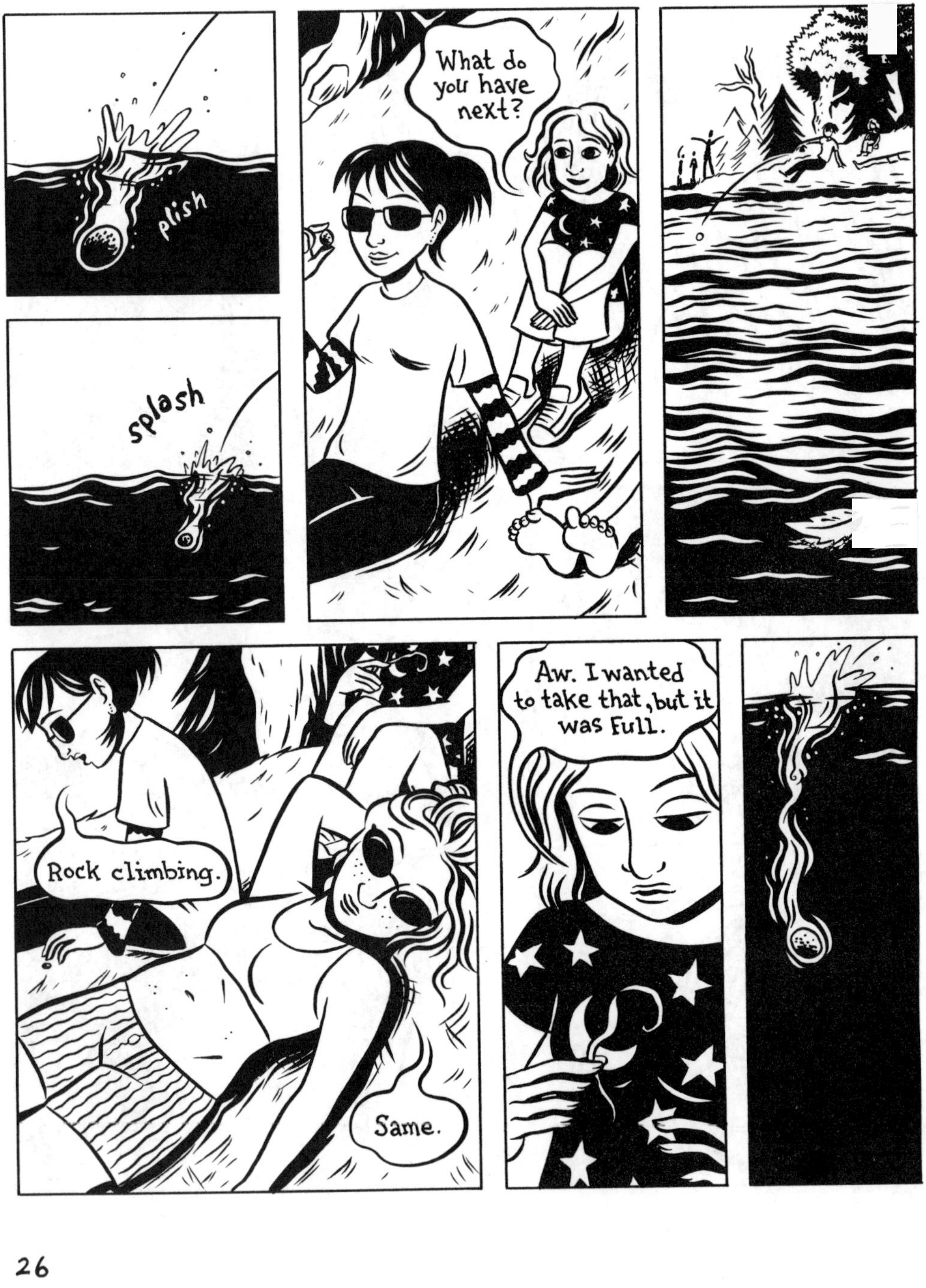
plish
splash
What do you have next?
Rock climbing.
Same.
Aw. I wanted to take that, but it was full.

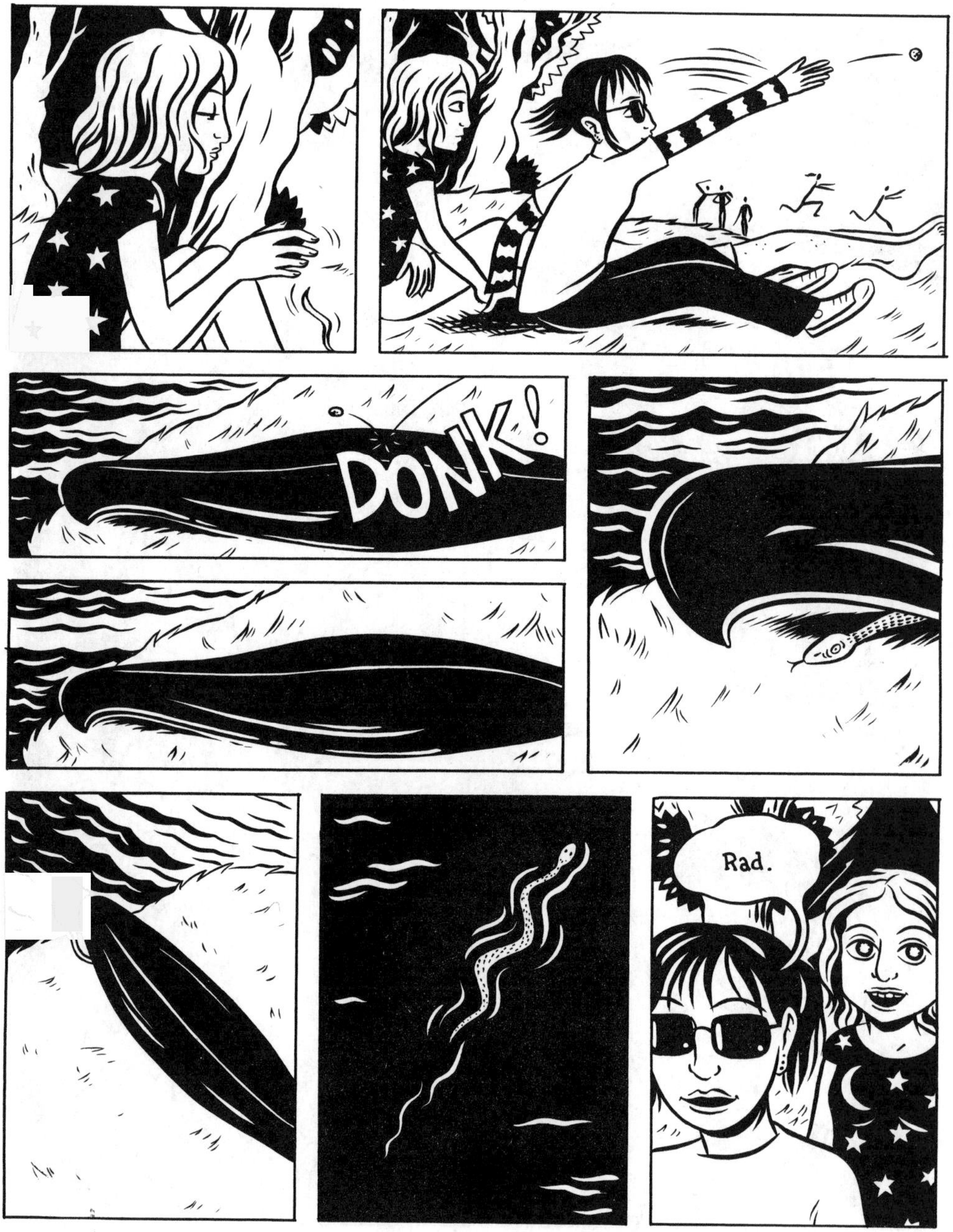
DONK!
Rad.

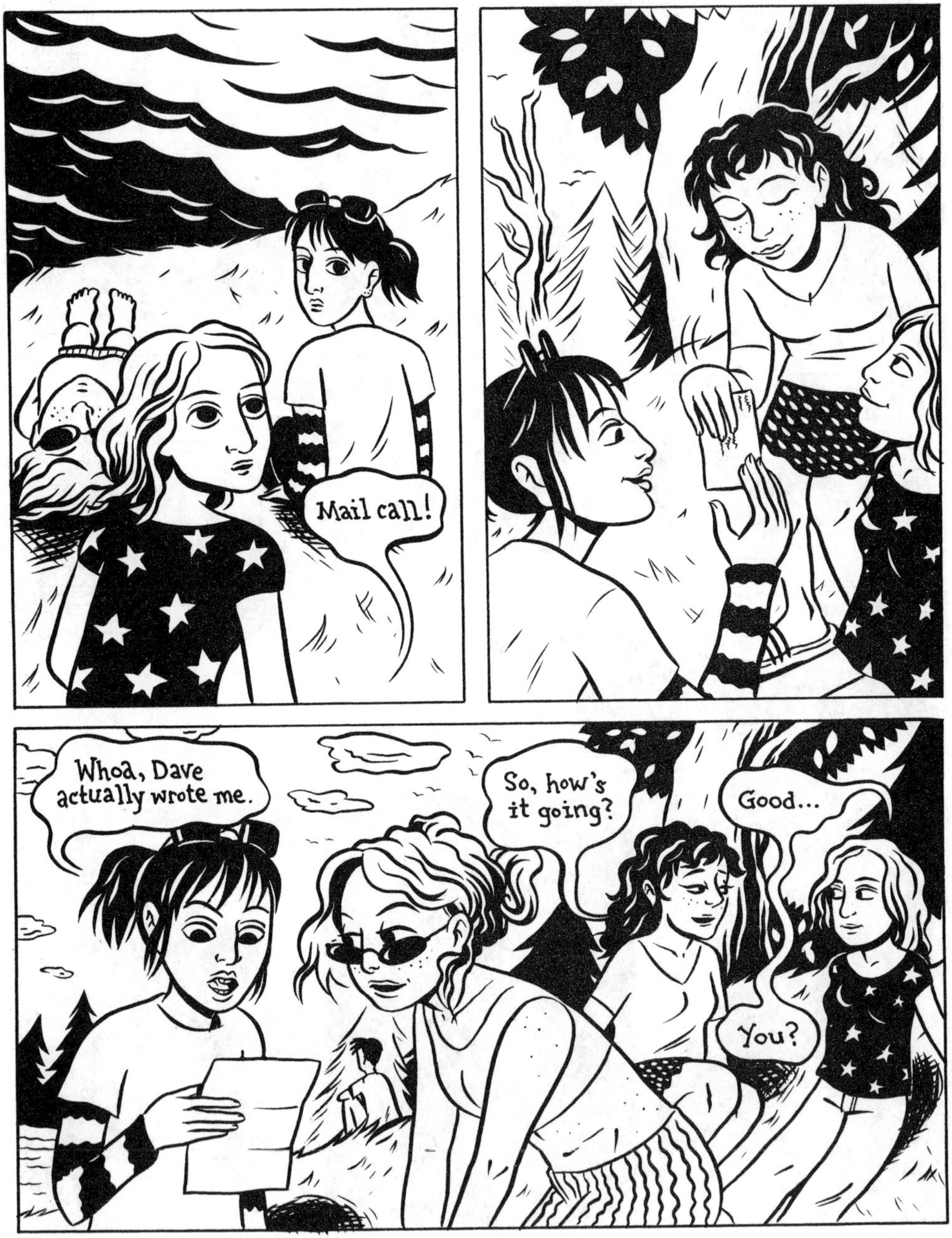
Mail call!
Whoa, Dave actually wrote me.
So, how's it going?
Good...
You?

Good.

Weird.

I keep remembering how it's my last summer as a camper. IF I come back next year, I'll have to be a counselor, but I'll have college in the Fall, so I don't know...

God, I always forget how old you are.

Ancient.

Why do you even hang out with me?

It's your youthful exuberance, Abby. You keep me vital—finger on the pulse of our generation.

Also, you have no sense of irony.

AUUJUUUUGH!!

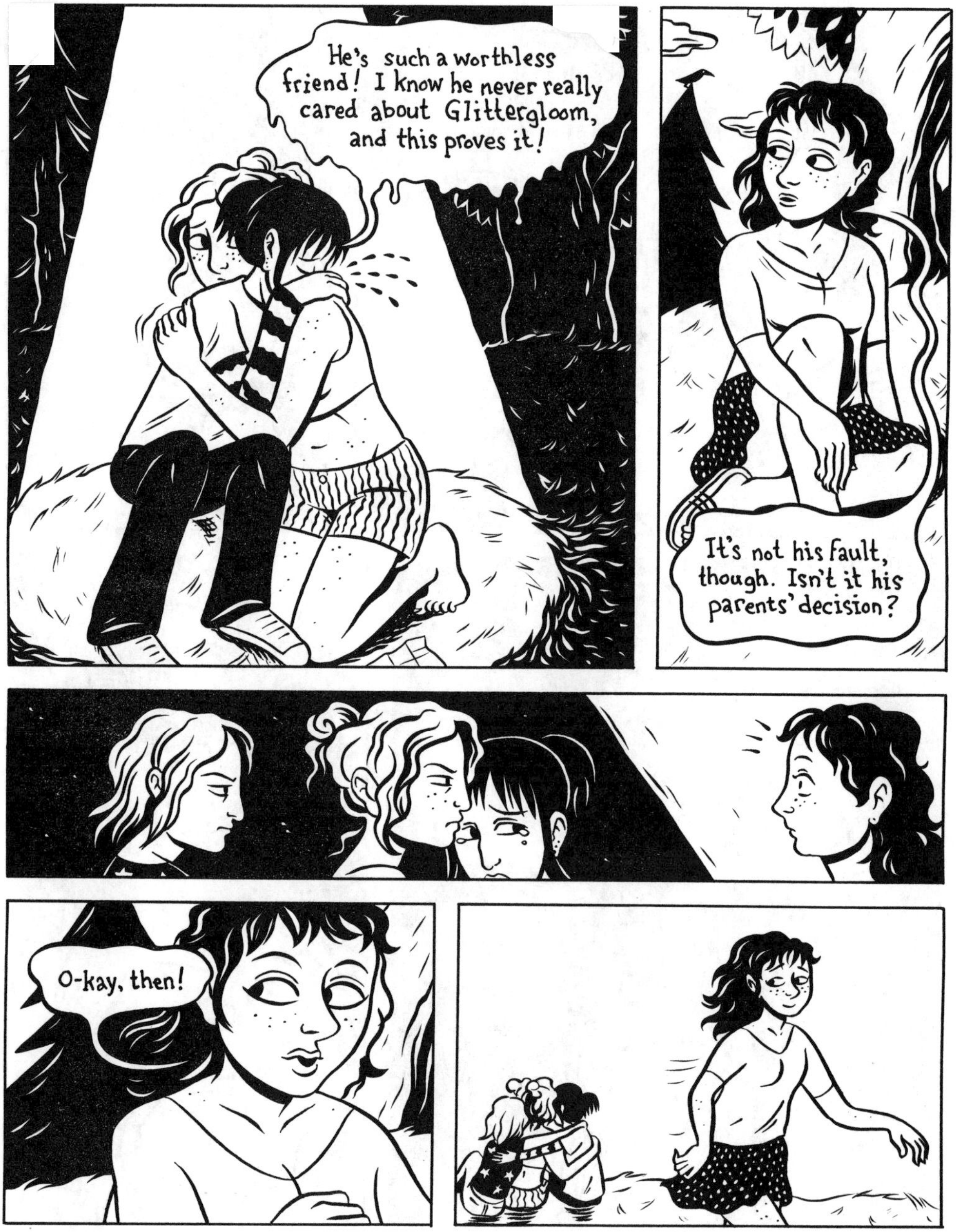
He's such a worthless friend! I know he never really cared about Glittergloom, and this proves it!
It's not his fault, though. Isn't it his parents' decision?
O-kay, then!

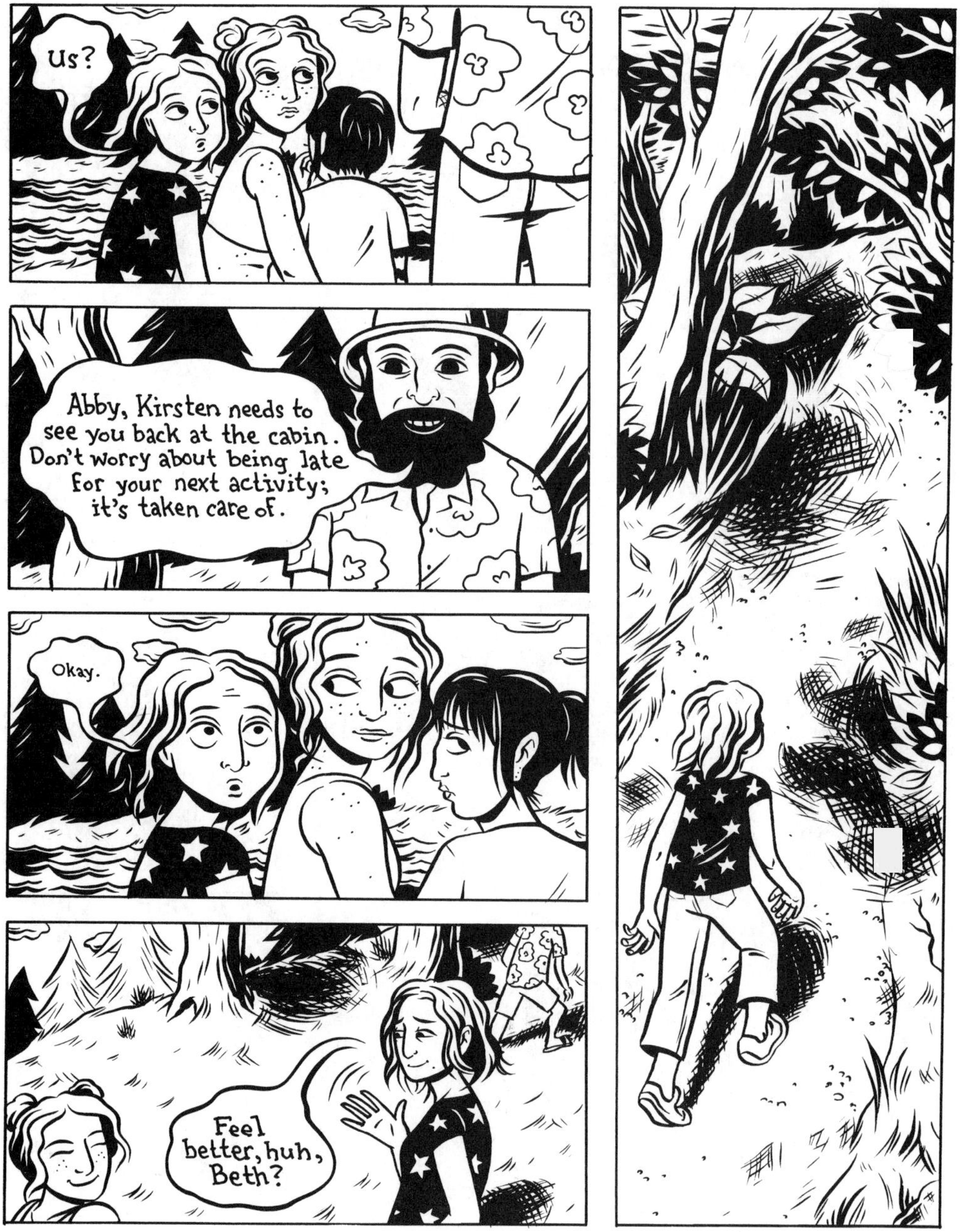
Us?
Abby, Kirsten needs to see you back at the cabin. Don't worry about being late for your next activity; it's taken care of.
Okay.
Feel better, huh, Beth?

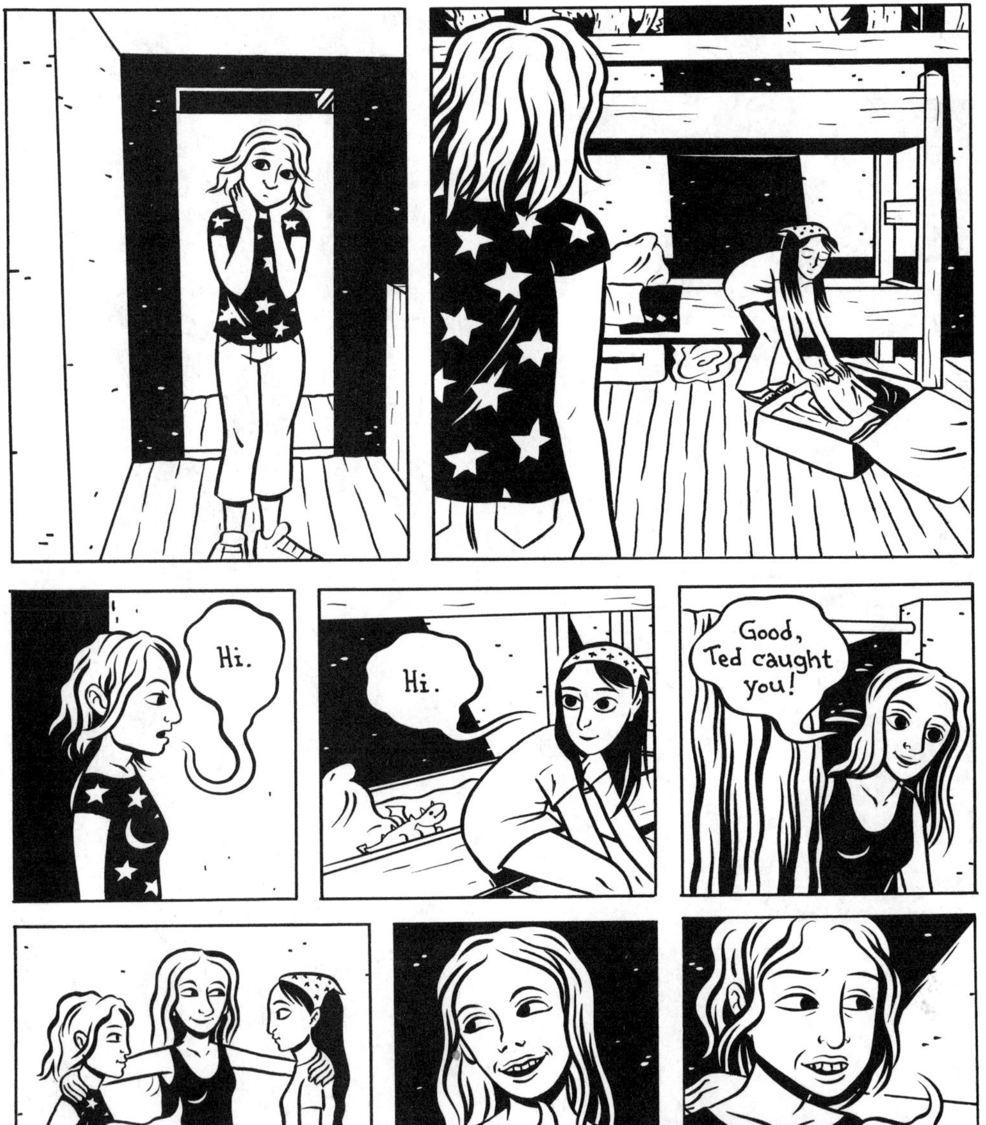
Hi.
Hi.
Good, Ted caught you!
This is Shasta, your new bunkmate.
Shasta, this is Abby. I'm sure you guys will get along great!
Yeah.

I have that too!

Really??
Outlaw Queen of Minas is my favorite book ever!

This is my fourth time reading it.

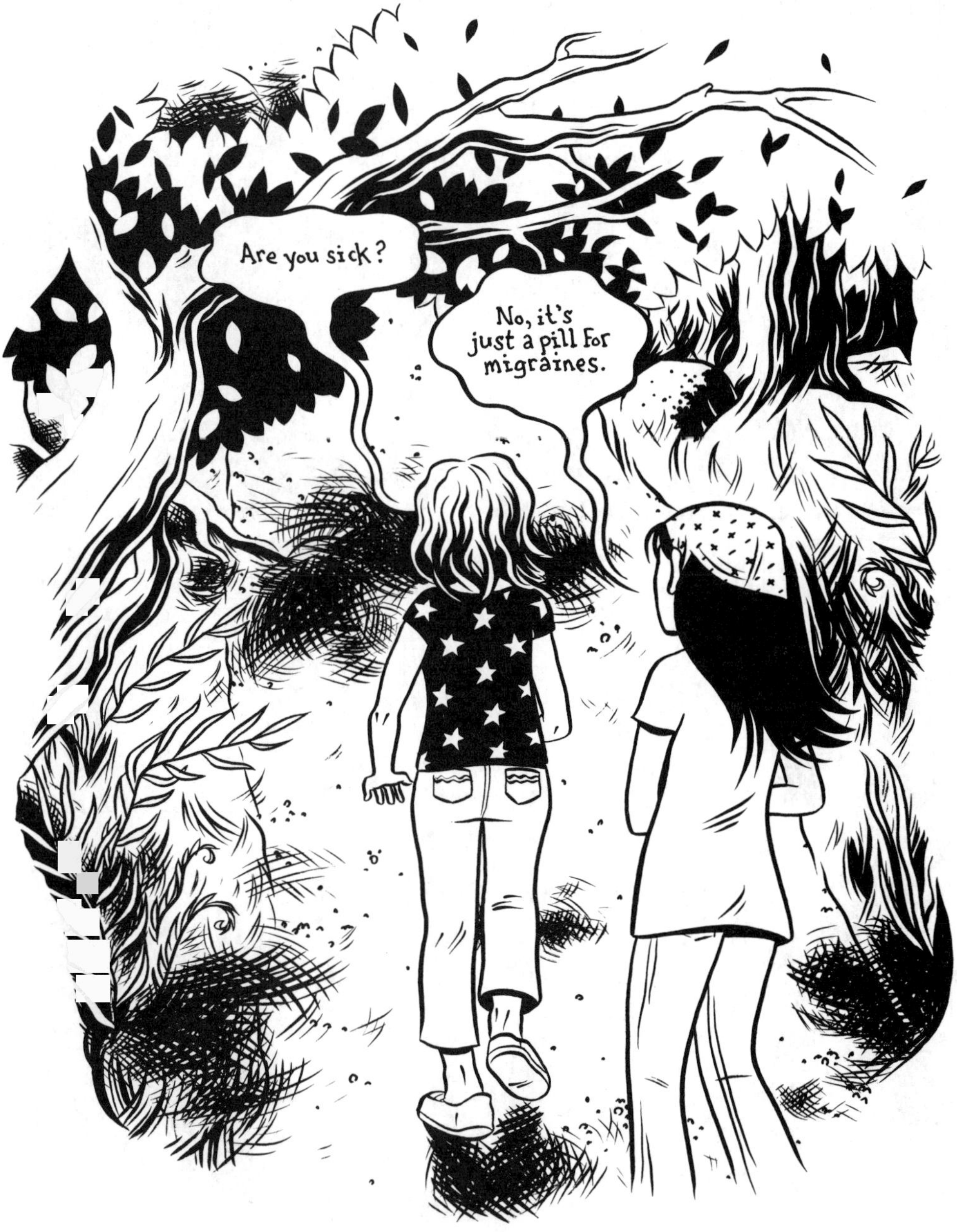
Are you sick?
No, it's just a pill for migraines.

...so I'm going to turn y'all loose in a minute. See how many different kinds of leaves you can collect.

And remember, leaves, not branches! Don't let me catch you dismembering the trees!

Look, sourwood!

Want some? It's good.

Isn't it, like, sour?

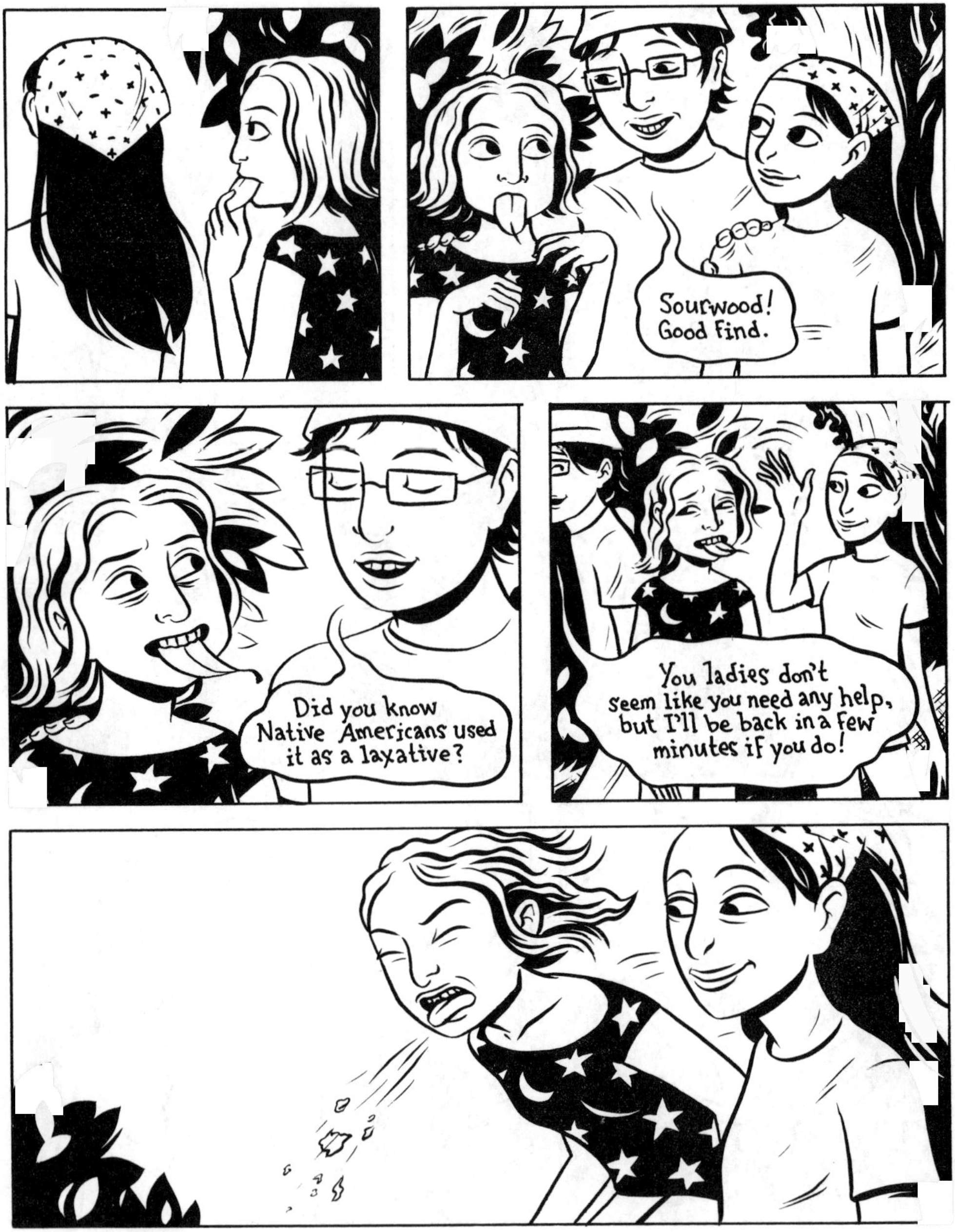
Sourwood! Good find.
Did you know Native Americans used it as a laxative?
You ladies don't seem like you need any help, but I'll be back in a few minutes if you do!

So, how can your mom not know you have a boy-friend?

Matt lives in New Jersey.

Is he your pen pal?

Huh?

Noooo! God! We talk on IM.

Really?

Yeah...?

OH MY GOD

Are you from some weird, wholesome family with no computer?

We have a computer. I just don't like it much.

43

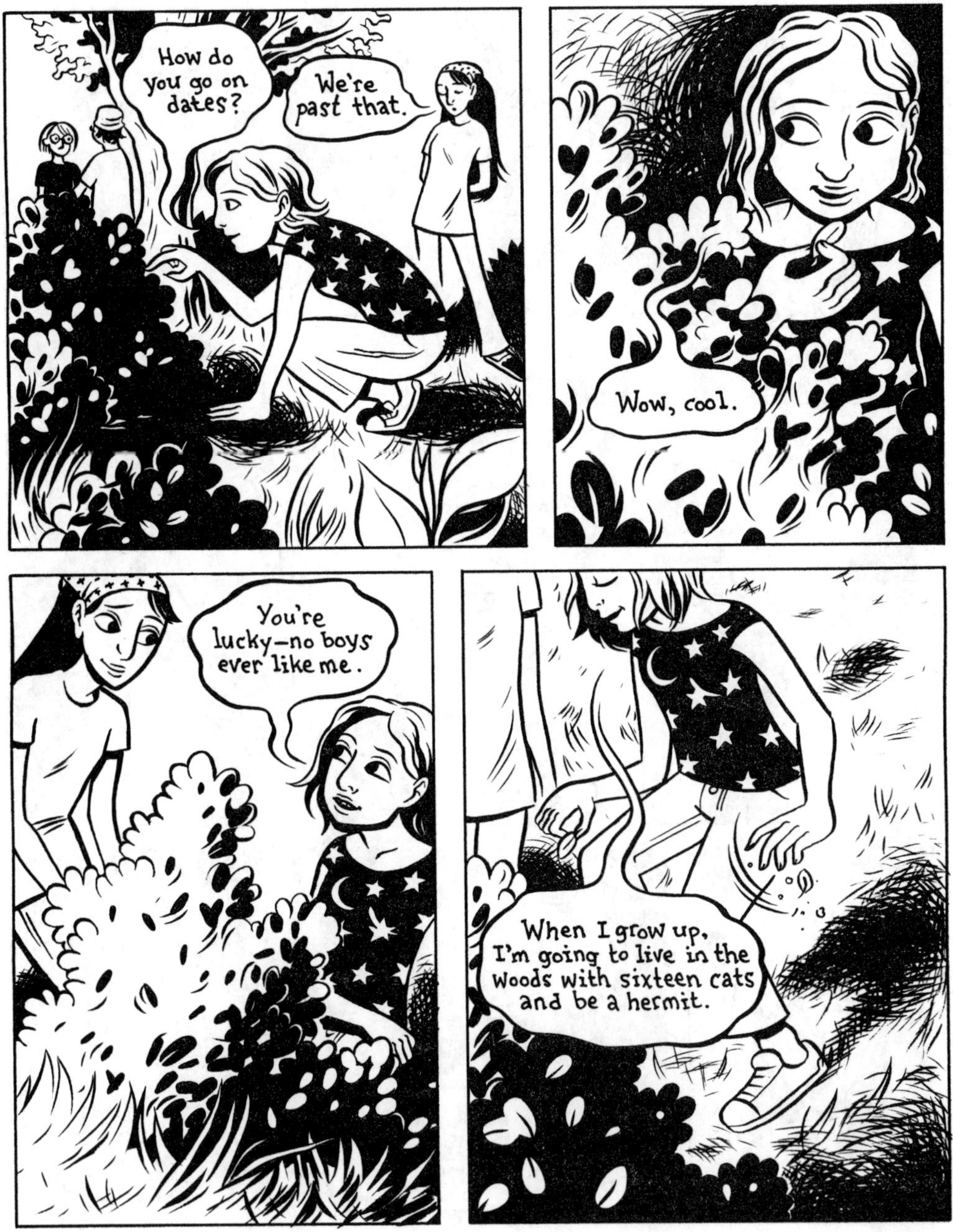
How do you go on dates?
We're past that.
Wow, cool.
You're lucky—no boys ever like me.
When I grow up, I'm going to live in the woods with sixteen cats and be a hermit.

Later

So, are you the new Deni?

?

I'm the new Shasta....

Like the cola?

Like the mountain.

?

In California?

Right. Cool.

45

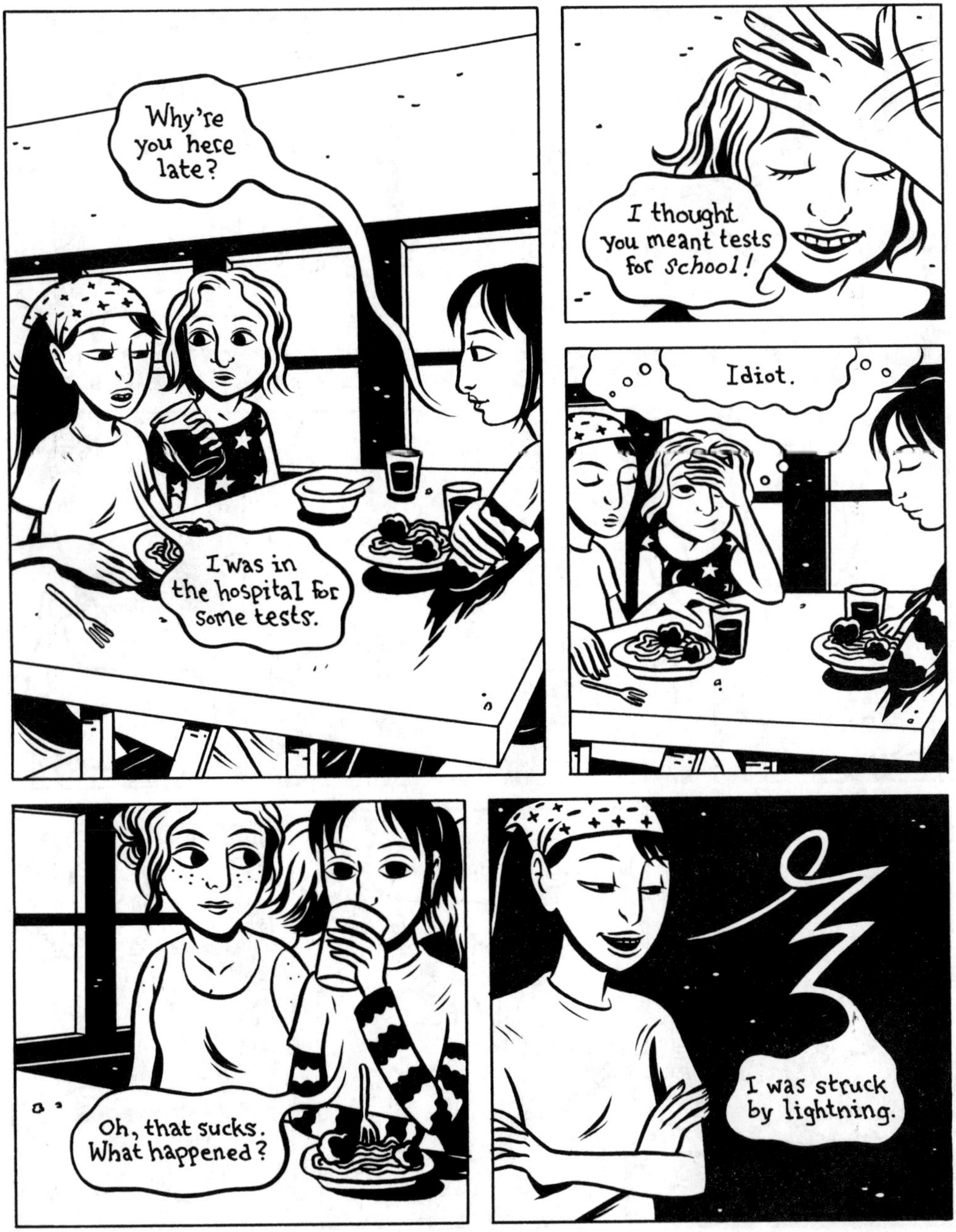
Why're you here late?
I was in the hospital for some tests.
I thought you meant tests for school!
Idiot.
Oh, that sucks. What happened?
I was struck by lightning.

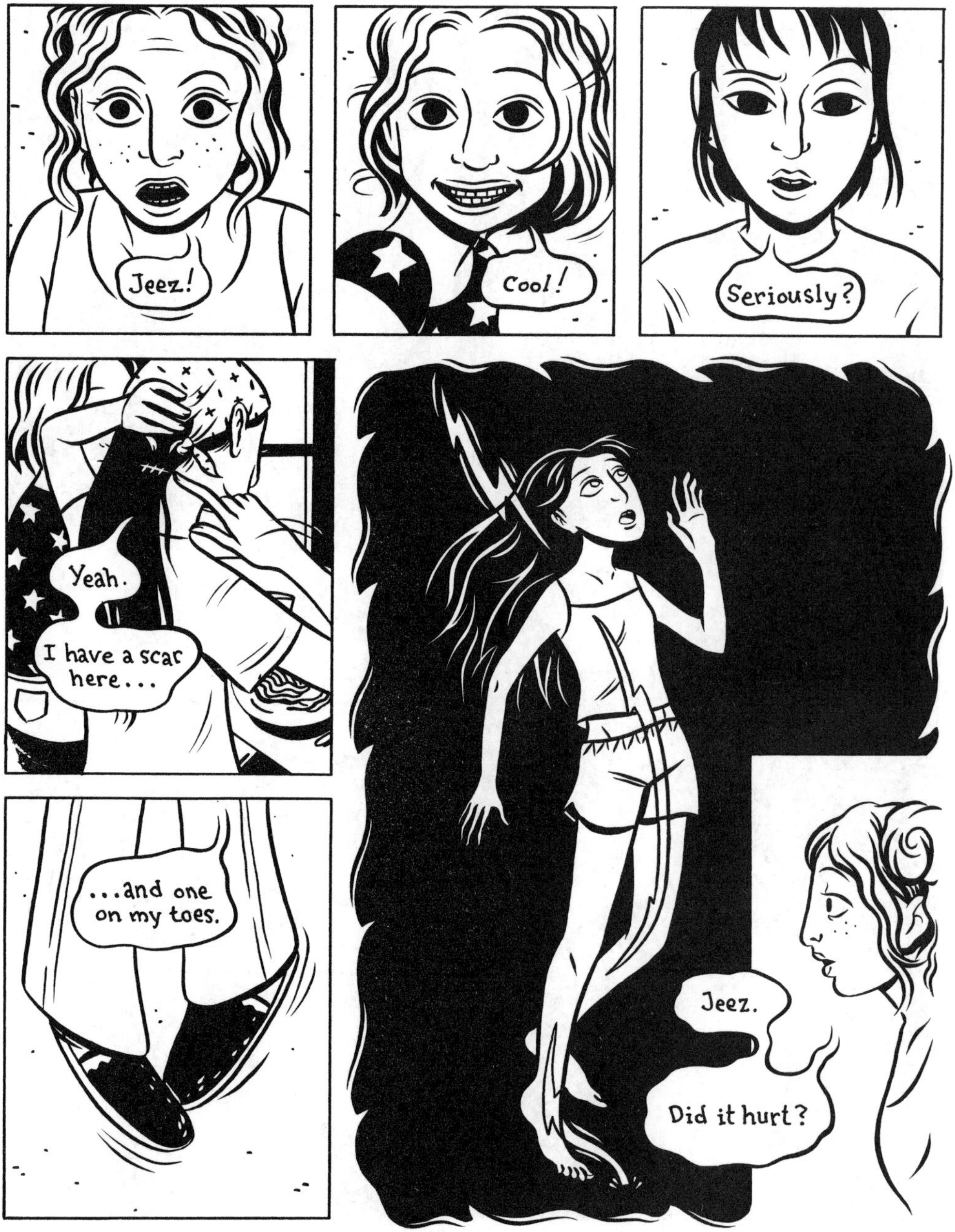
Jeez!
Cool!
Seriously?
Yeah.
I have a scar here...
...and one on my toes.
Jeez.
Did it hurt?

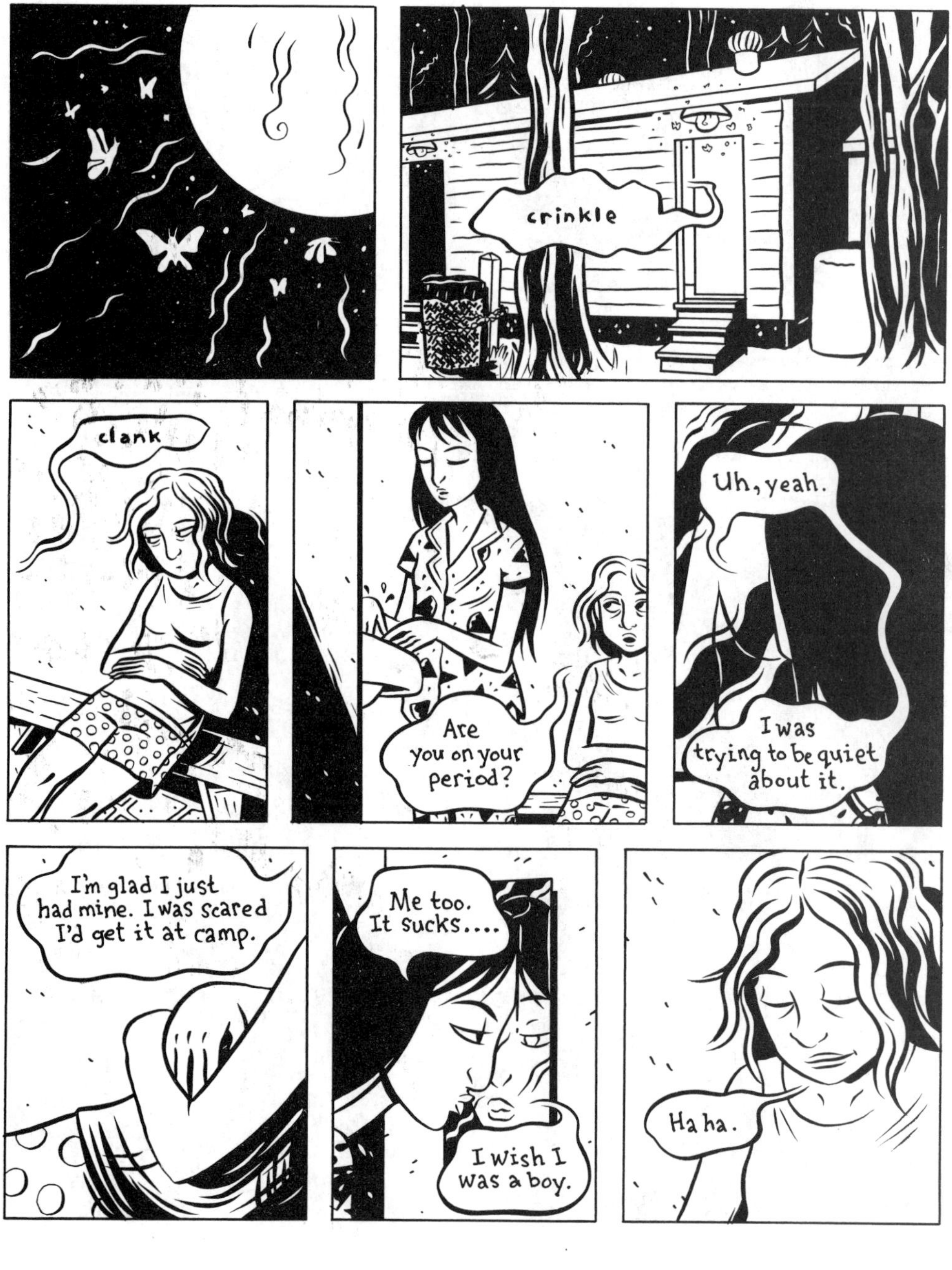
crinkle
clank
Are you on your period?
Uh, yeah.
I was trying to be quiet about it.
I'm glad I just had mine. I was scared I'd get it at camp.
Me too. It sucks....
I wish I was a boy.
Ha ha.

What's it like having a boyfriend?

It *SUCKS!*

Um.

I practically never get to text him or *anything* because it's too expensive and my stupid *mom* would spaz out.

I can't wait till Matt's eighteen and he can move to Florida. We'll be together all the time!

Lately he's a *jerk*, though. He says there aren't any good schools in Florida. He wants to go to NYU.

Grr!

At least you guys found each other, right?

Yeah.

He's my *soulmate*. You know?

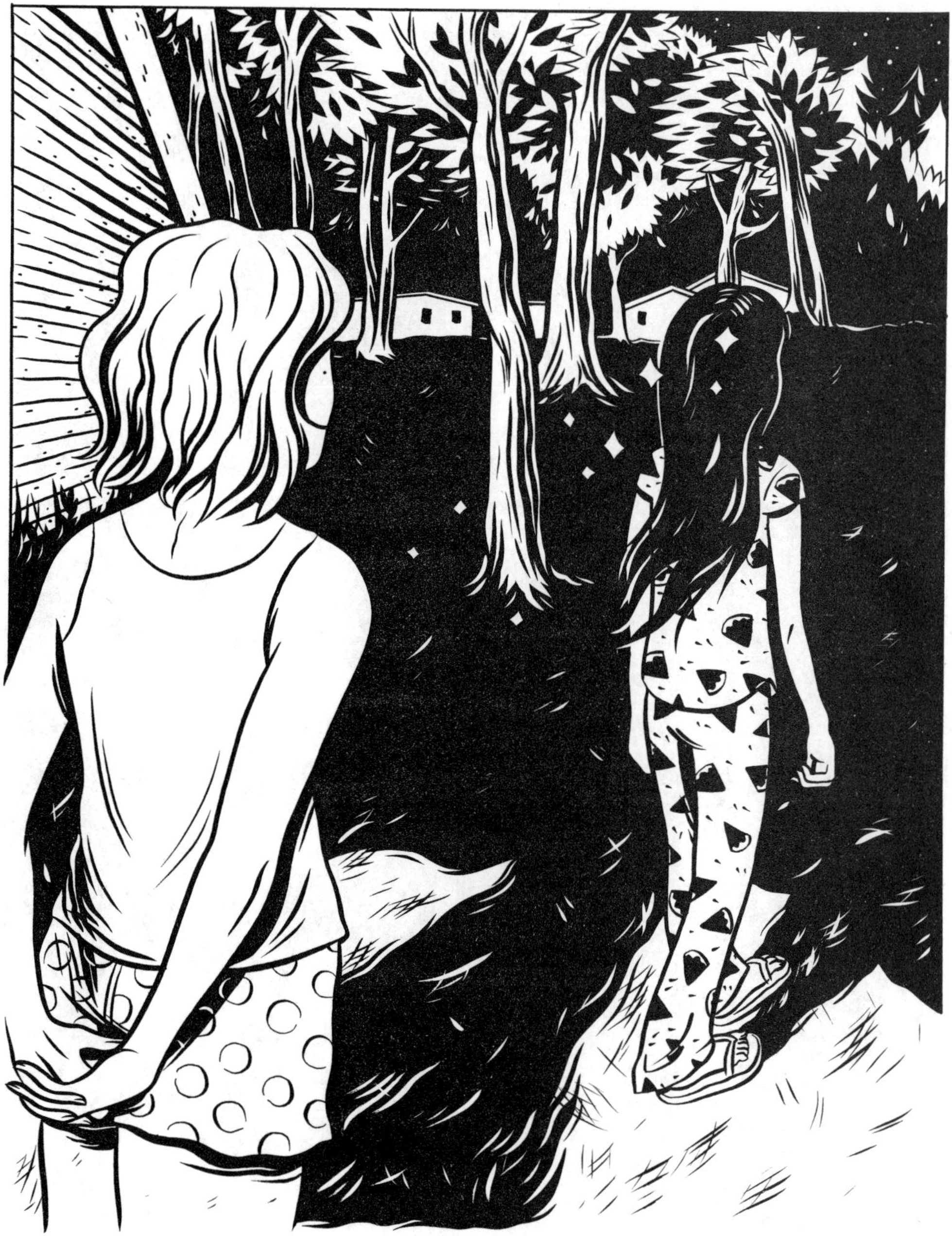

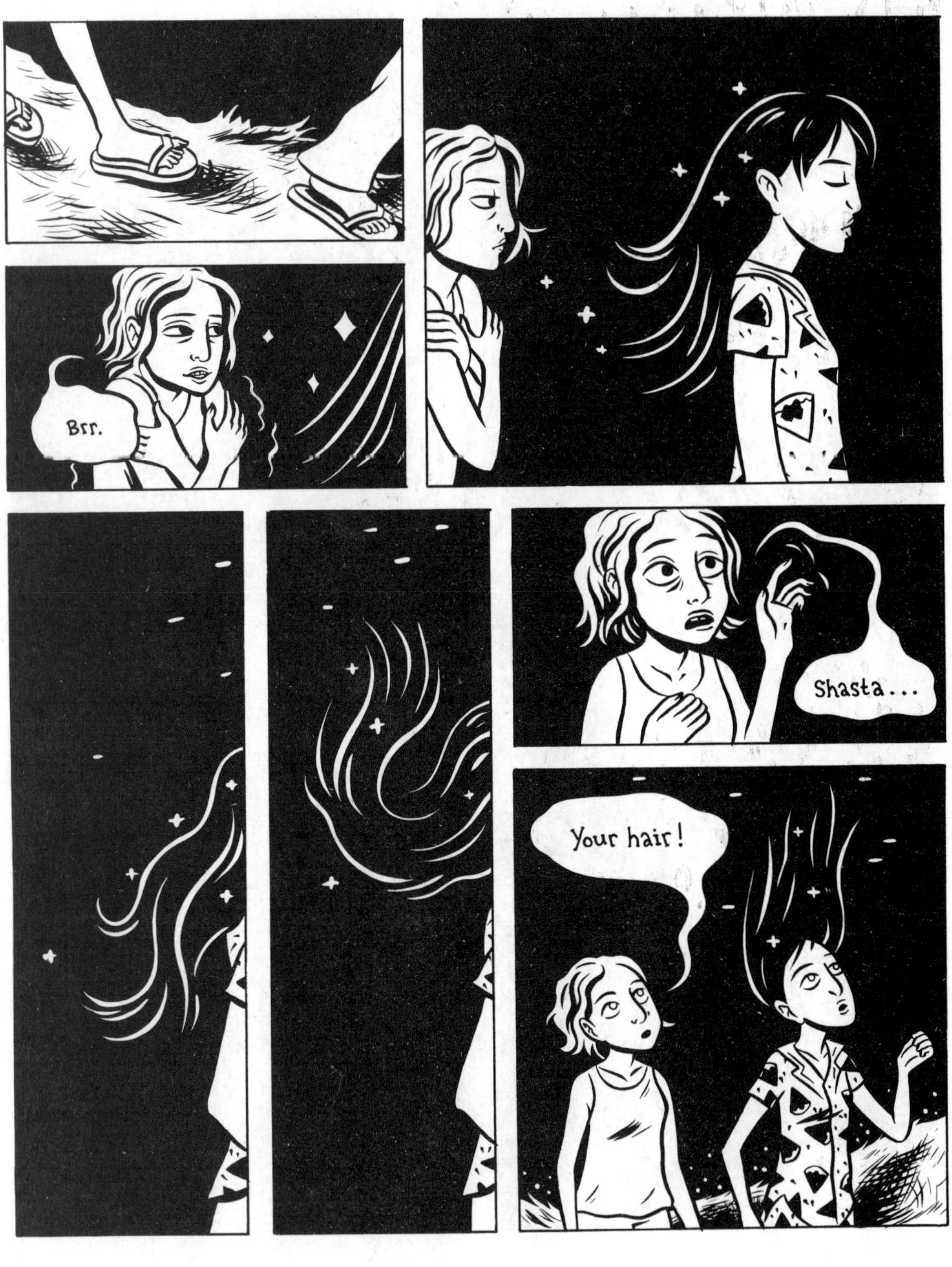
Brr.
Shasta...
Your hair!

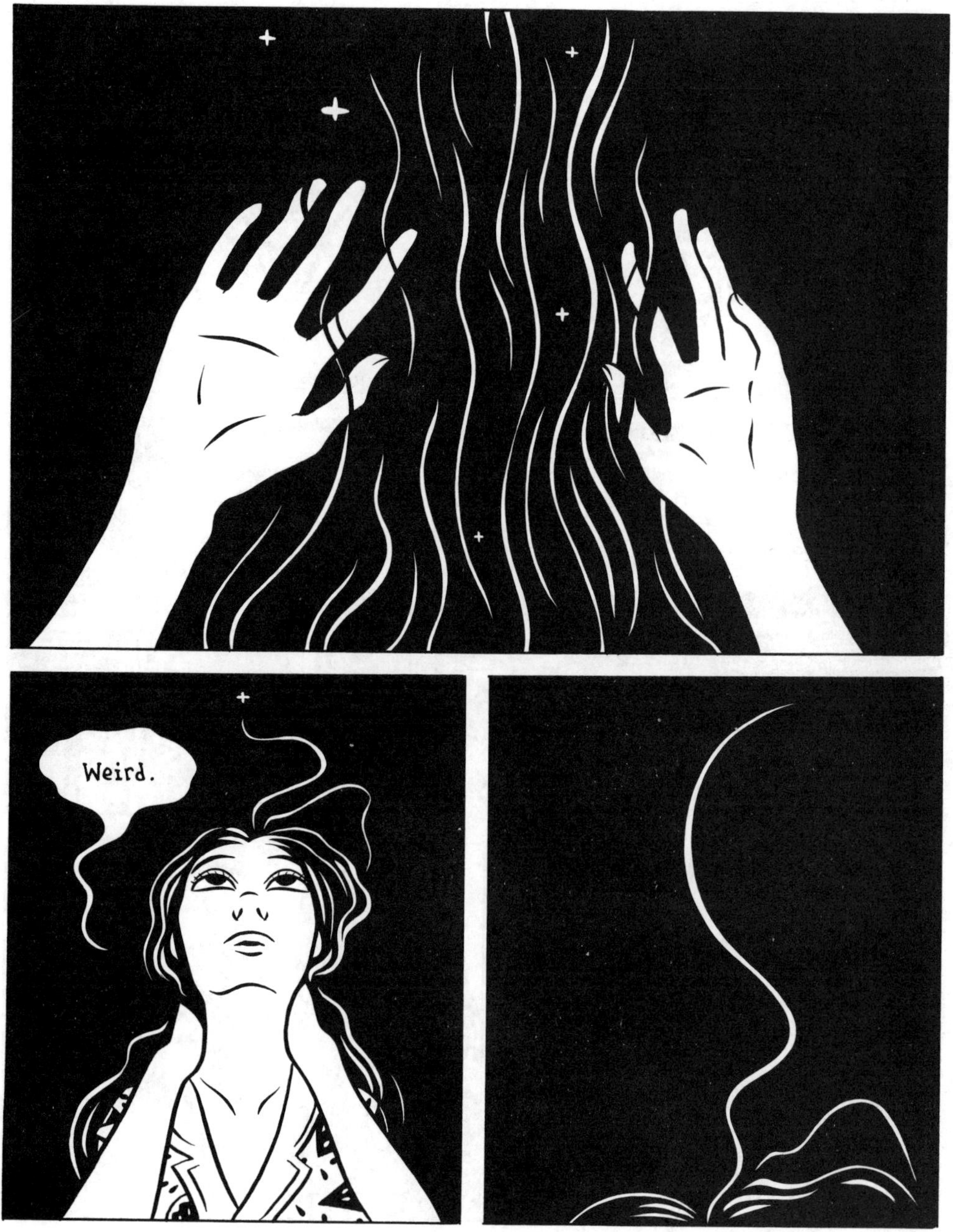
Weird.

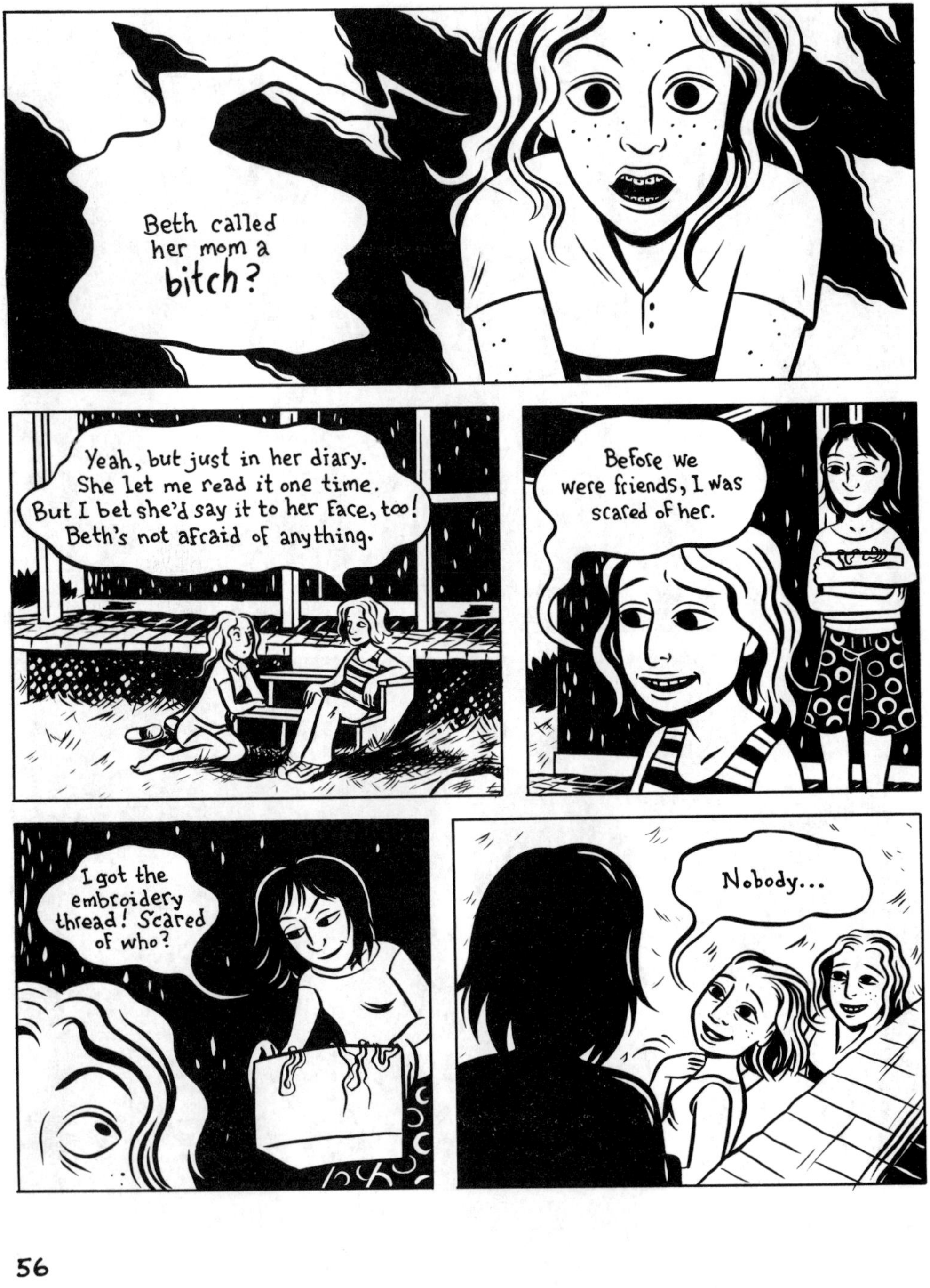
Beth called her mom a bitch?
Yeah, but just in her diary. She let me read it one time. But I bet she'd say it to her face, too! Beth's not afraid of anything.
Before we were friends, I was scared of her.
I got the embroidery thread! Scared of who?
Nobody...

beth ?

how to make a friendship bracelet

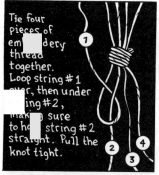

Tie four pieces of embroidery thread together. Loop string #1 over, then under string #2, making sure to hold string #2 straight. Pull the knot tight.

1

2 3 4

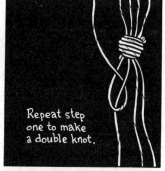

Repeat step one to make a double knot.

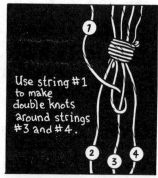

Use string #1 to make double knots around strings #3 and #4.

1

2 3 4

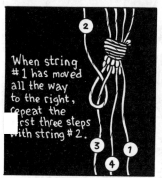

When string #1 has moved all the way to the right, repeat the first three steps with string #2.

2

3 1
4

Continue until you have a bracelet long enough for your wrist.

Knot the end of your bracelet. You're finished!

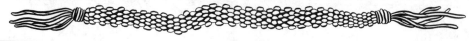

I was scared of you at first! I thought you'd be mean, or else really nerdy.

Oh, thanks.

I wish Shasta'd get chiggers and go home. You have, like, the *worst* luck in bunkmates.

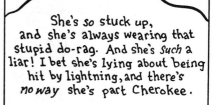

She's *so* stuck up, and she's always wearing that stupid do-rag. And she's *such* a liar! I bet she's lying about being hit by lightning, and there's *no way* she's part Cherokee.

?

Lay *off*, Beth! I'm just trying to be *nice* to her.

Okay, calm down! It's not like I'm talking about *you!*

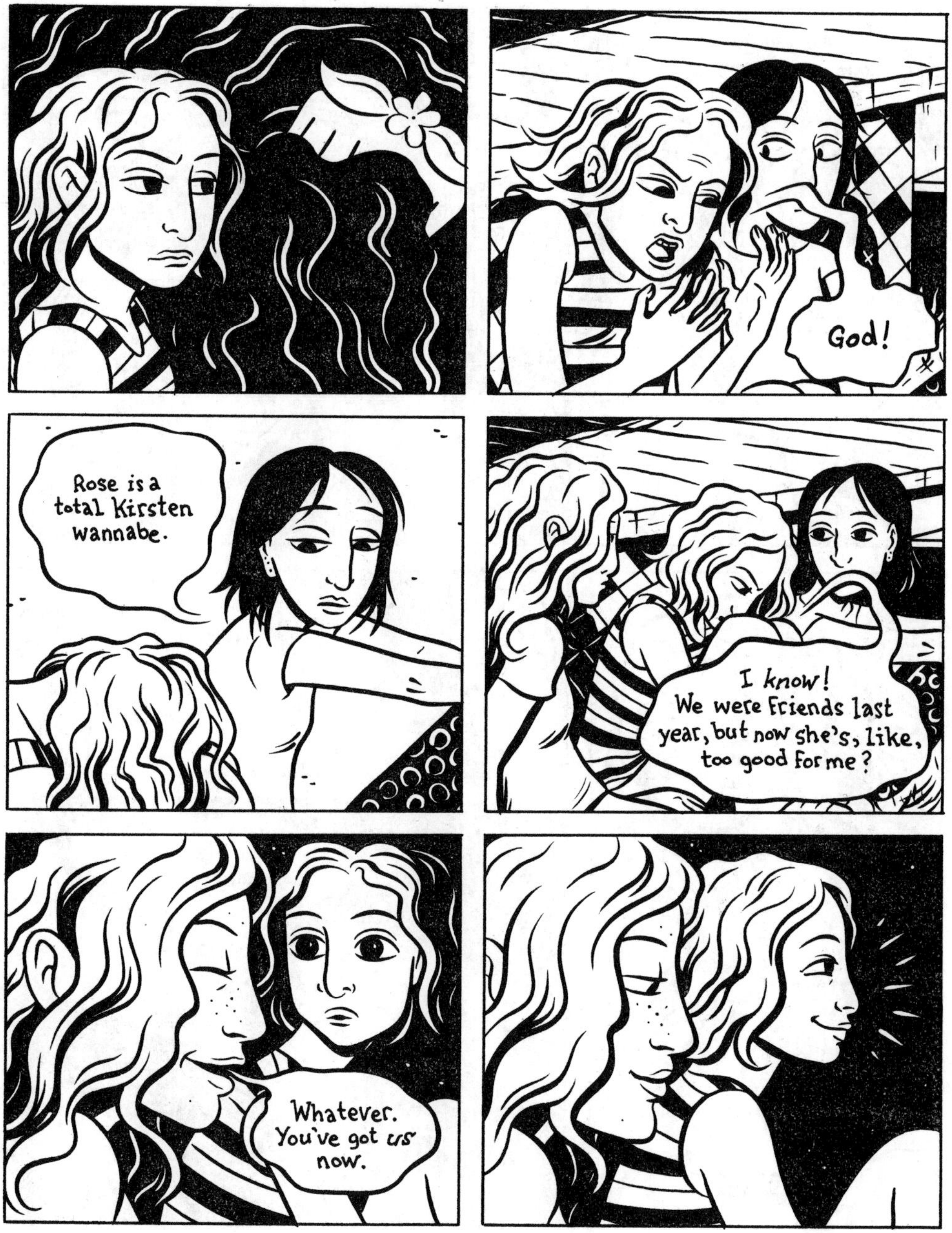
God!
Rose is a total Kirsten wannabe.
I know! We were friends last year, but now she's, like, too good for me?
Whatever. You've got us now.

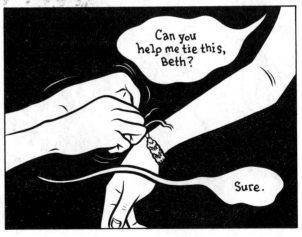

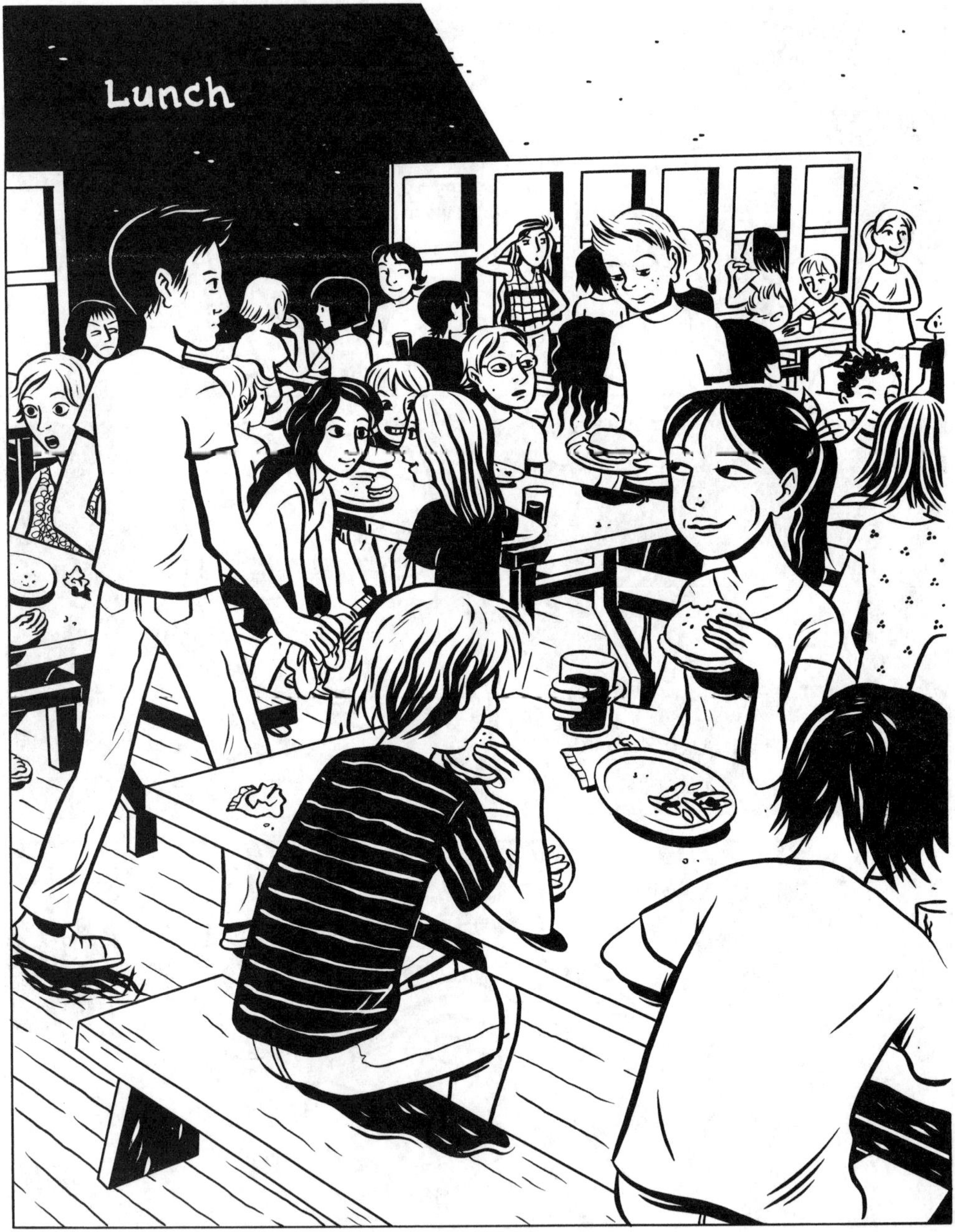
Lunch

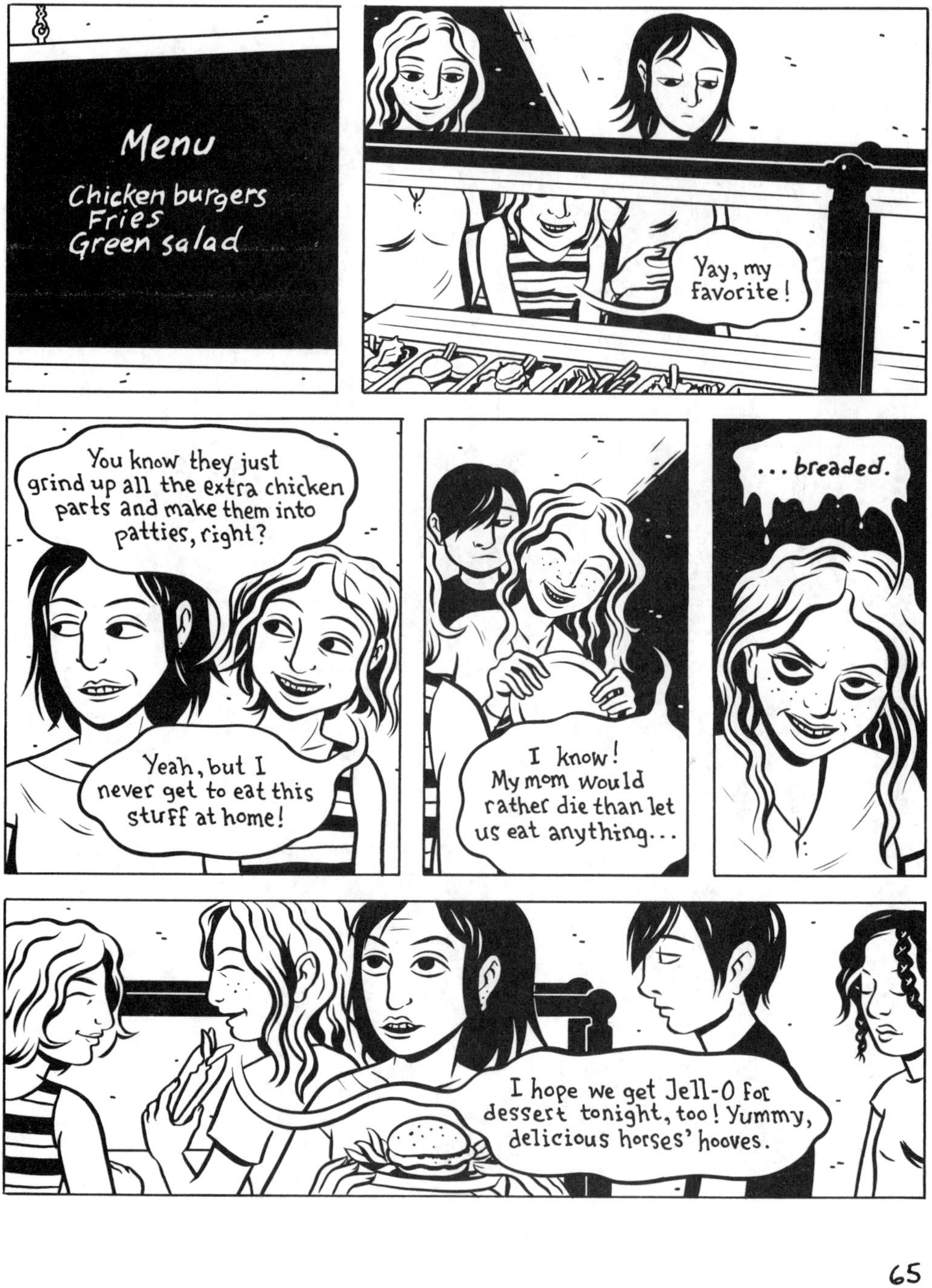
Menu
Chicken burgers
Fries
Green salad
Yay, my favorite!
You know they just grind up all the extra chicken parts and make them into patties, right?
Yeah, but I never get to eat this stuff at home!
I know! My mom would rather die than let us eat anything...
...breaded.
I hope we get Jell-O for dessert tonight, too! Yummy, delicious horses' hooves.

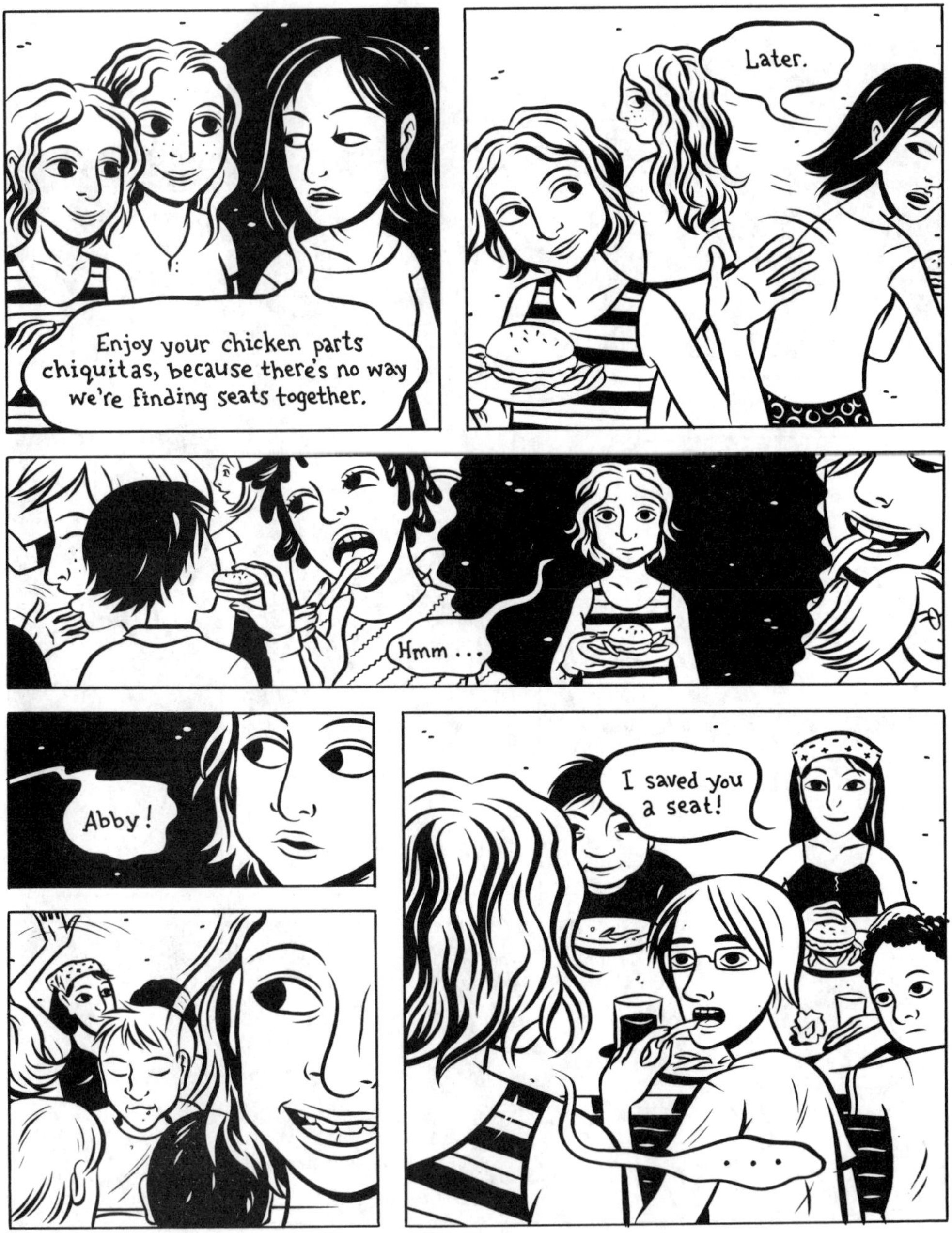
Enjoy your chicken parts chiquitas, because there's no way we're finding seats together.
Later.
Hmm . . .
Abby!
I saved you a seat!
. . .

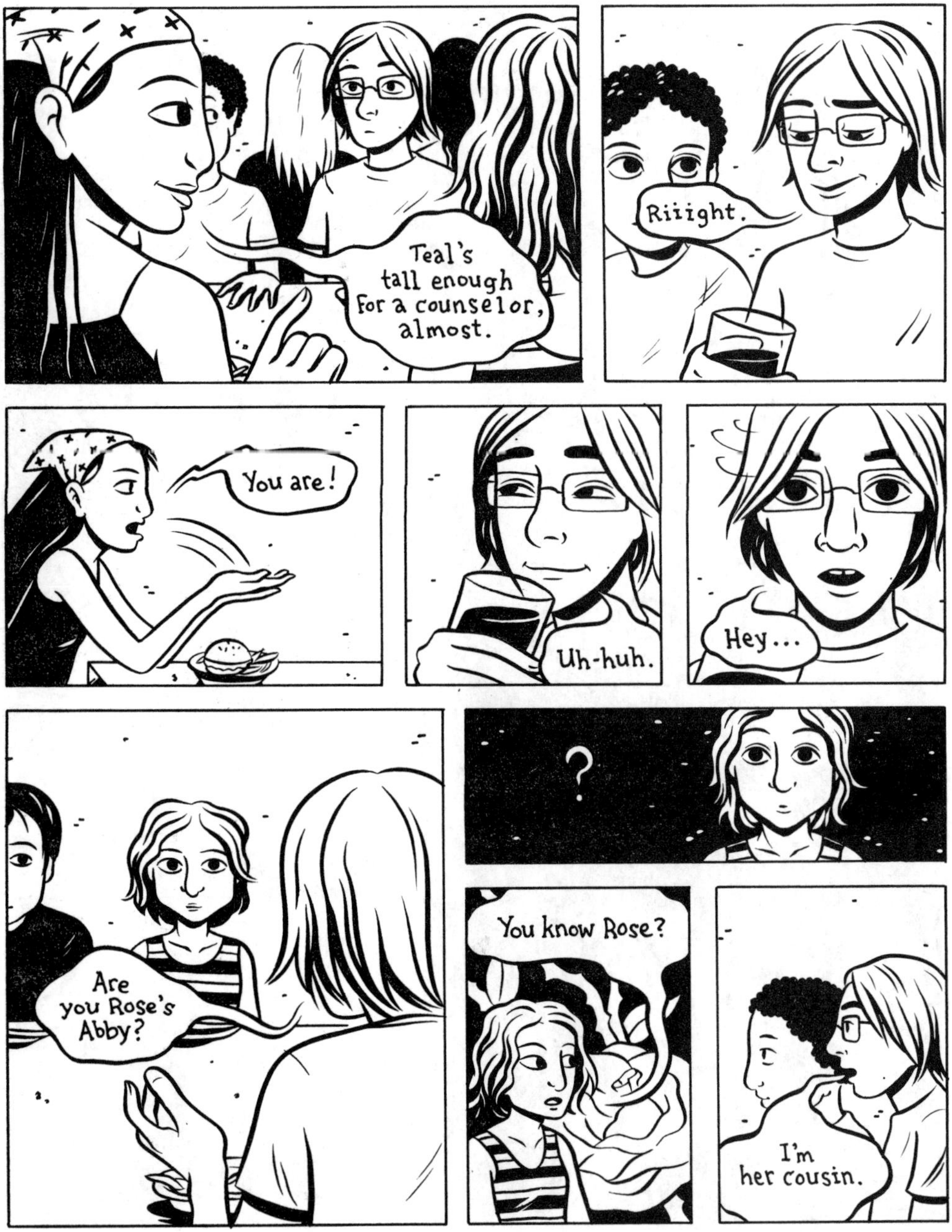
Teal's tall enough for a counselor, almost.
Riiight.
You are!
Uh-huh.
Hey...
?
Are you Rose's Abby?
You know Rose?
I'm her cousin.

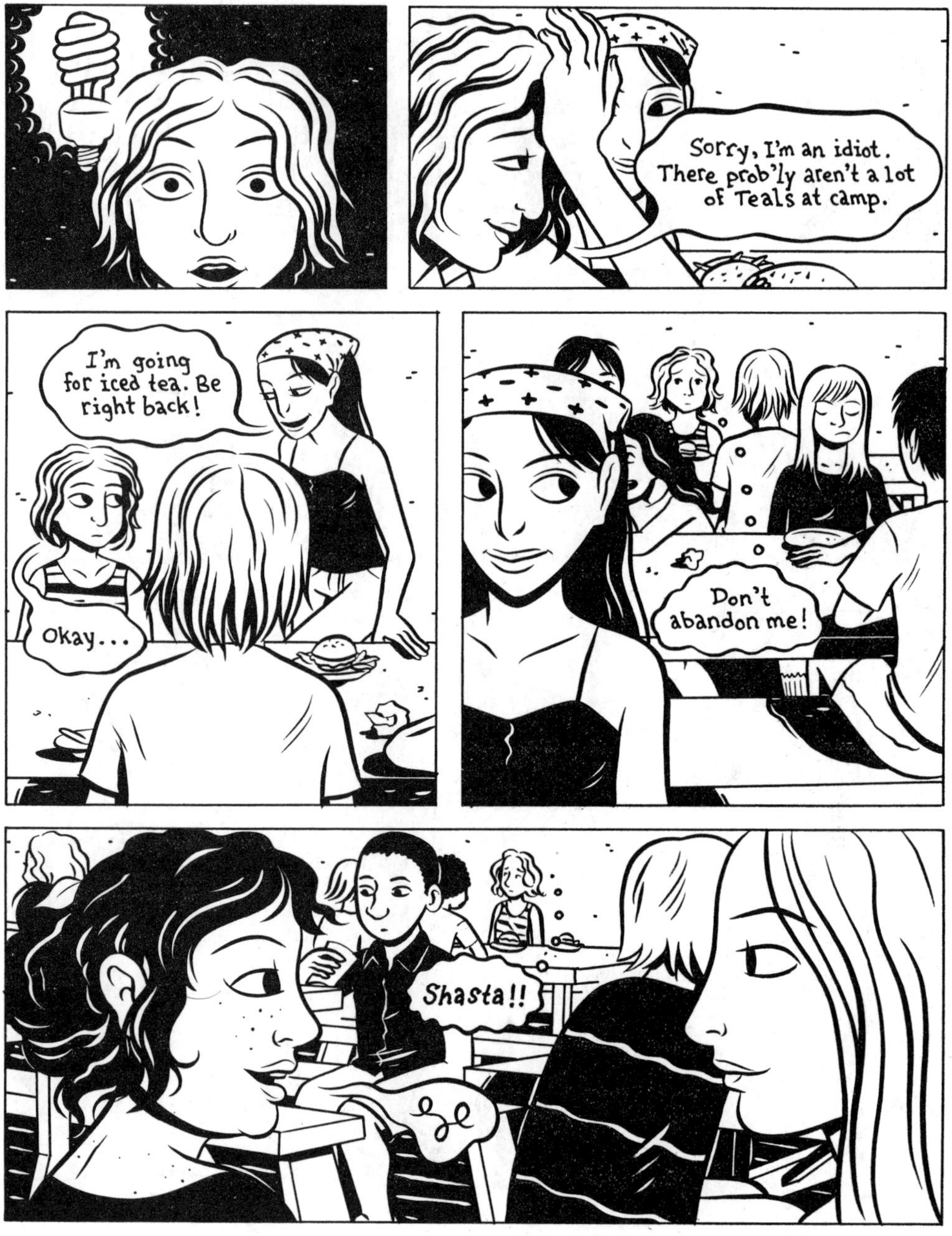
Sorry, I'm an idiot. There prob'ly aren't a lot of Teals at camp.
I'm going for iced tea. Be right back!
Okay...
Don't abandon me!
Shasta!!

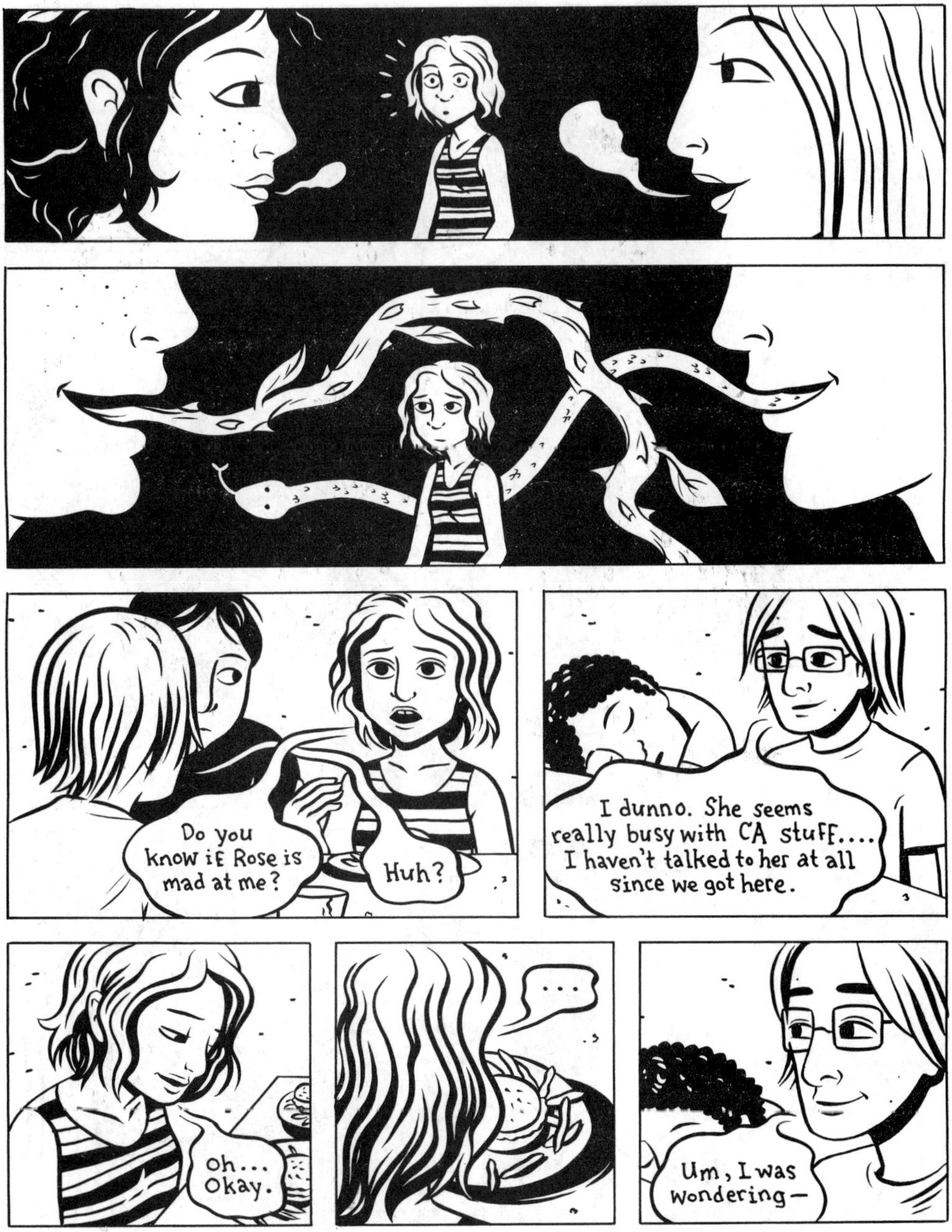
Do you know if Rose is mad at me?
Huh?
I dunno. She seems really busy with CA stuff.... I haven't talked to her at all since we got here.
Oh... Okay.
...
Um, I was wondering—

75

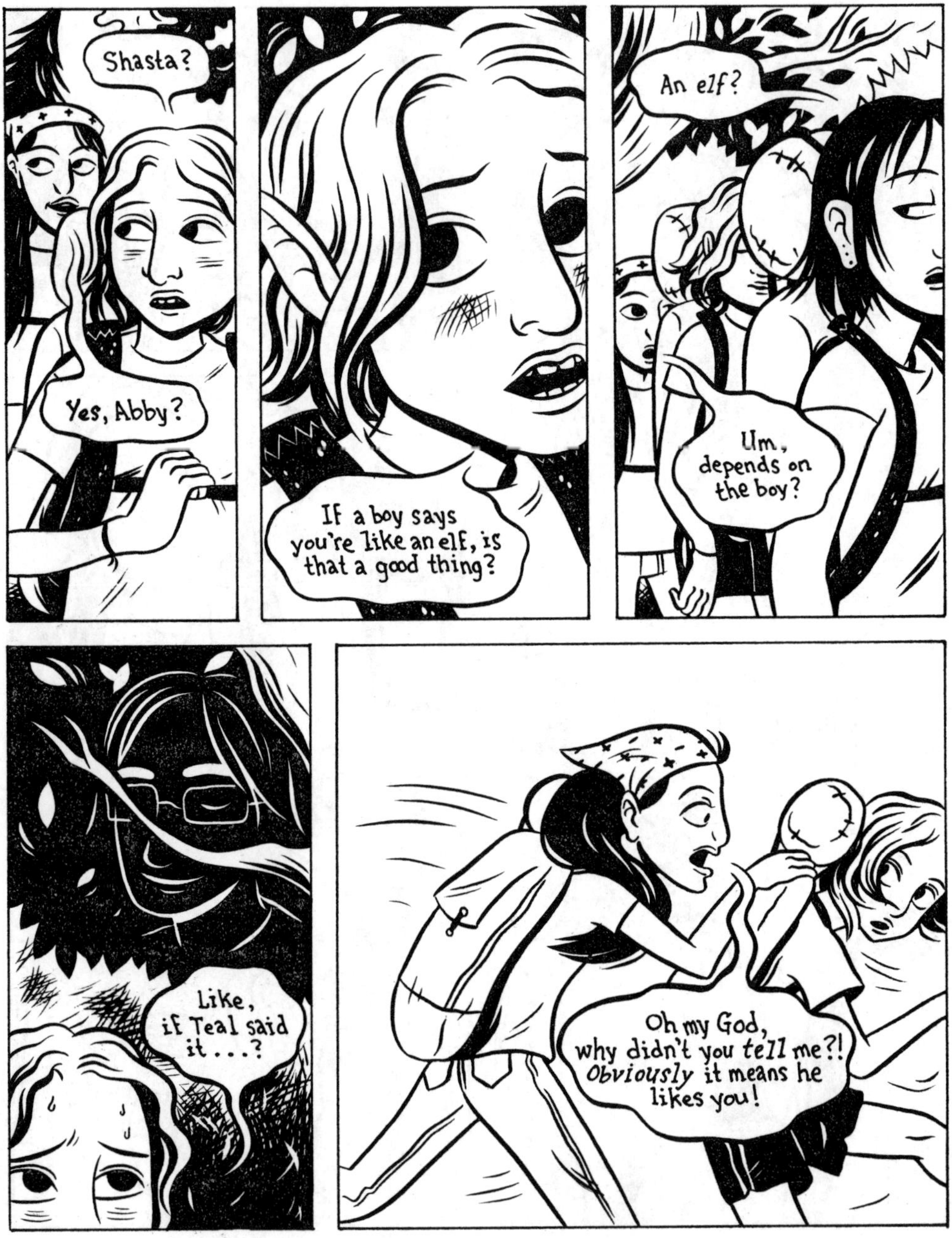
Shasta?
Yes, Abby?
If a boy says you're like an elf, is that a good thing?
An elf?
Um, depends on the boy?
Like, if Teal said it . . .?
Oh my God, why didn't you *tell* me?! *Obviously* it means he likes you!

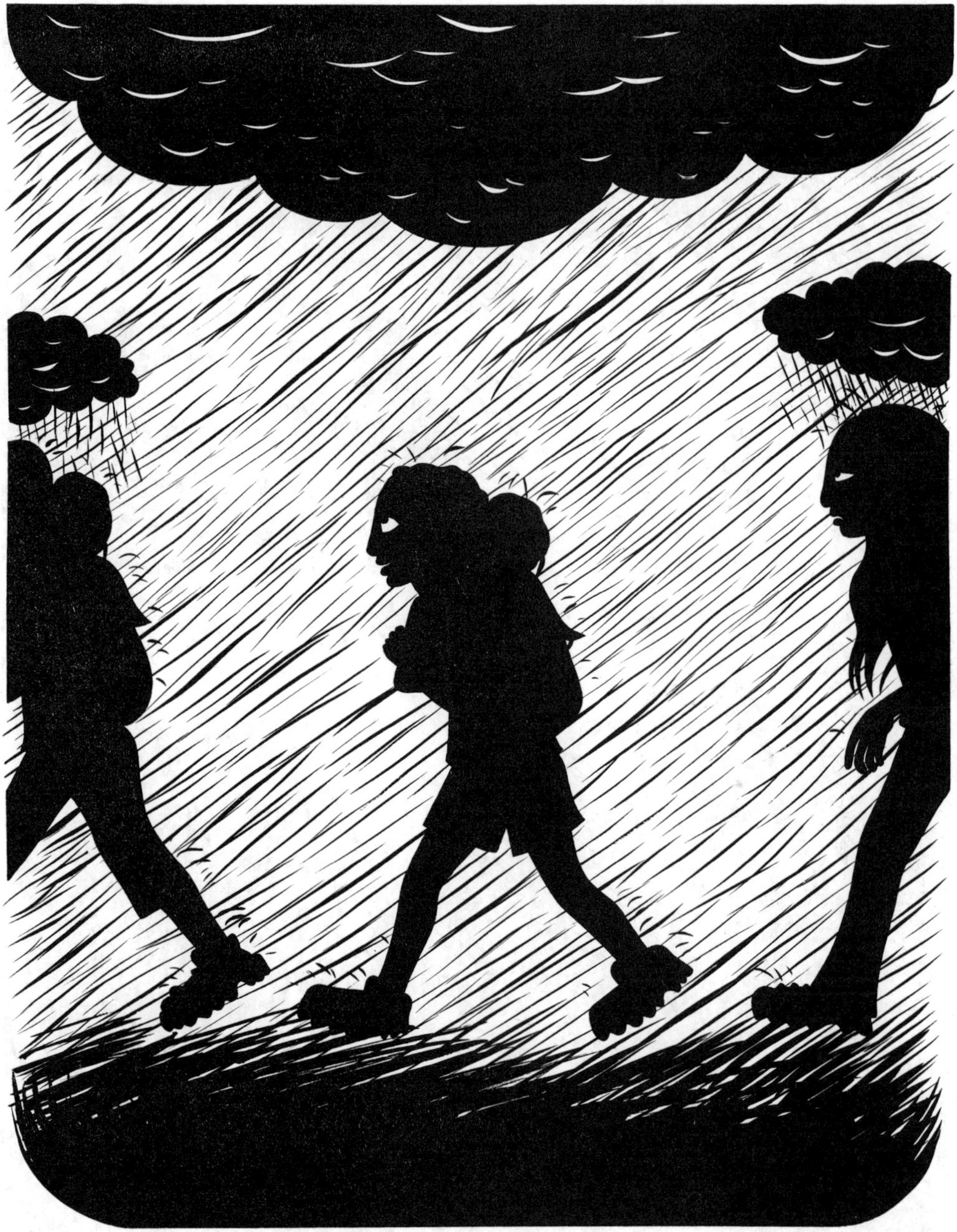

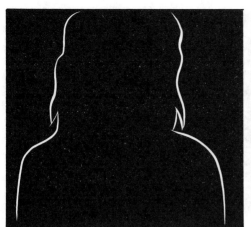

In olden times, during the Civil War, there was a boy named Timothy Blake, who was a scout for the Union. One night he was in the mountains—not far from here—spying on a Confederate regiment, when he was caught and taken prisoner.

When morning came, they blindfolded him and dragged him out into the meadow and tied him to a tree. And then—

BANG!

They shot off his head with a cannon.

Do you know that after they guillotined people in the French Revolution, the heads in the baskets would talk to each other?

Shut up, Zoë!

His head went flying off and fell in the bushes, and they couldn't find it.

giggle

snicker

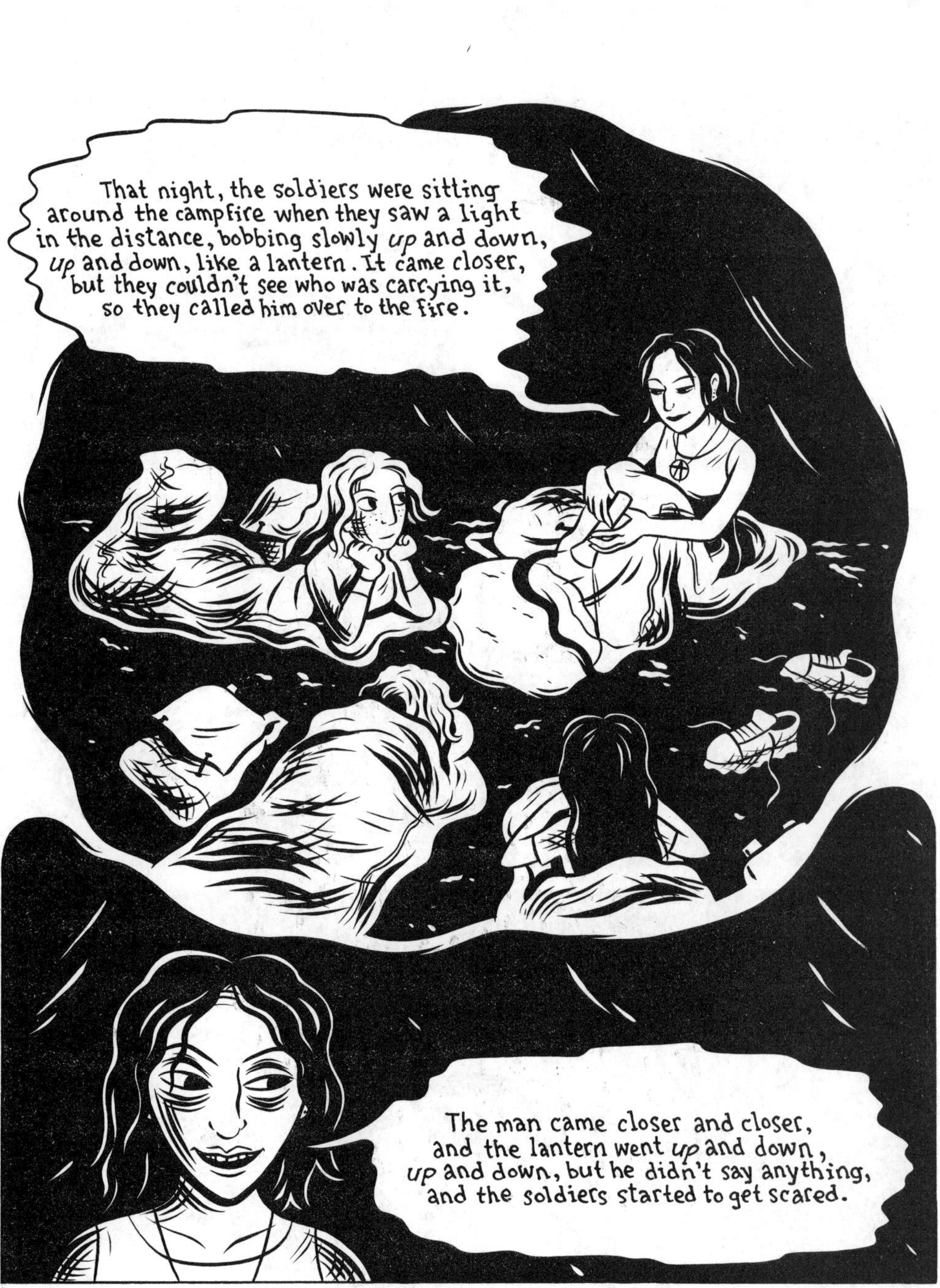
That night, the soldiers were sitting around the campfire when they saw a light in the distance, bobbing slowly *up* and down, *up* and down, like a lantern. It came closer, but they couldn't see who was carrying it, so they called him over to the fire.
The man came closer and closer, and the lantern went *up* and down, *up* and down, but he didn't say anything, and the soldiers started to get scared.

85

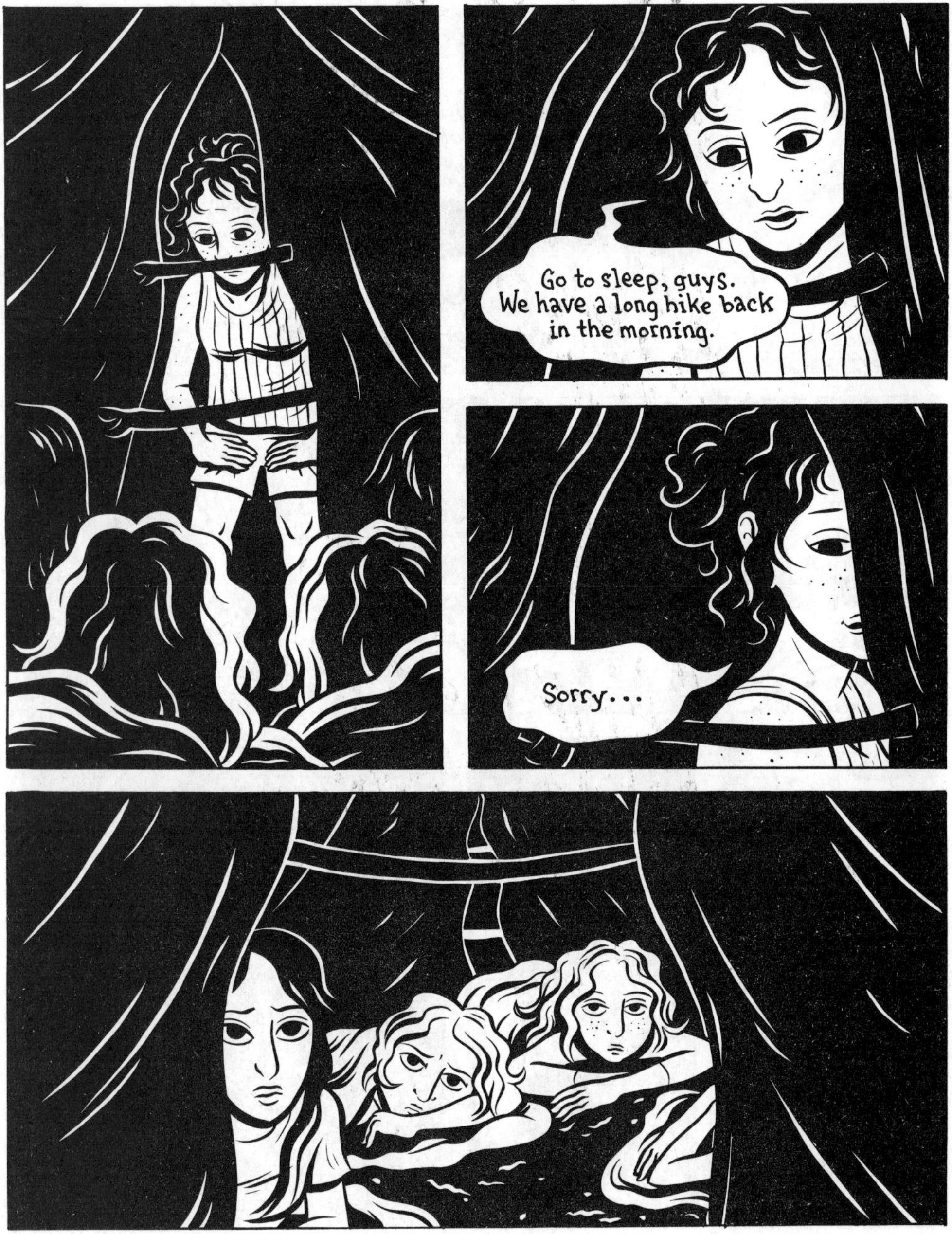
Go to sleep, guys. We have a long hike back in the morning.
Sorry...

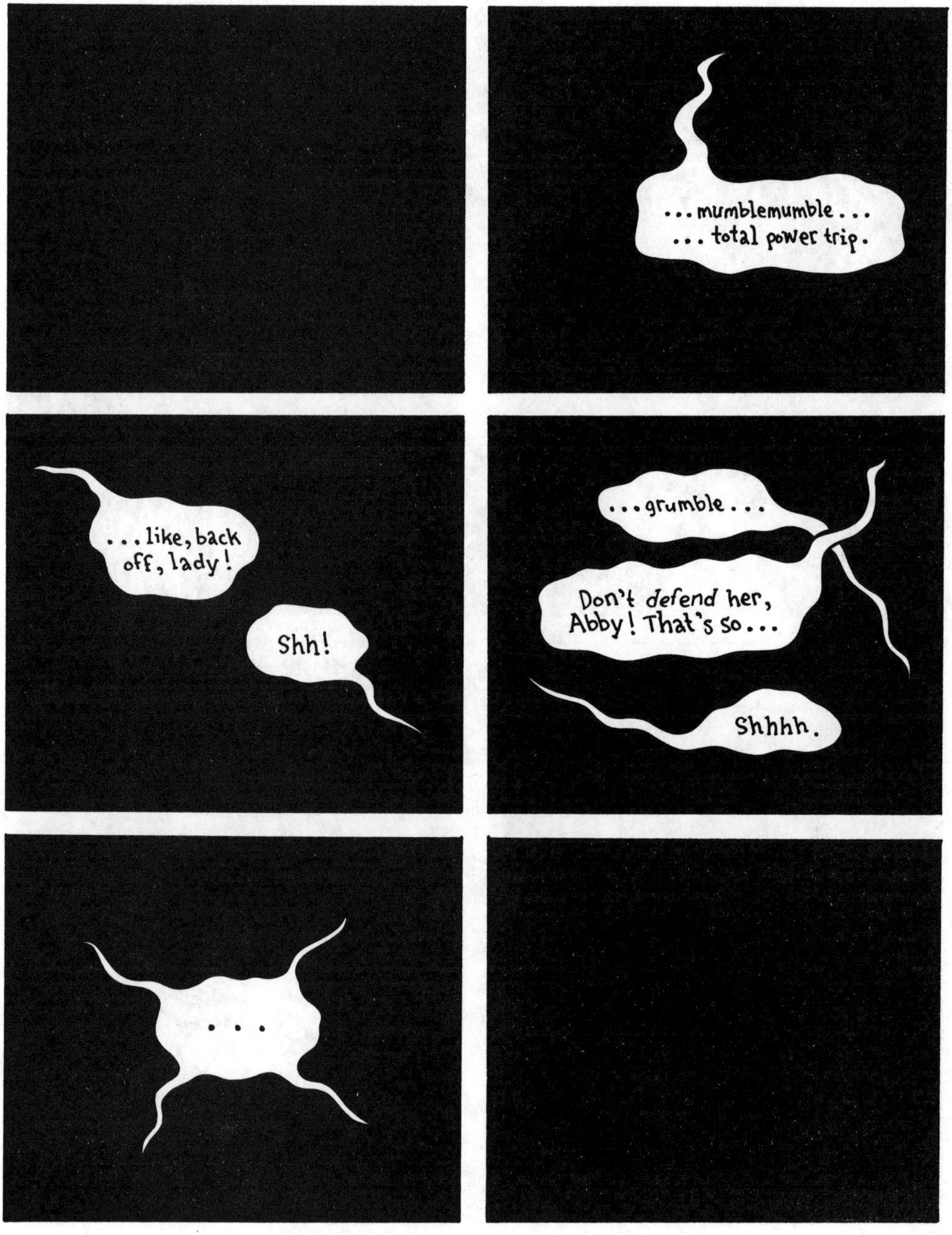
...mumblemumble...
...total power trip.
...like, back off, lady!
Shh!
...grumble...
Don't defend her, Abby! That's so...
Shhhh.
...

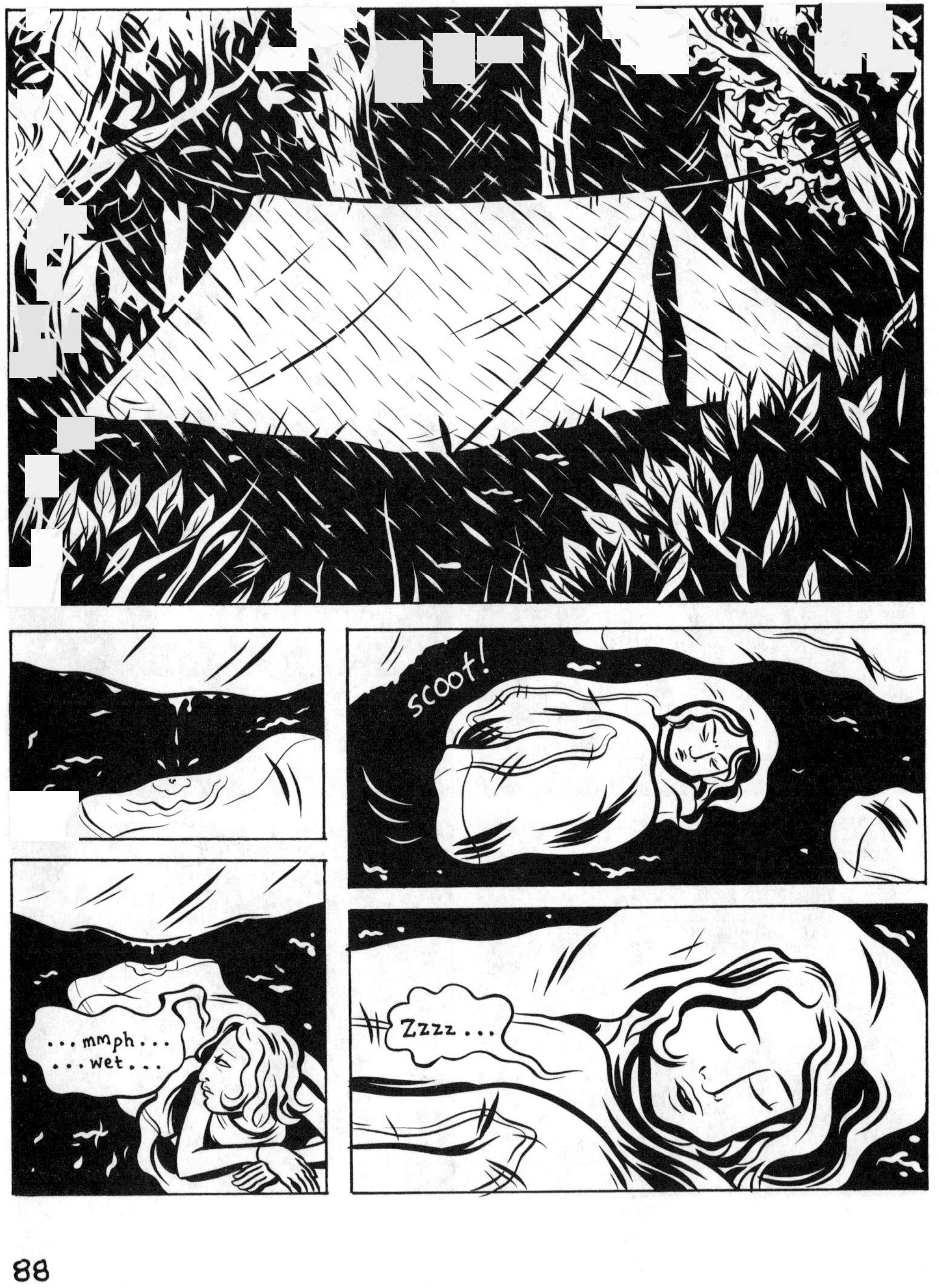
scoot!
...mmph...
...wet...
Zzzz...

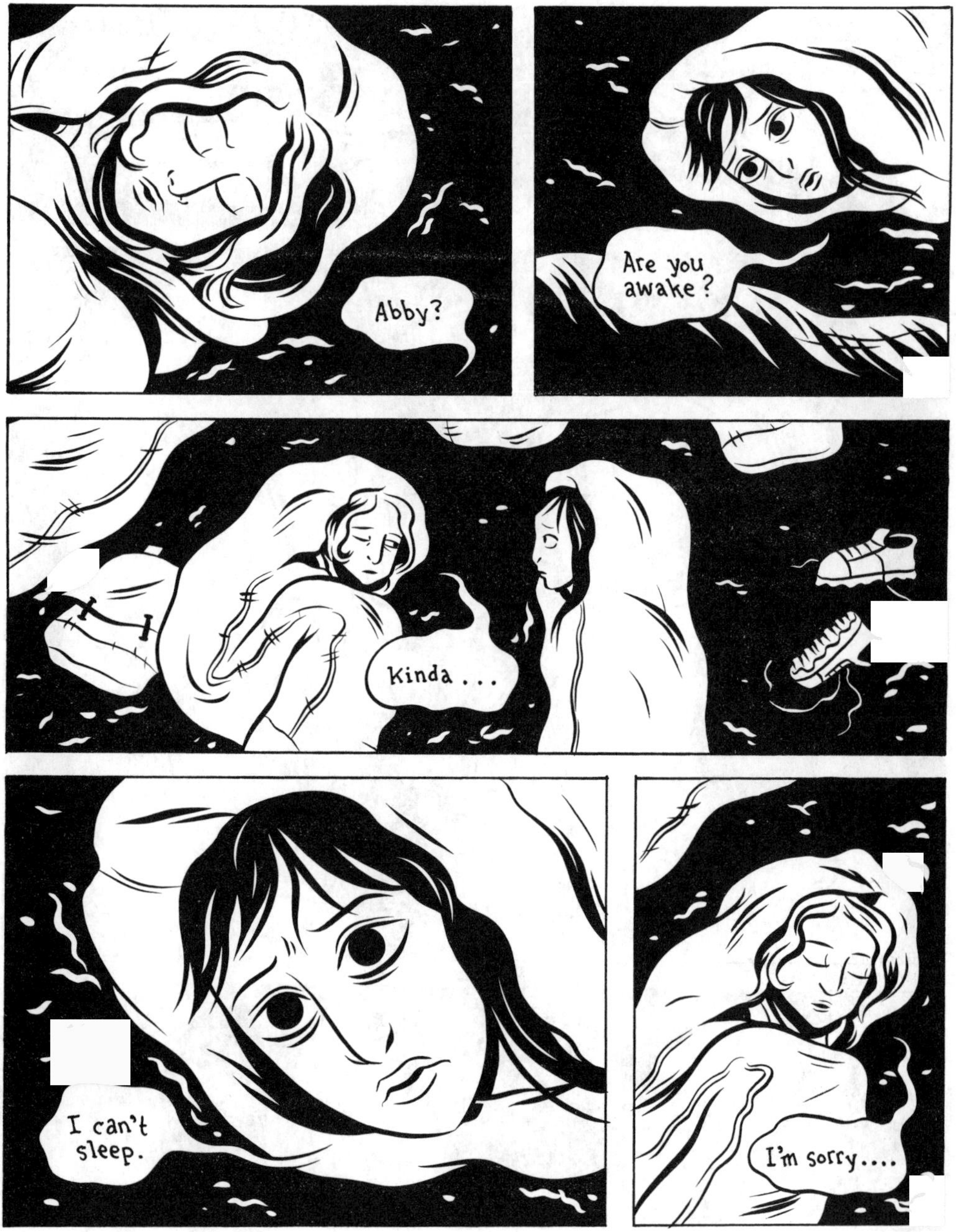
Abby?
Are you awake?
Kinda . . . .
I can't sleep.
I'm sorry....

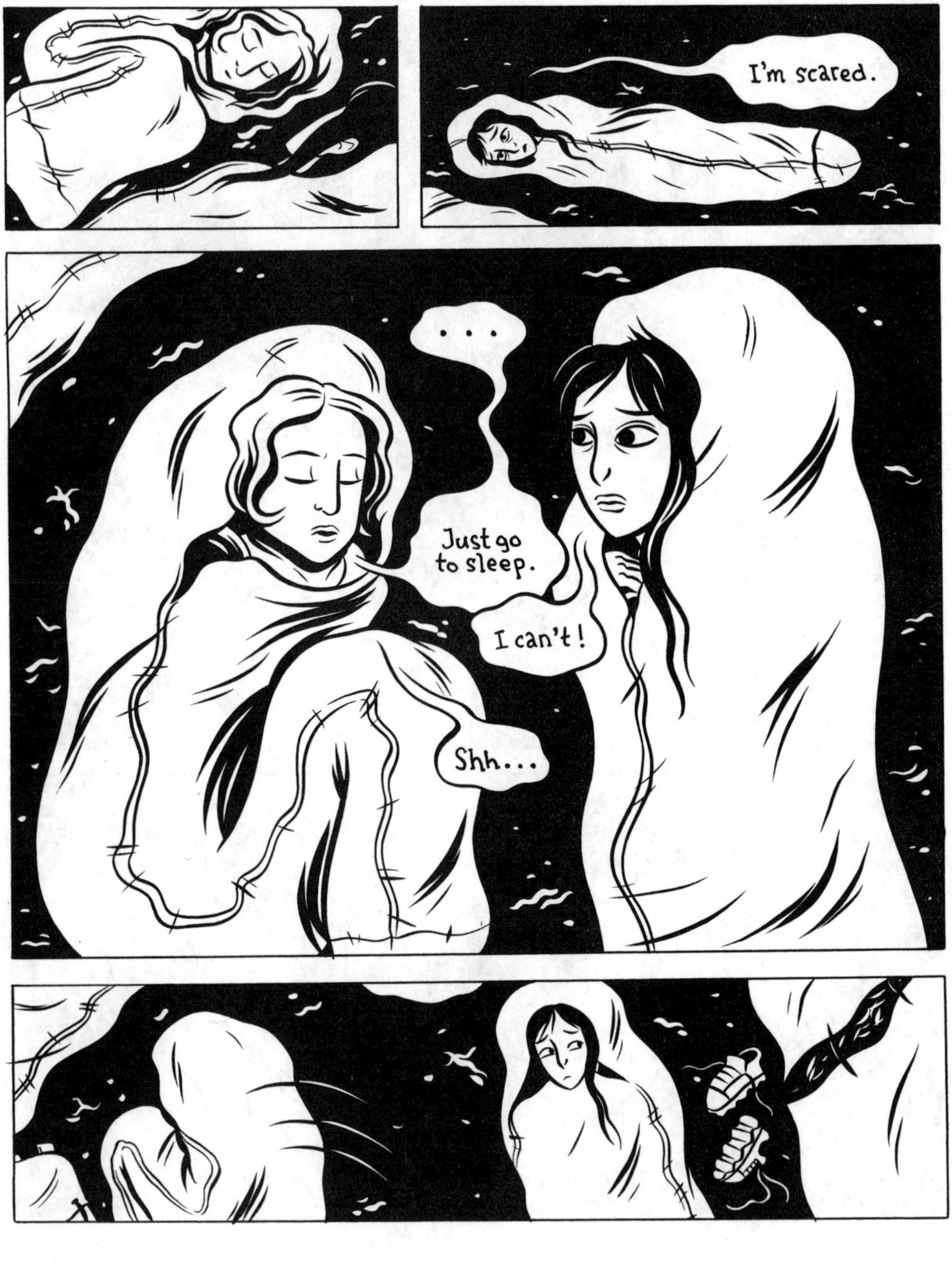
I'm scared.
. . .
Just go to sleep.
I can't!
Shh...

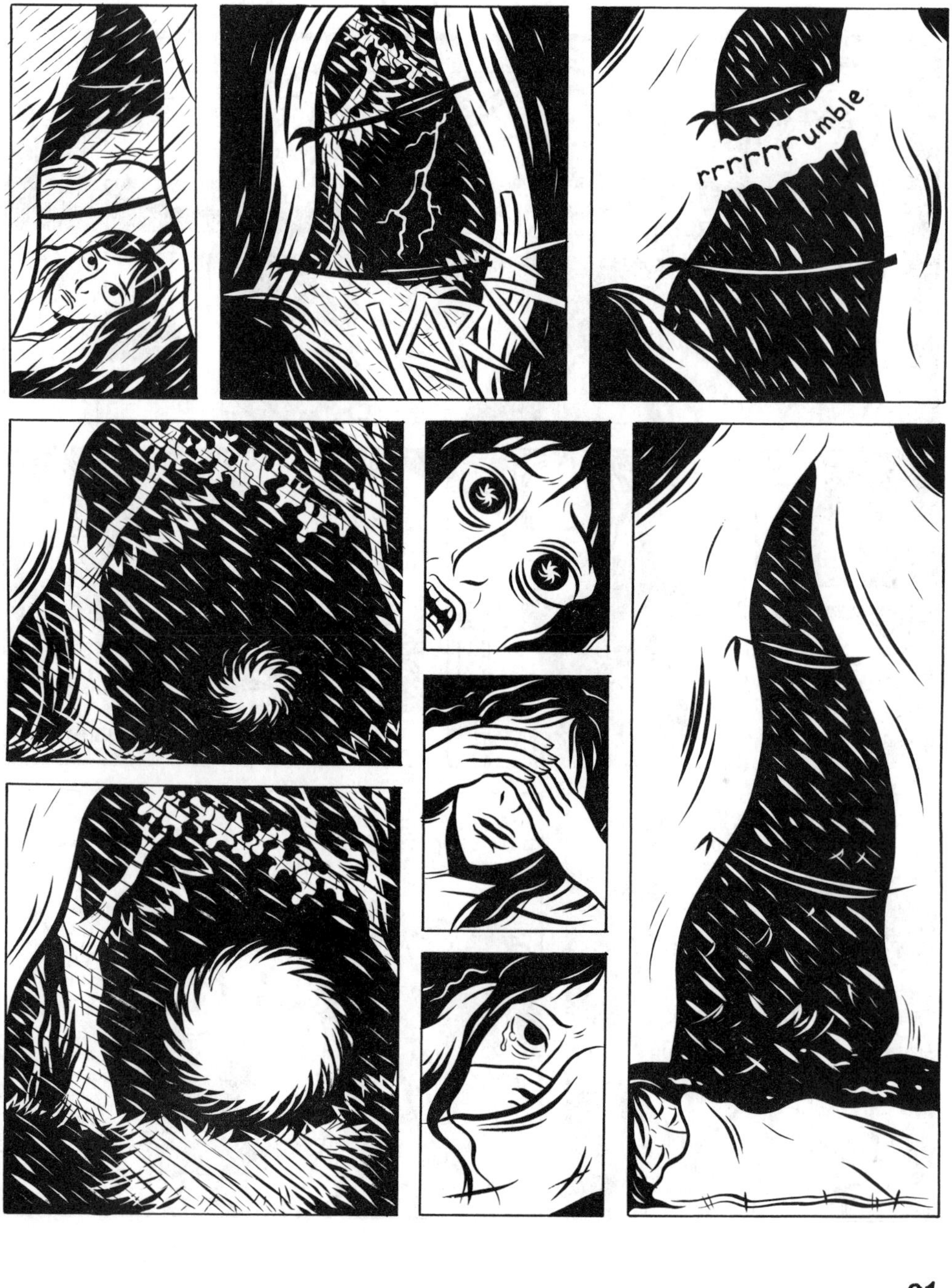
rrrrrrumble

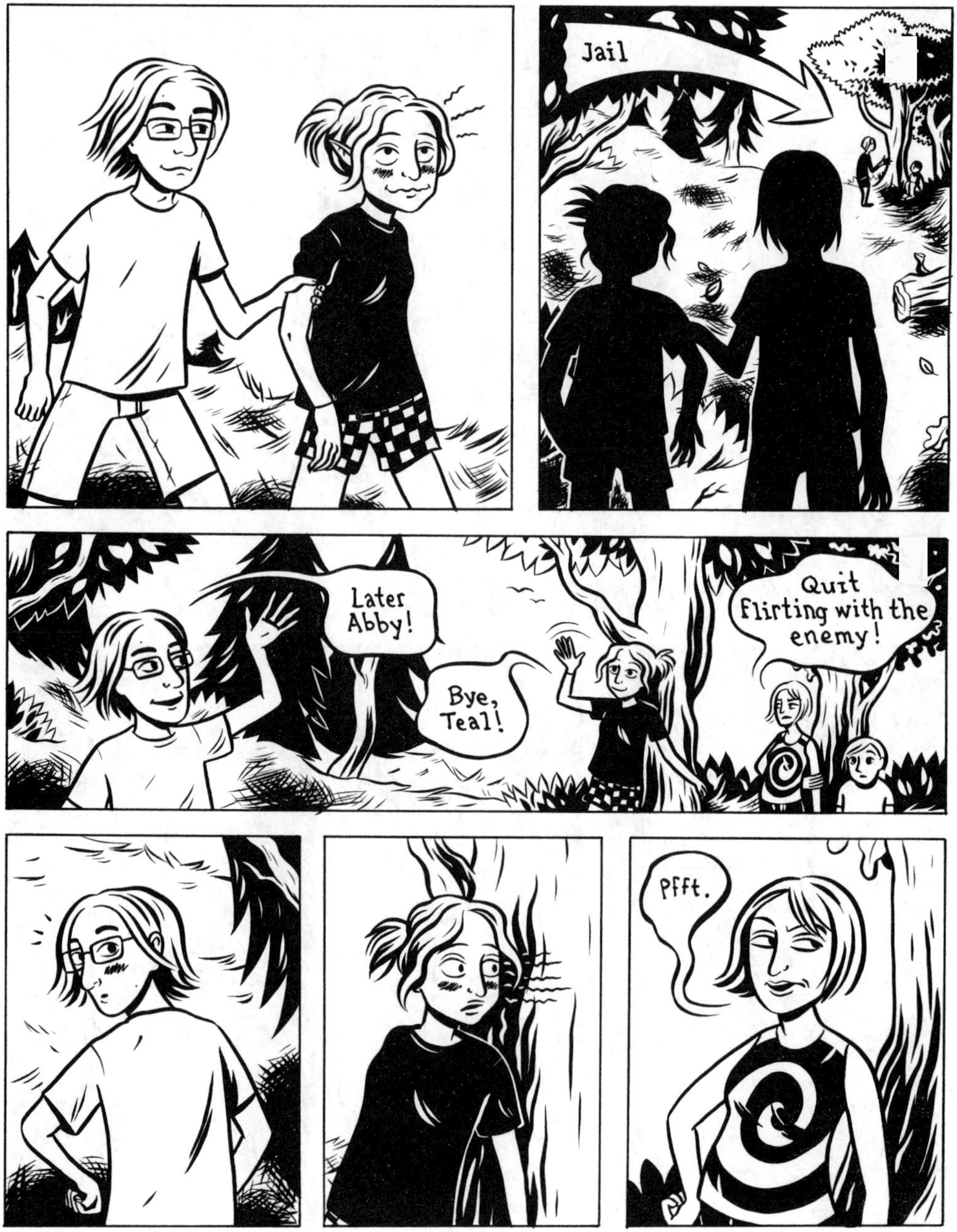
Jail
Later Abby!
Bye, Teal!
Quit flirting with the enemy!
Pfft.

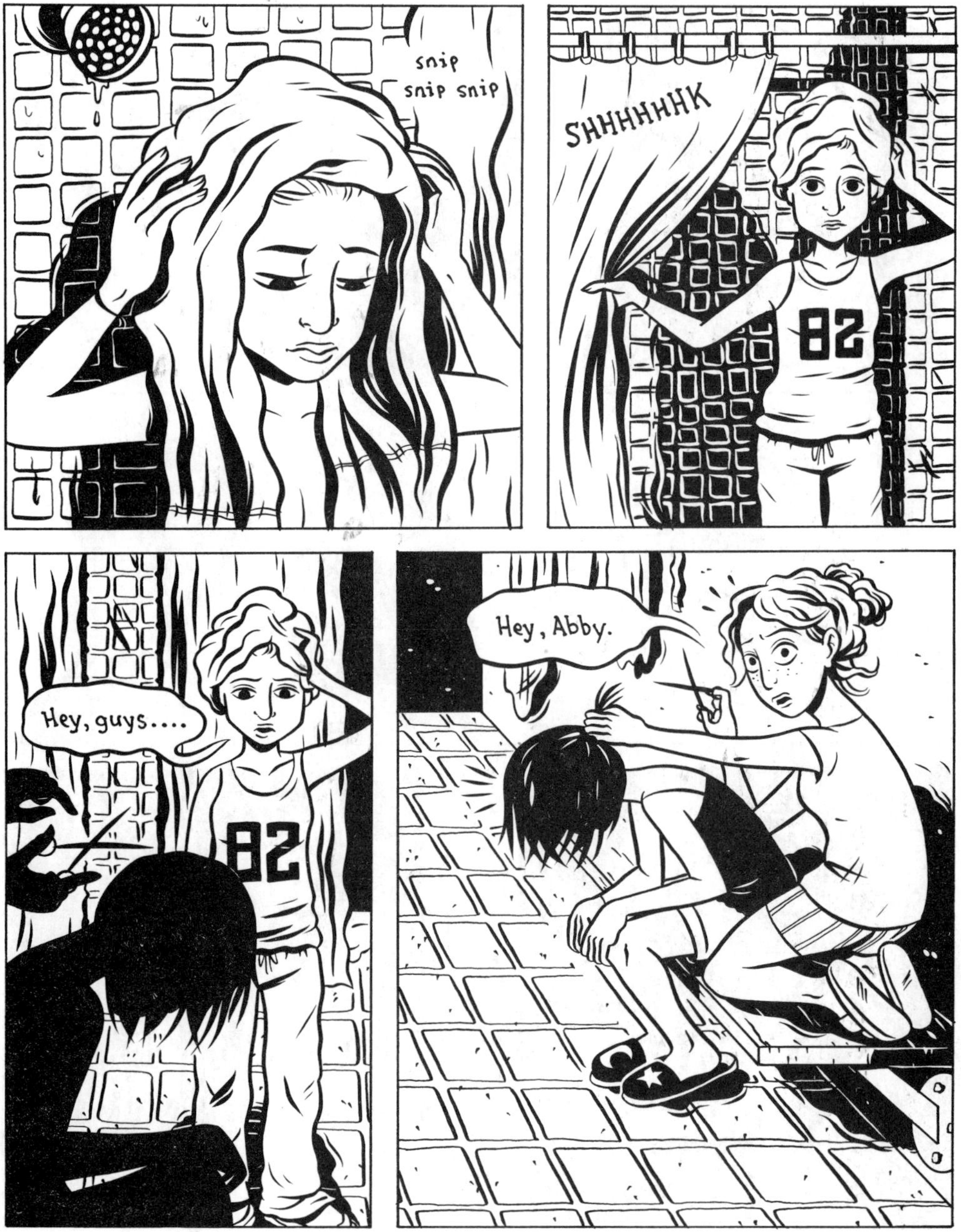
snip
snip snip
SHHHHHHK
Hey, guys....
Hey, Abby.

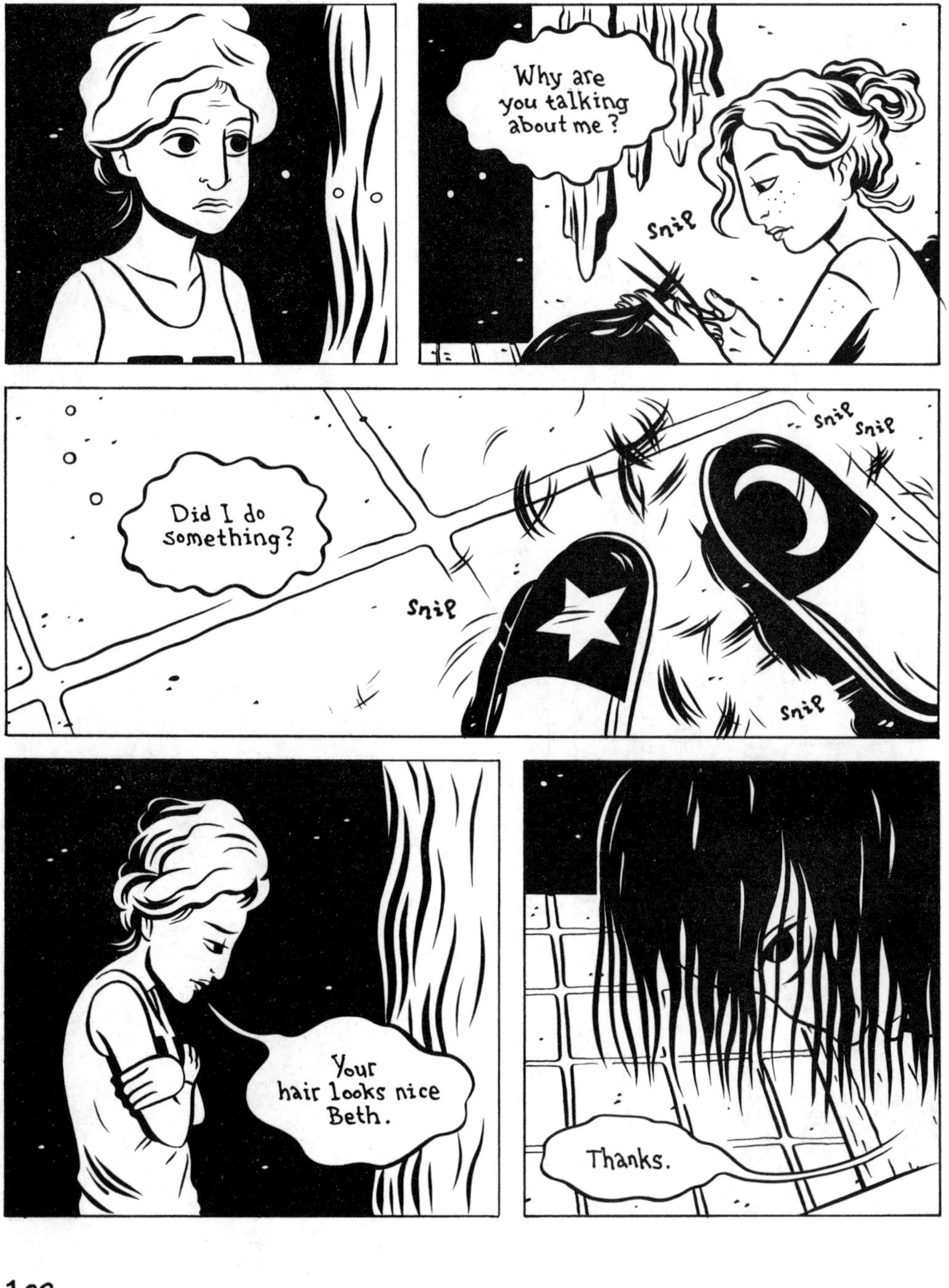
Why are you talking about me?
Snip
Did I do something?
Snip
Snip
Snip
Snip
Your hair looks nice Beth.
Thanks.

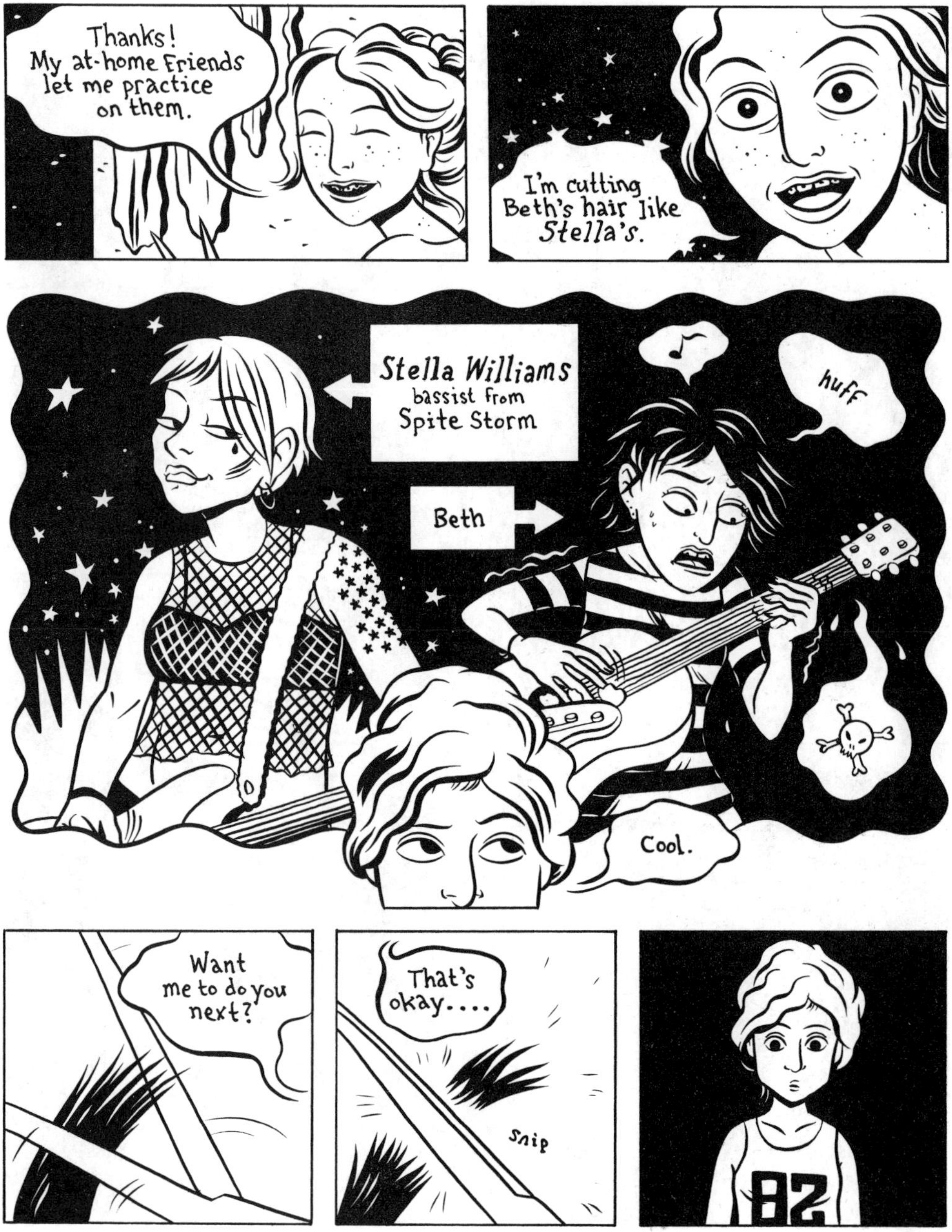
Thanks! My at-home Friends let me practice on them.
I'm cutting Beth's hair like Stella's.
Stella Williams bassist from Spite Storm
huff
Beth
Cool.
Want me to do you next?
That's okay....
snip
82

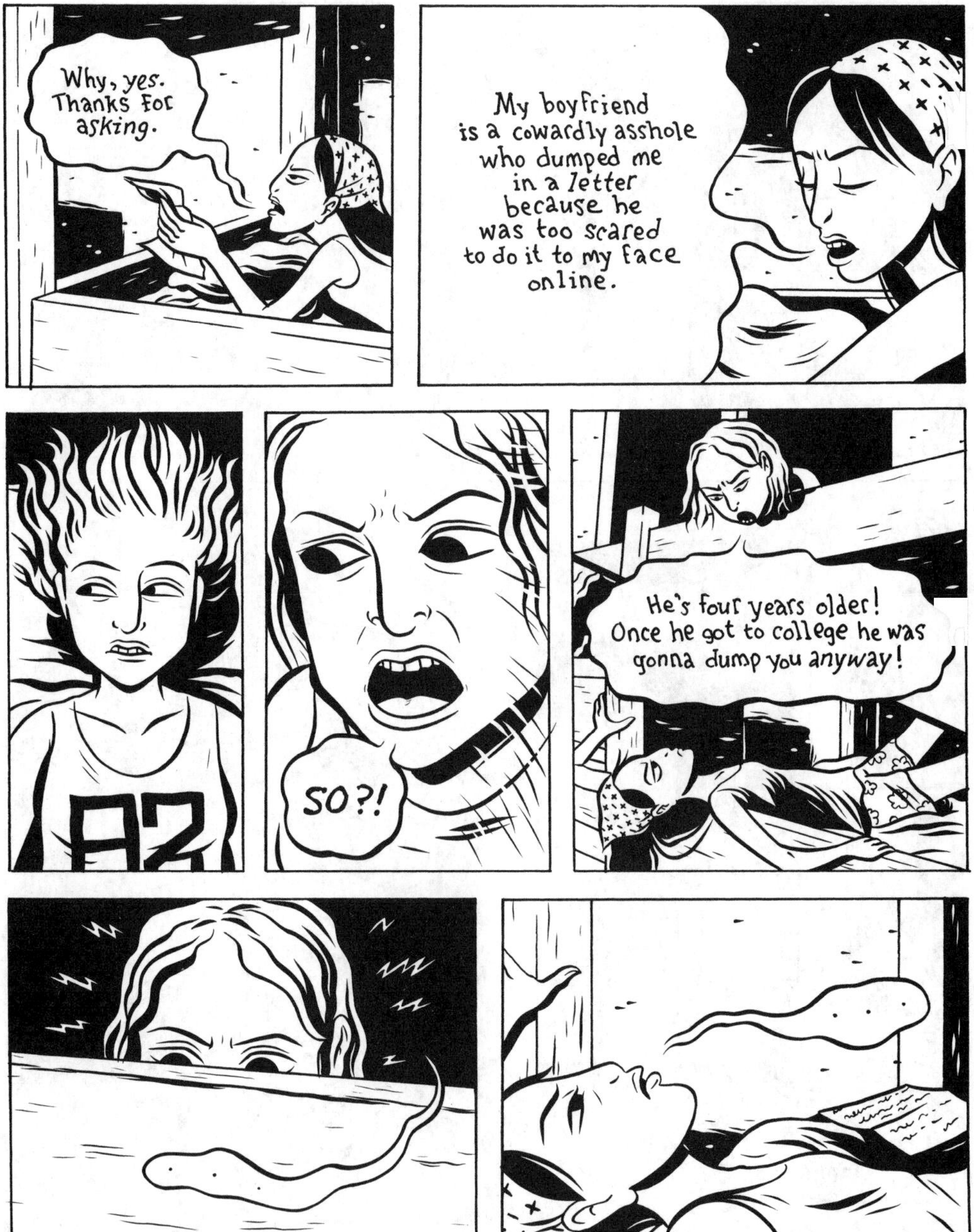
Why, yes. Thanks for asking.
My boyfriend is a cowardly asshole who dumped me in a letter because he was too scared to do it to my face online.
SO?!
He's four years older! Once he got to college he was gonna dump you anyway!

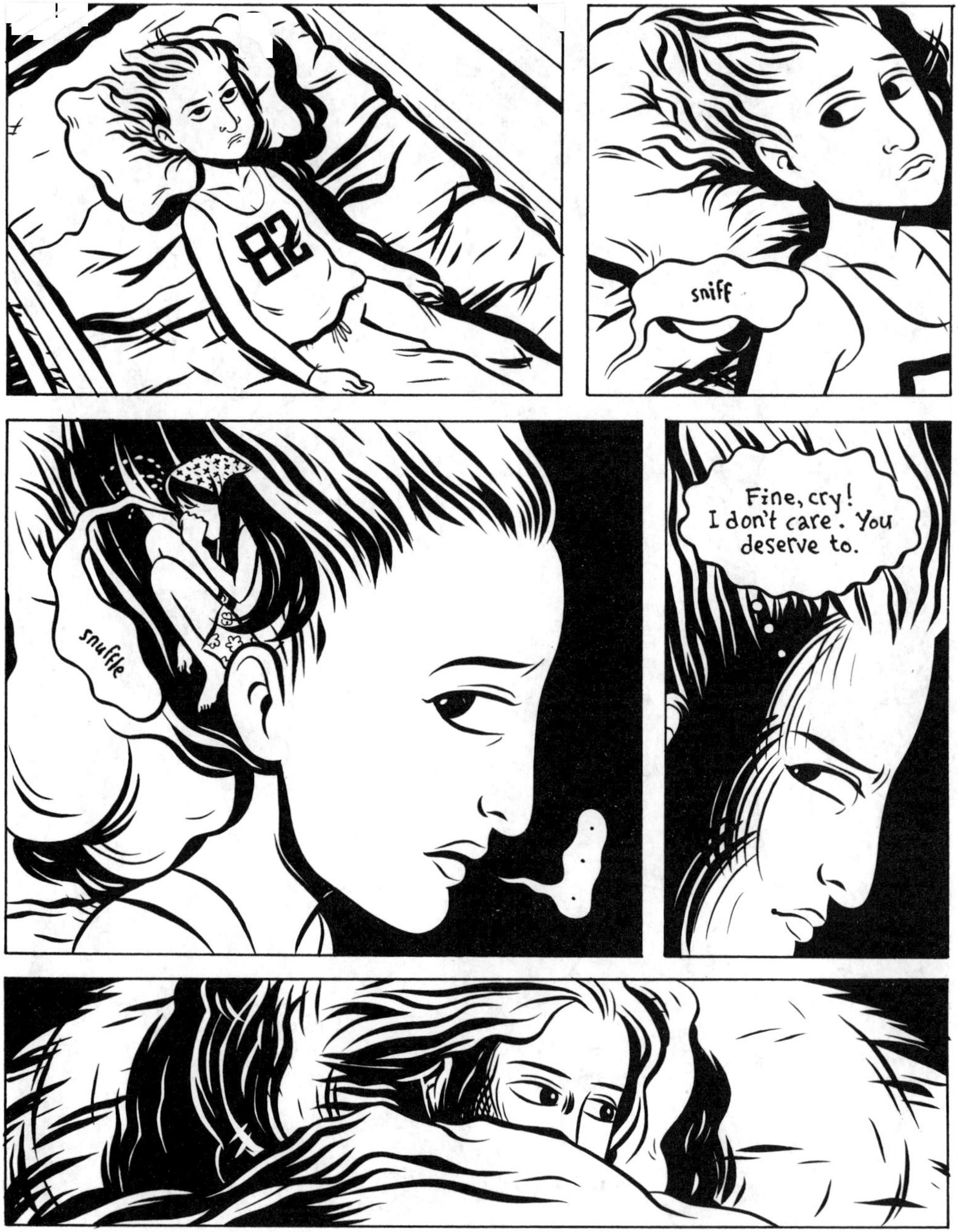
sniff
snuffle
Fine, cry! I don't care. You deserve to.

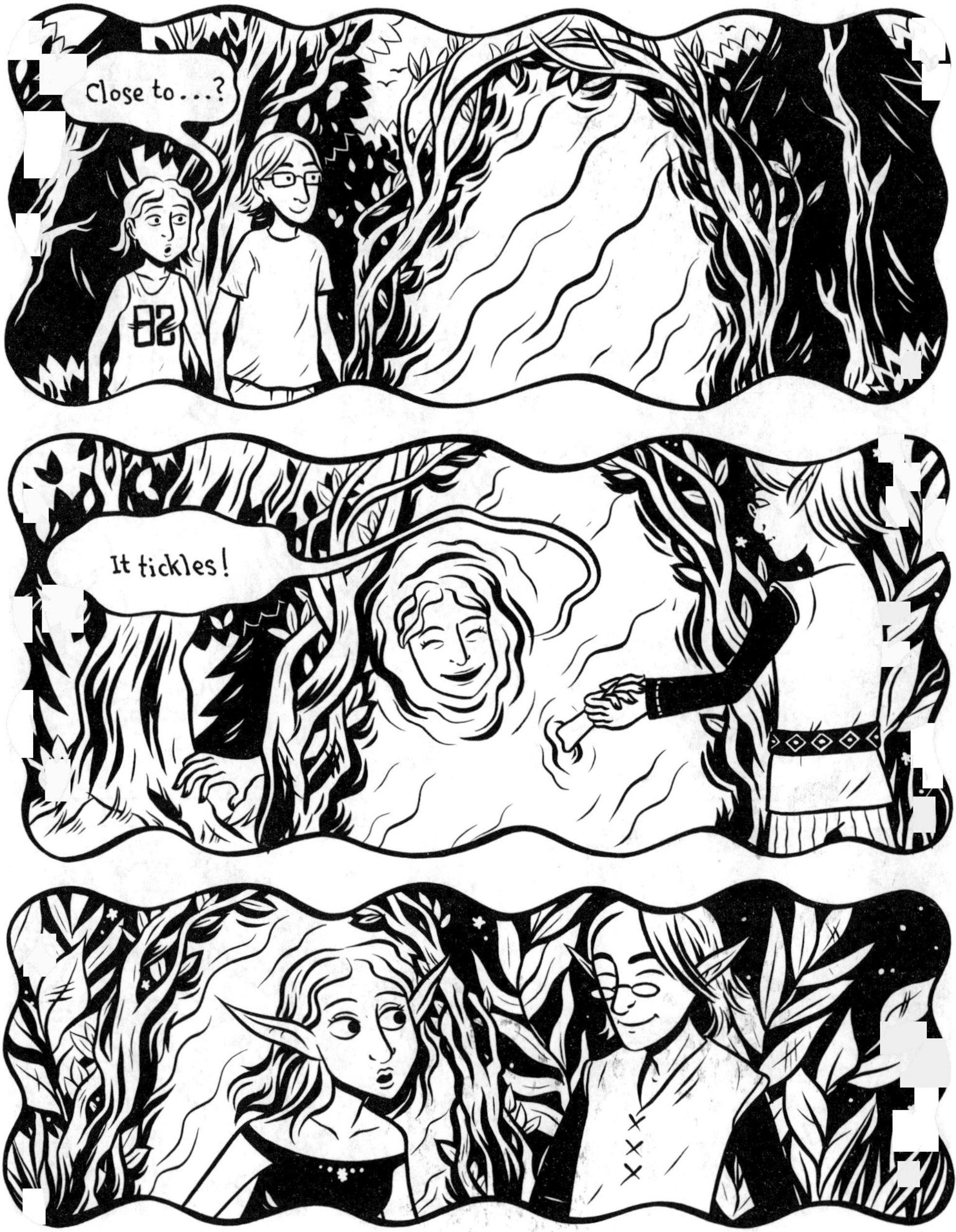
Close to . . . ?
It tickles!

It went under the bed!
I told you! It's after me.
I-

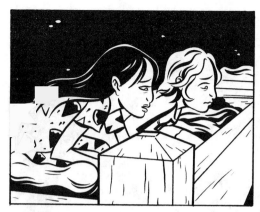

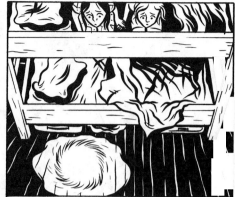

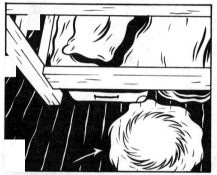

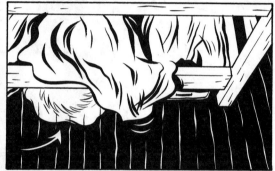

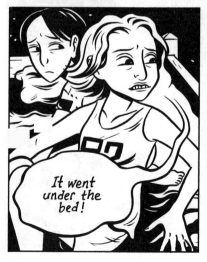

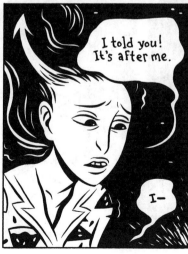

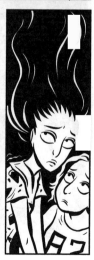

Are you sure you don't want to come in? I have an extra swimsuit.
Nah...
Oh, right... You can't do *anything*.
Don't be like that. It's not my fault!
You came on the hike, though! This is easier than hiking.
...
I'm still not supposed to.
Shasta, *stop*.
Just admit you don't want to.

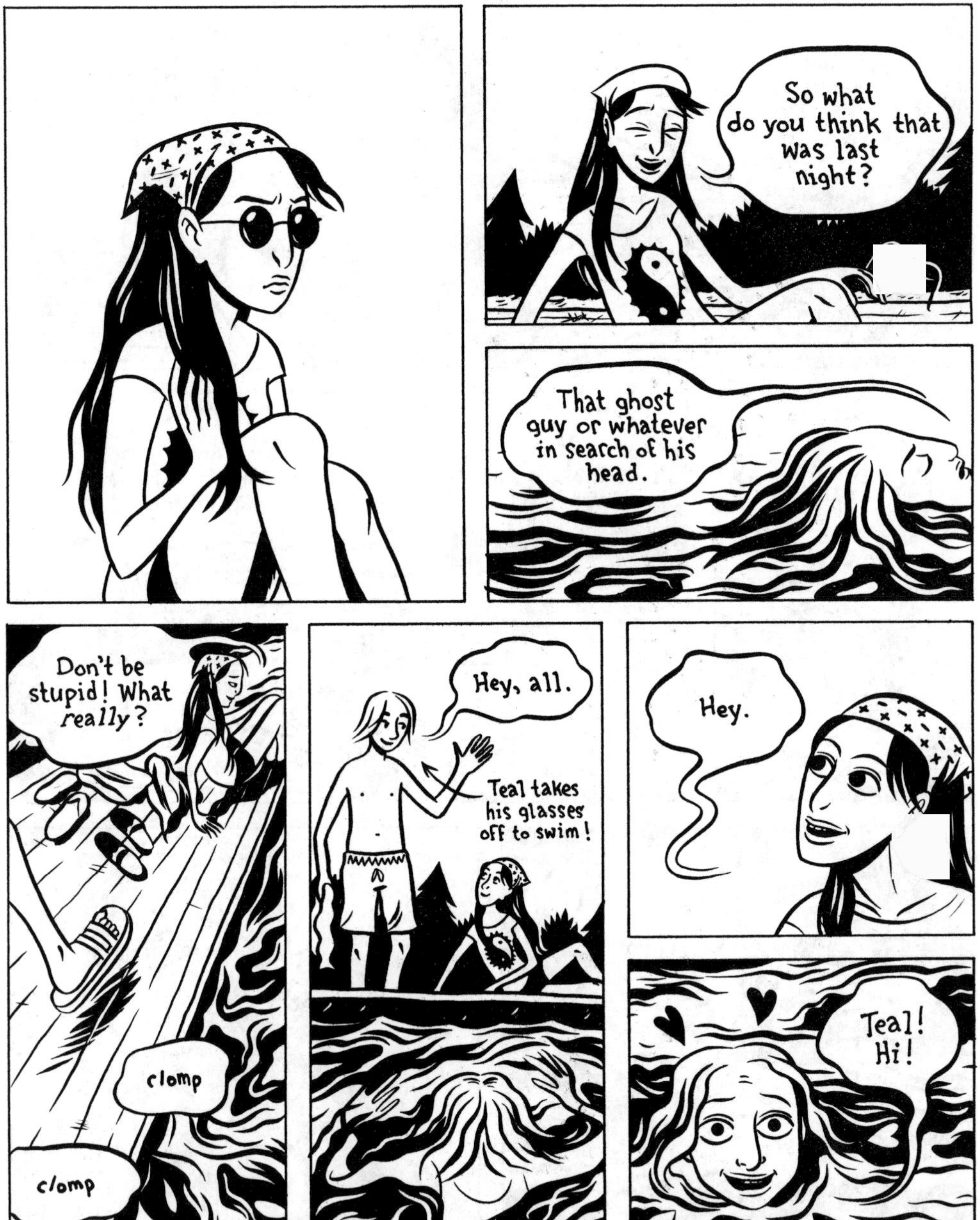
So what do you think that was last night?
That ghost guy or whatever in search of his head.
Don't be stupid! What *really*?
clomp
clomp
Hey, all.
Teal takes his glasses off to swim!
Hey.
Teal! Hi!

*DM: Dungeon Master

Crap! I forgot my towel.

On the dock?

Yeah... I better go get it.

We'll come—

We'll cover for you with Kirsten and meet you at the dining hall. That way no one gets in trouble.

Thanks! I'll be right back!

He likes me! I know it!
Te
clomp
clomp
Teal!
Teal!

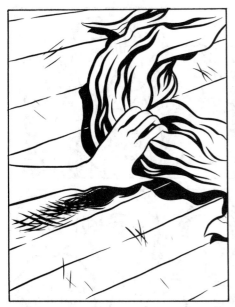

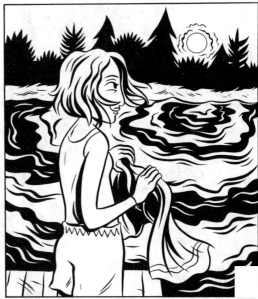

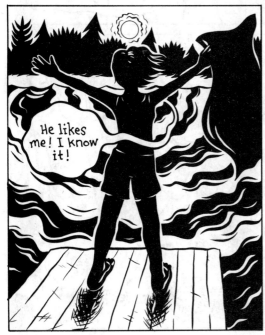

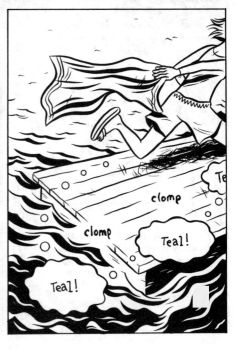

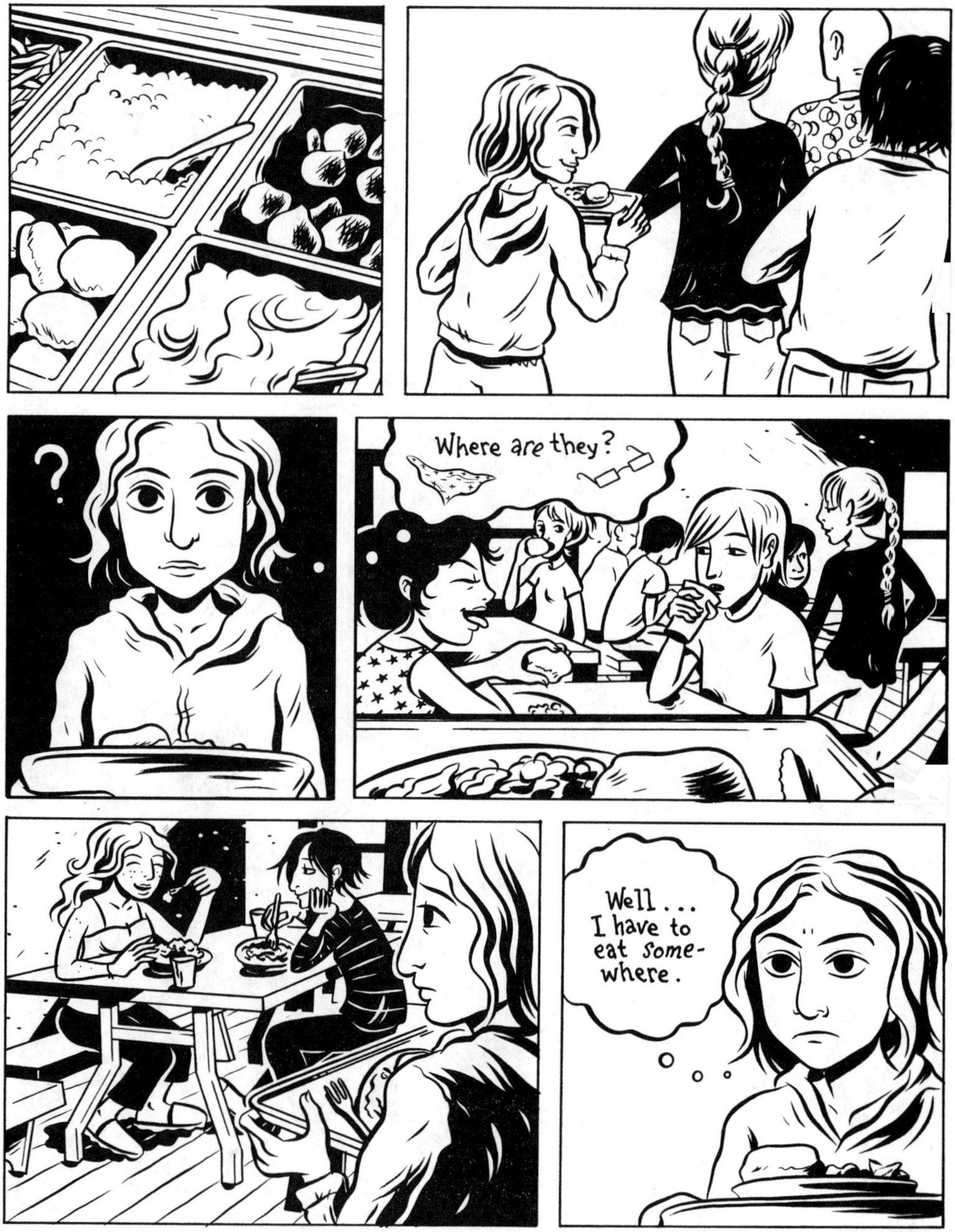
Where are they?
Well... I have to eat some-where.

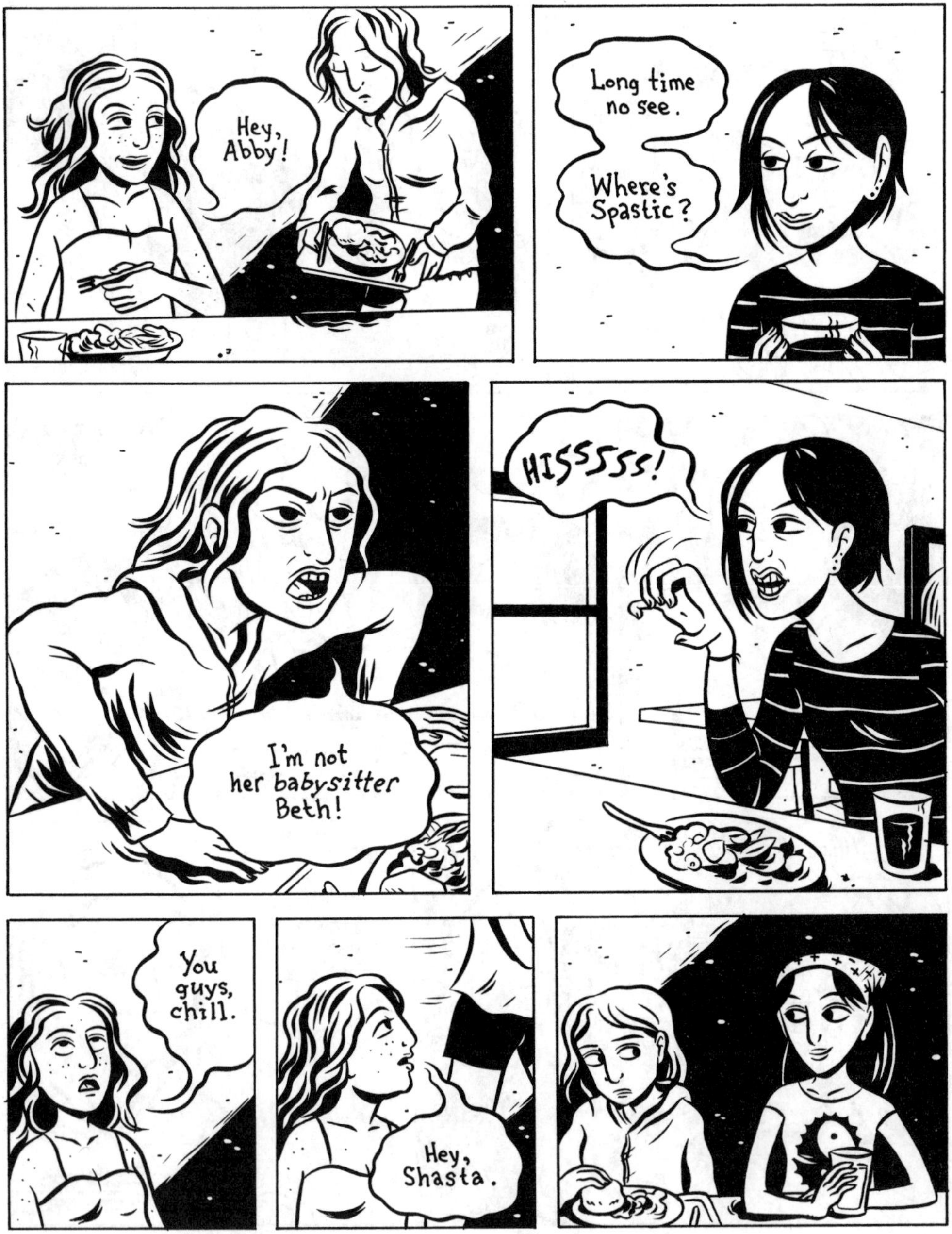
Hey, Abby!
Long time no see.
Where's Spastic?
I'm not her babysitter Beth!
HISSSSS!
You guys, chill.
Hey, Shasta.

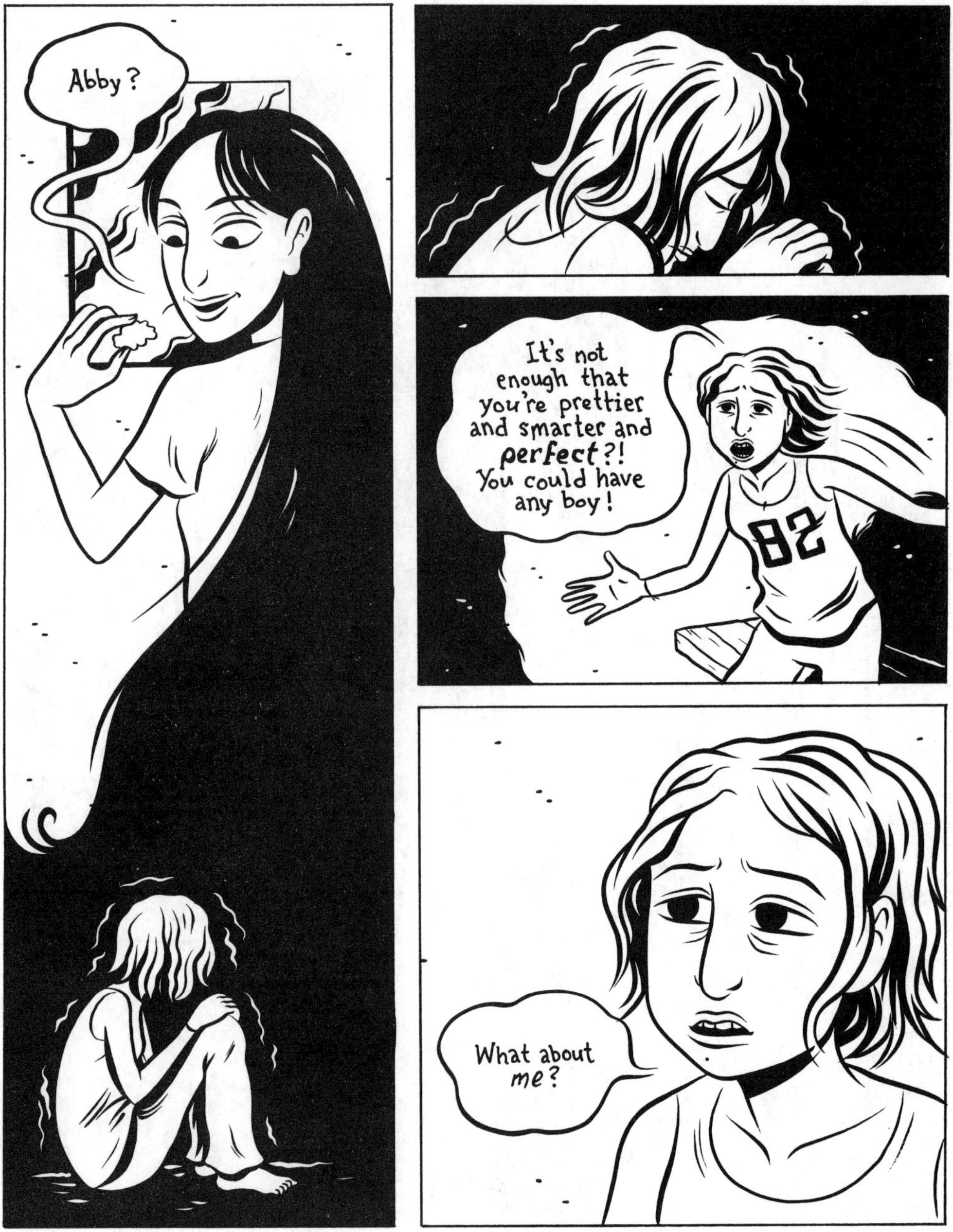
Abby?
It's not enough that you're prettier and smarter and *perfect*?! You could have any boy!
82
What about *me*?

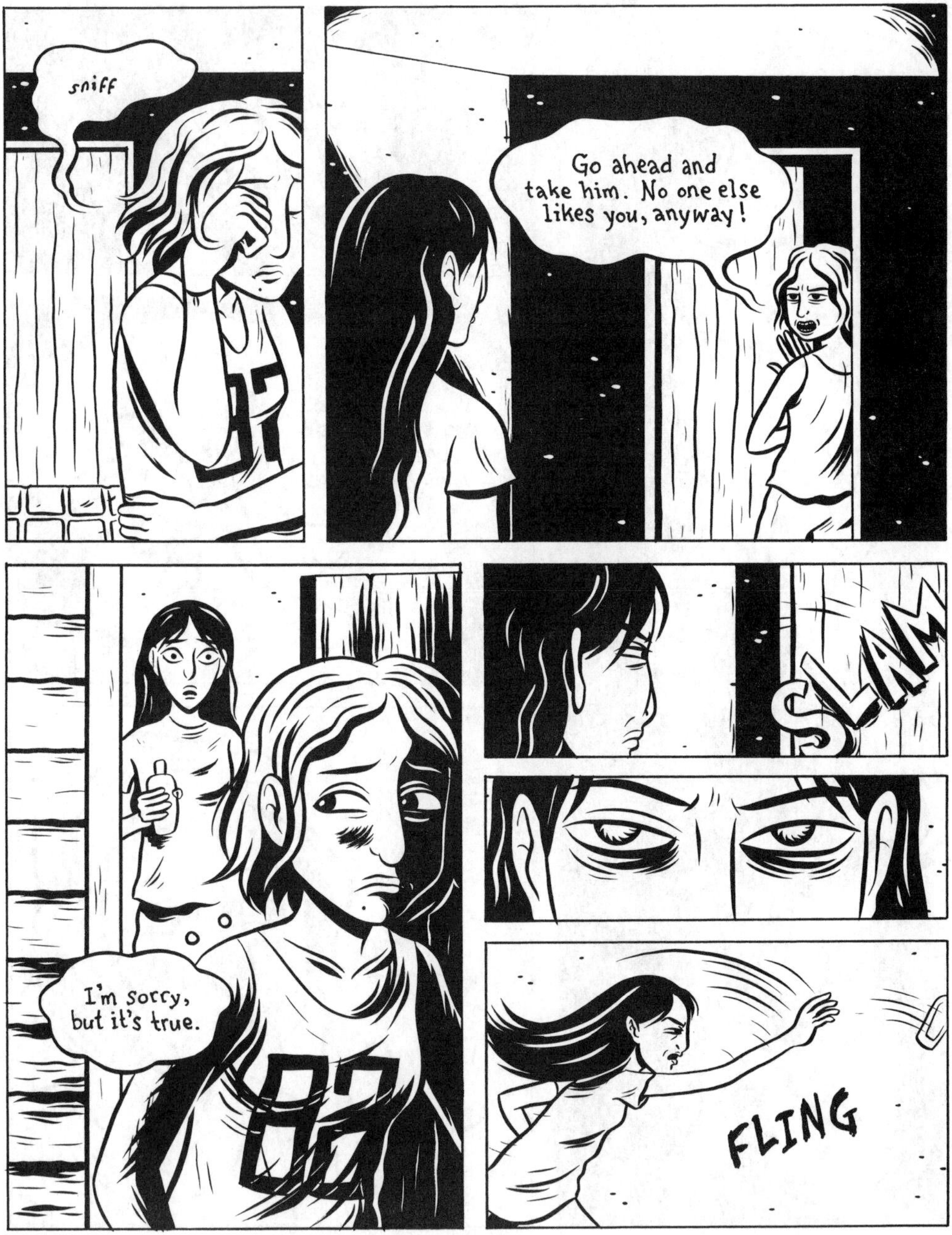
sniff
Go ahead and take him. No one else likes you, anyway!
I'm sorry, but it's true.
SLAM
FLING

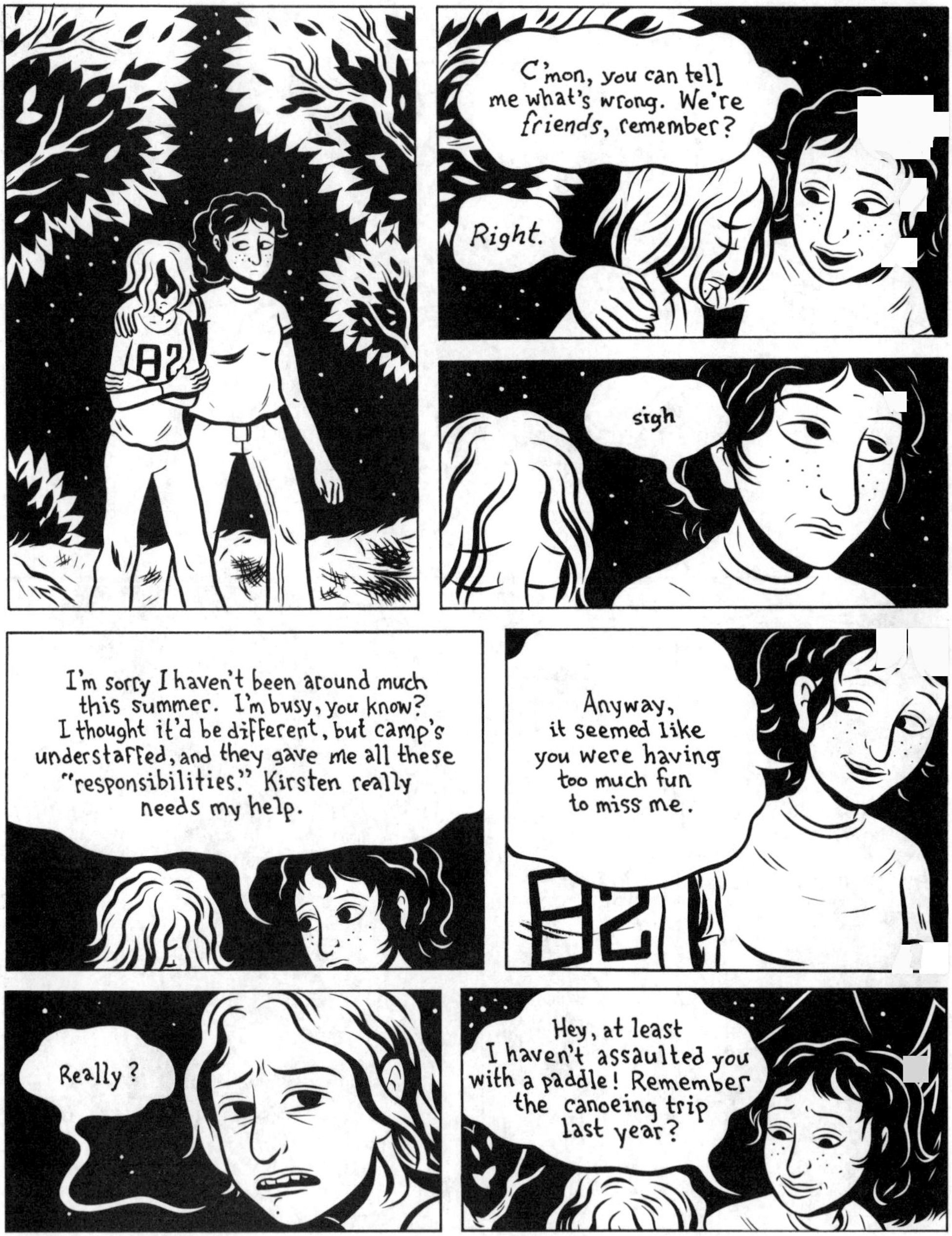
C'mon, you can tell me what's wrong. We're *friends*, remember?
Right.
sigh
I'm sorry I haven't been around much this summer. I'm busy, you know? I thought it'd be different, but camp's understaffed, and they gave me all these "responsibilities." Kirsten really needs my help.
Anyway, it seemed like you were having too much fun to miss me.
Really?
Hey, at least I haven't assaulted you with a paddle! Remember the canoeing trip last year?

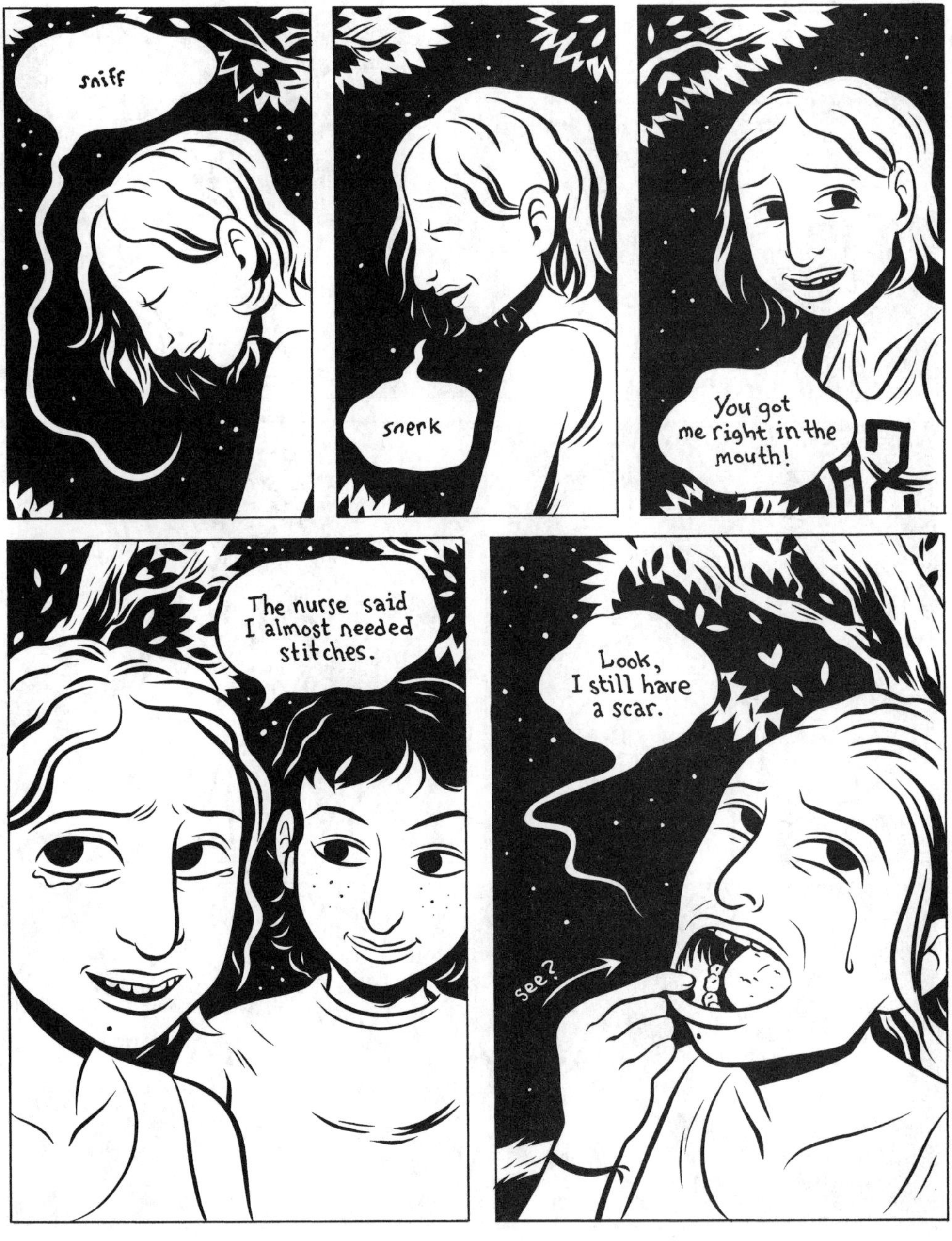
sniff
snerk
You got me right in the mouth!
The nurse said I almost needed stitches.
Look, I still have a scar.
see?

Hey, I kind of wanted to ask you something.

Uh-huh?

Um... Do you like Teal?

ha

ha

ha

He likes Shasta.

What are you talking about? That's BS, Abby!

Hang on....

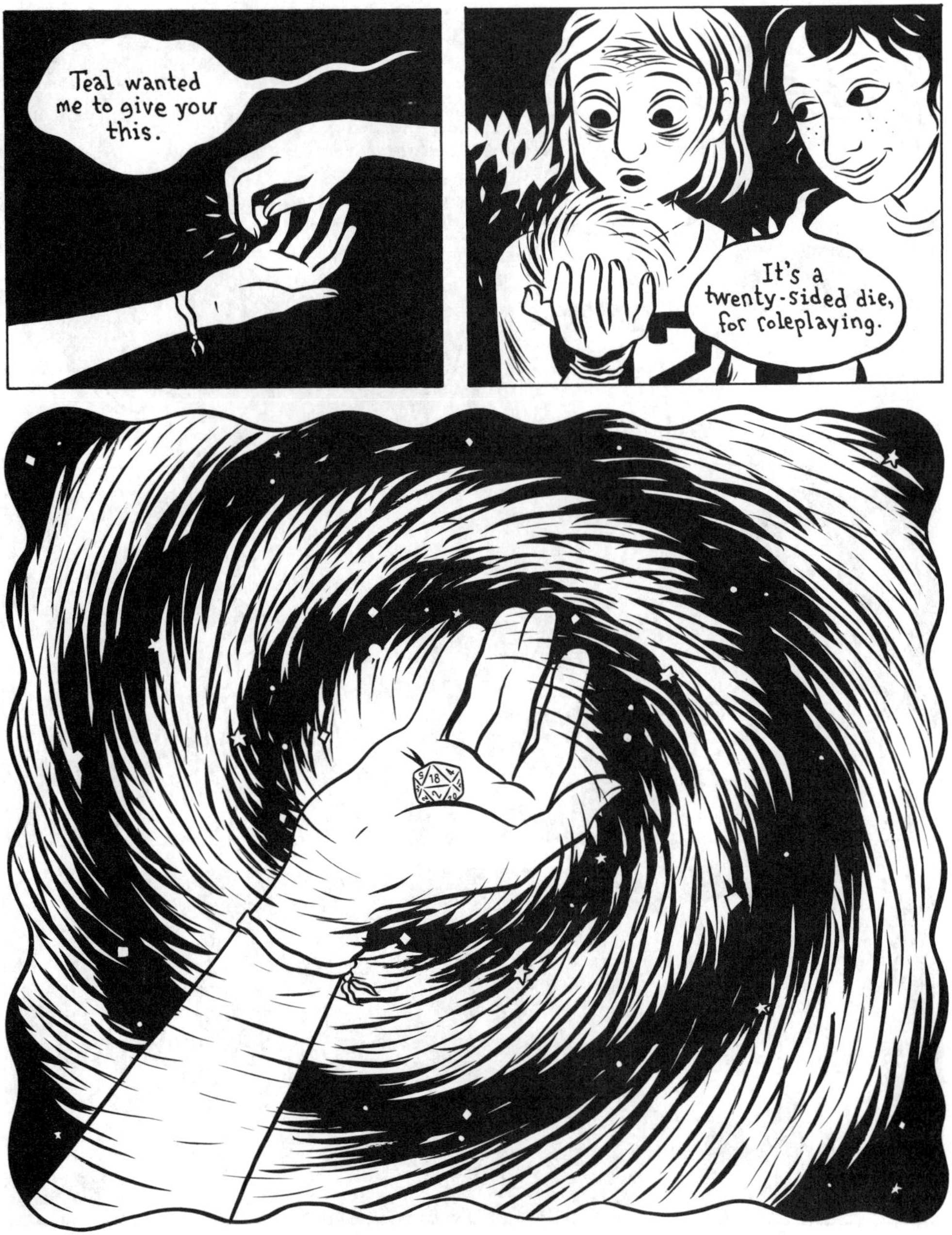
Teal wanted me to give you this.
It's a twenty-sided die, for roleplaying.
18

He also wants you to know that, uh, "will o' the wisps are attracted to areas with high amounts of electrical charge," whatever that means. I'm sure he meant it to be charming.

So what should I tell him? That you like him back?

NOD

He's a good guy *and* an awesome DM. Did I tell you how he invented two whole worlds?

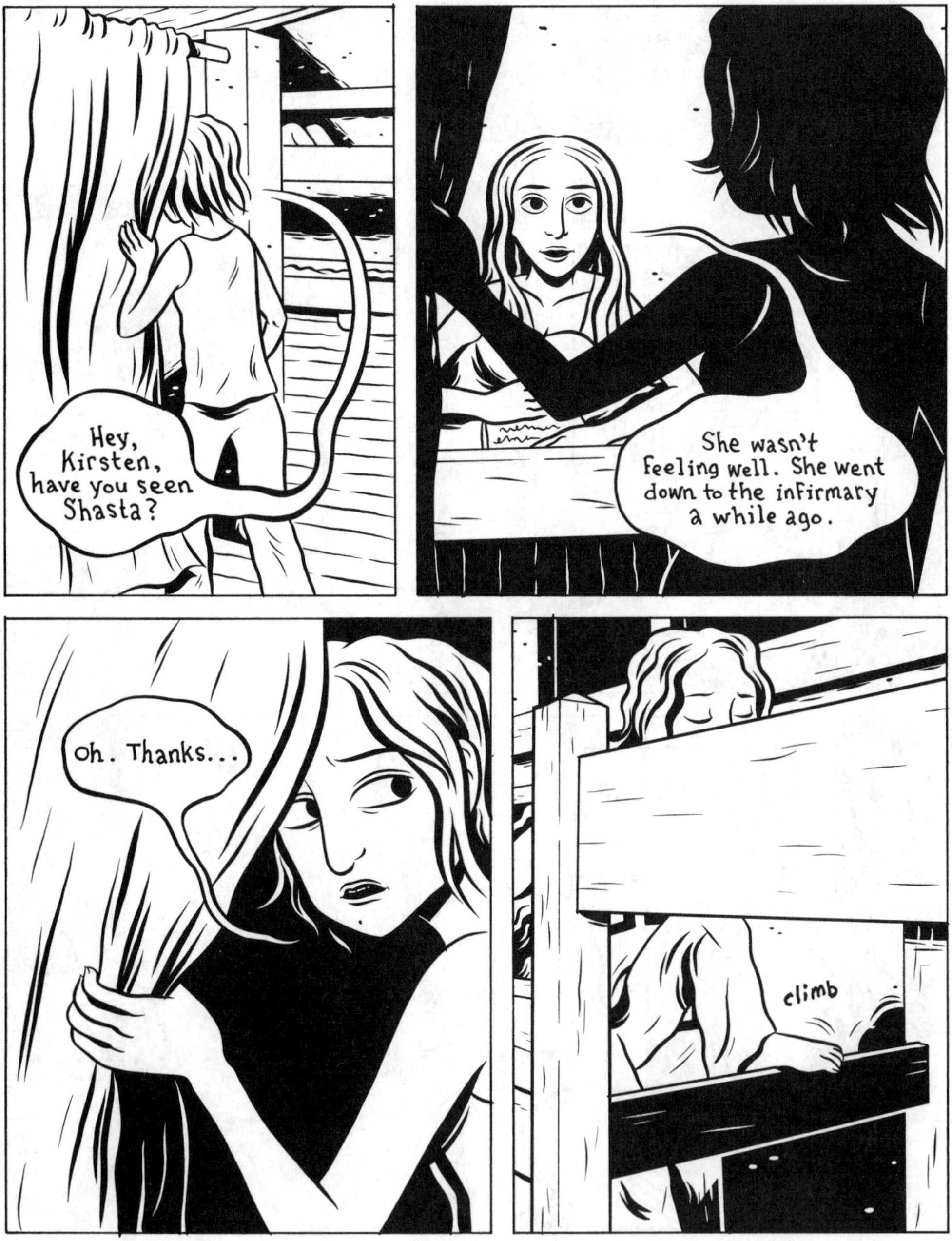
Hey, Kirsten, have you seen Shasta?
She wasn't feeling well. She went down to the infirmary a while ago.
Oh. Thanks...
climb

Dear Abby,

I'm sorry about what I said before. You're right, everyone hates me. Beth and Zoë hate me, my boyfriend hates me, and now you hate me. Sorry for being such a <u>bad</u> friend. I guess I deserve it.

I am going to look for the spooklight or whatever, to see what it wants. It's probably going to be dangerous, so don't look for me. Kirsten thinks I'm at the infirmary — ha ha.

Your friend,
Shasta

P.S.
Teal probably doesn't really like me. I think I just wanted to get you back for being a jerk about Matt.

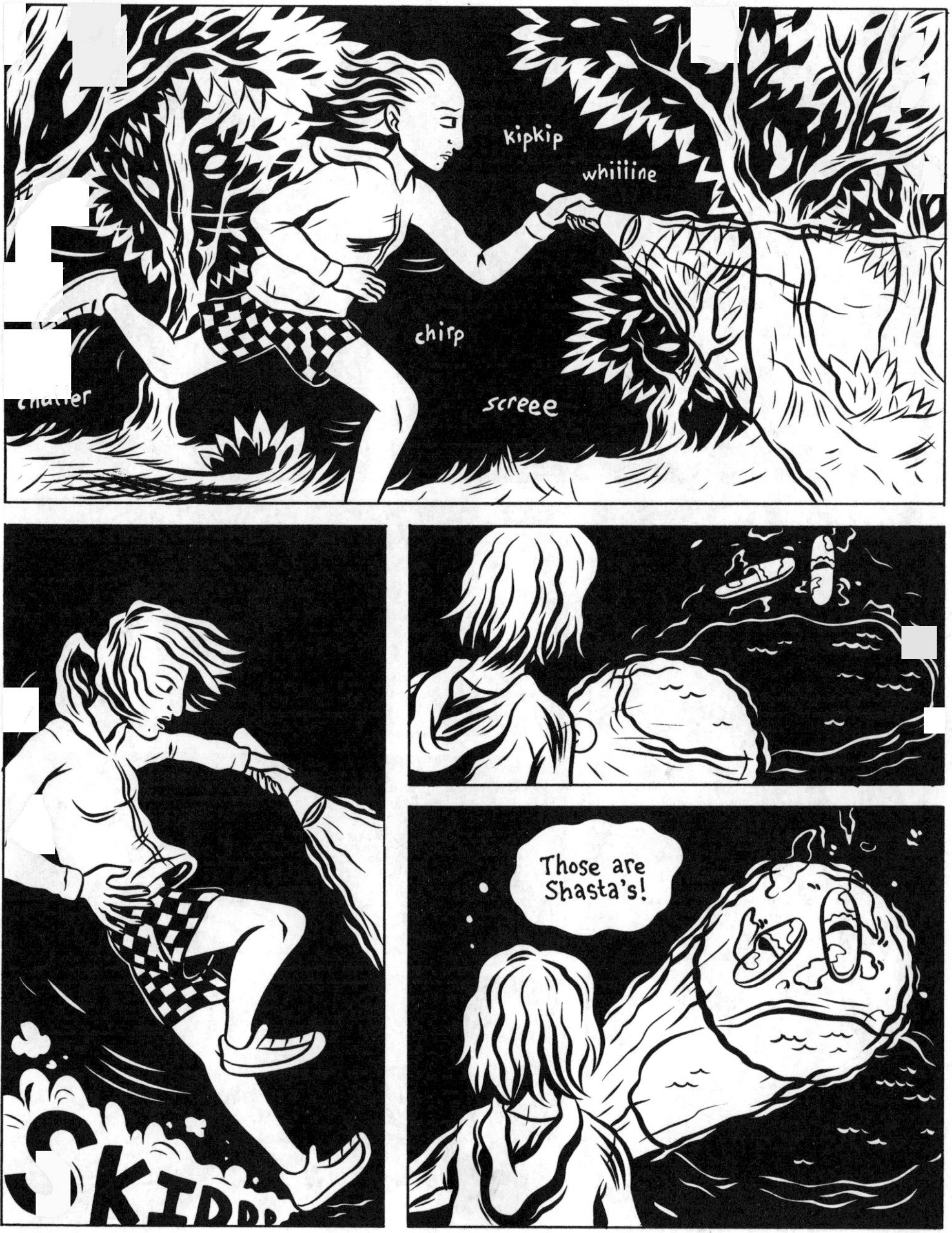
kipkip
whiiiine
chirp
chatter
screee
Those are Shasta's!

leap

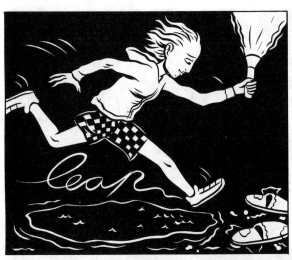

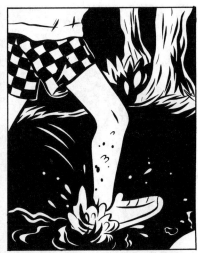

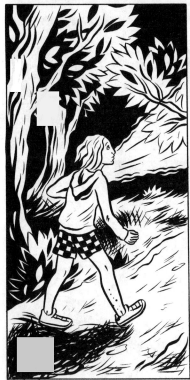

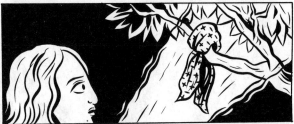

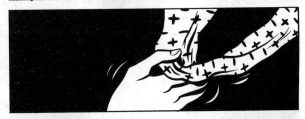

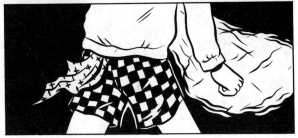

Shastaaaaaa!
Where are you?

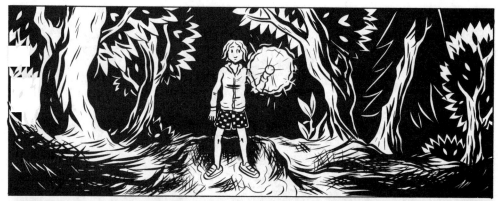

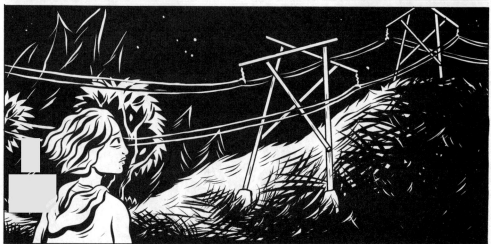

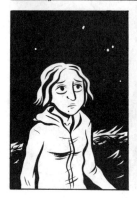

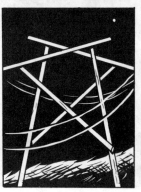

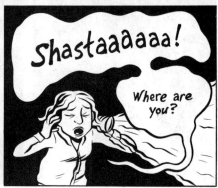

SHAASTAAA!!
Up here!
I found you!

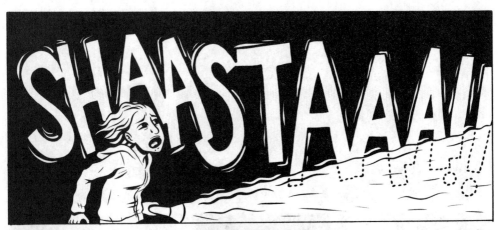

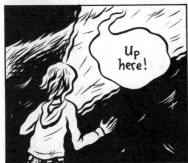

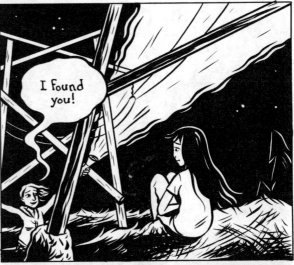

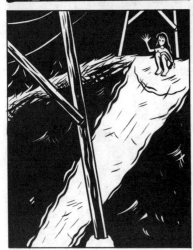

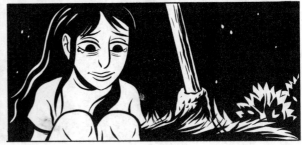

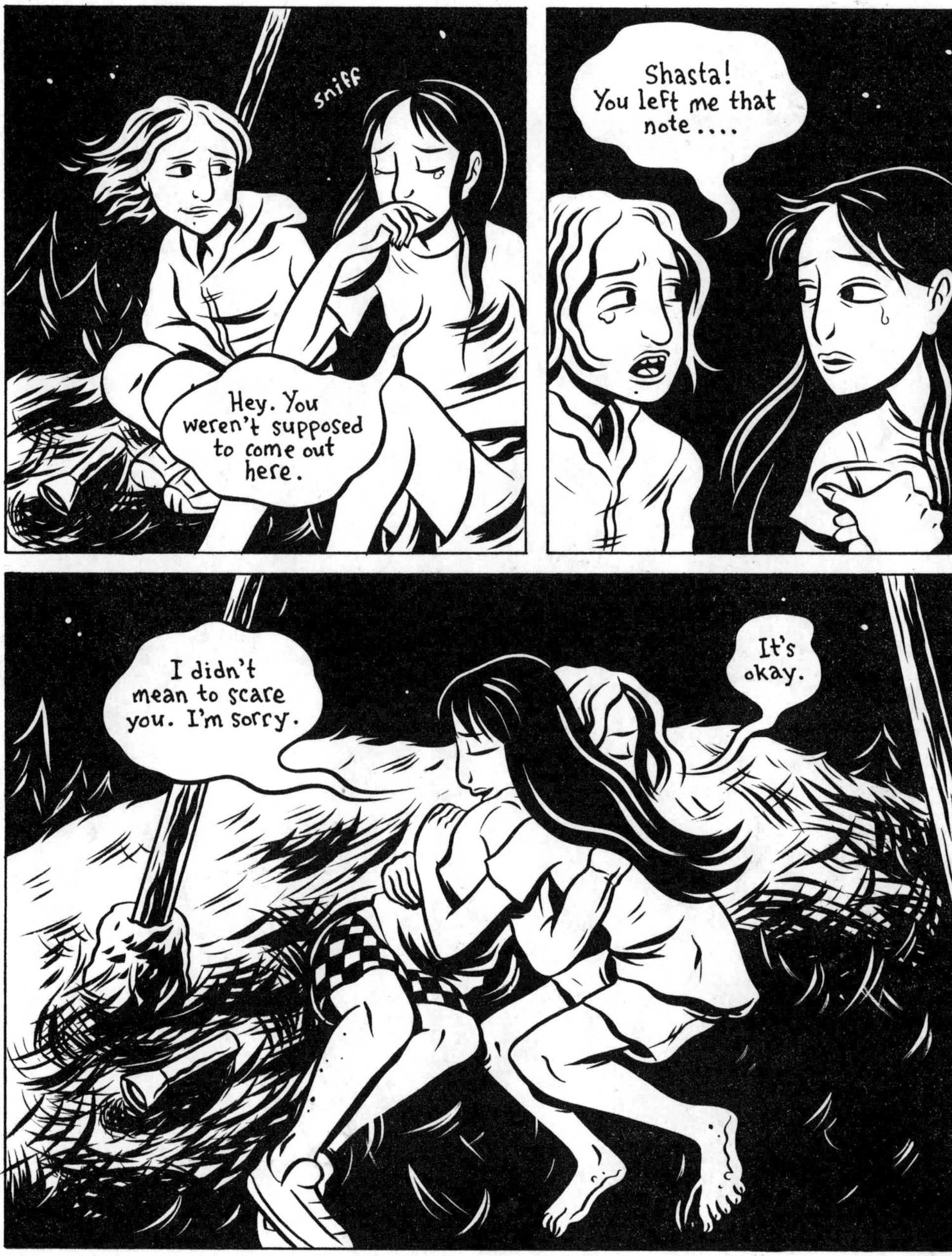
sniff
Hey. You weren't supposed to come out here.
Shasta! You left me that note....
I didn't mean to scare you. I'm sorry.
It's okay.

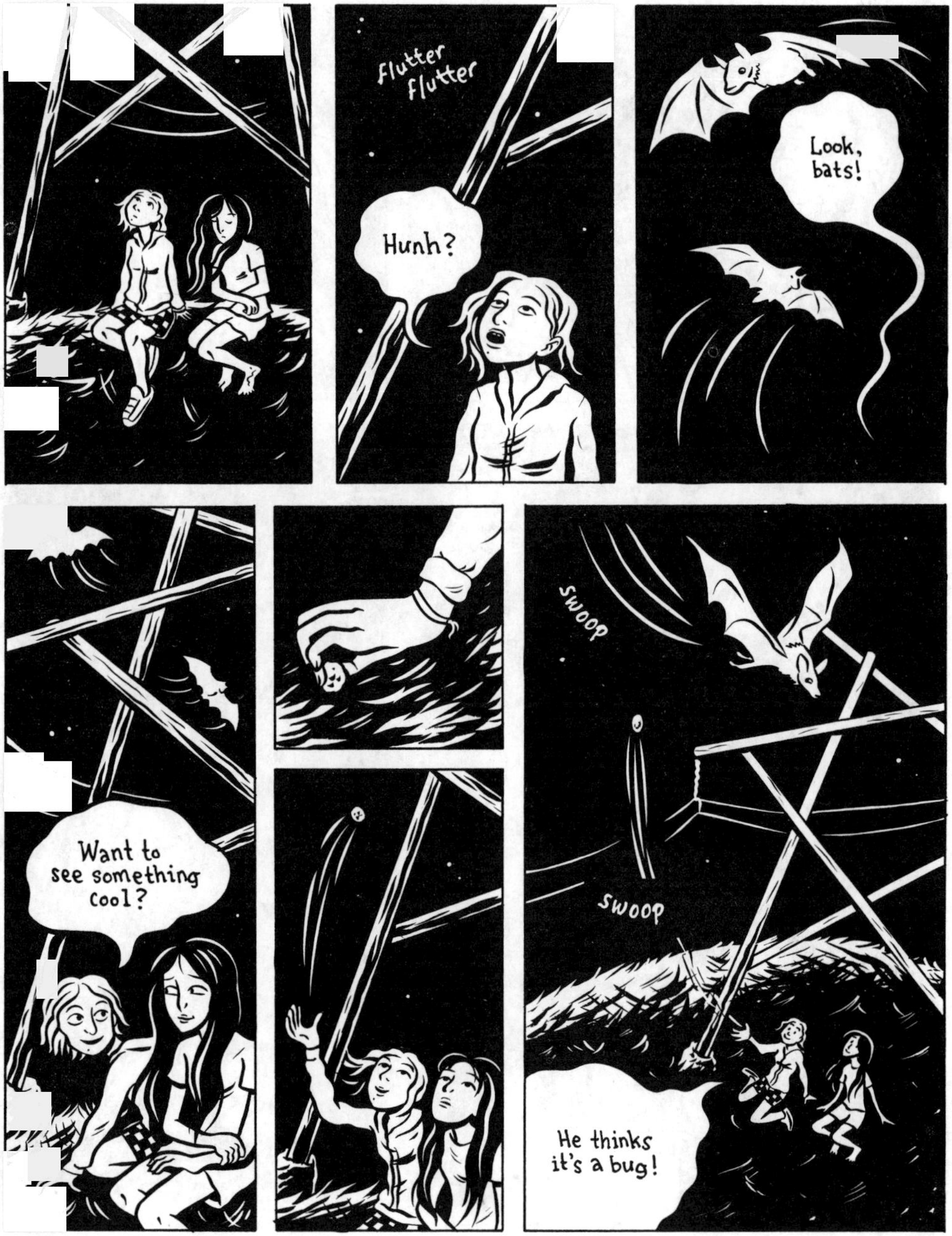
Flutter flutter
Hunh?
Look, bats!
Want to see something cool?
SWOOP
SWOOP
He thinks it's a bug!

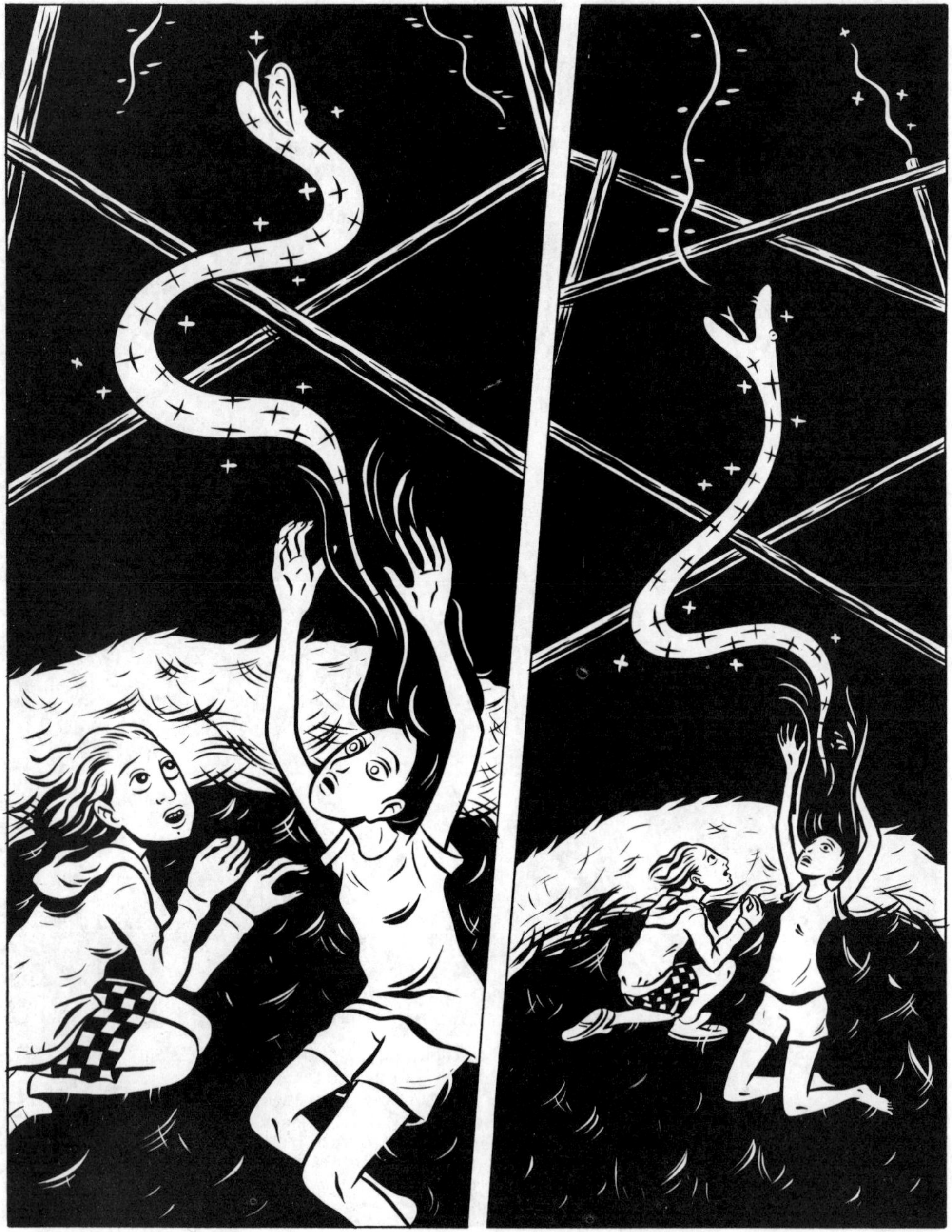

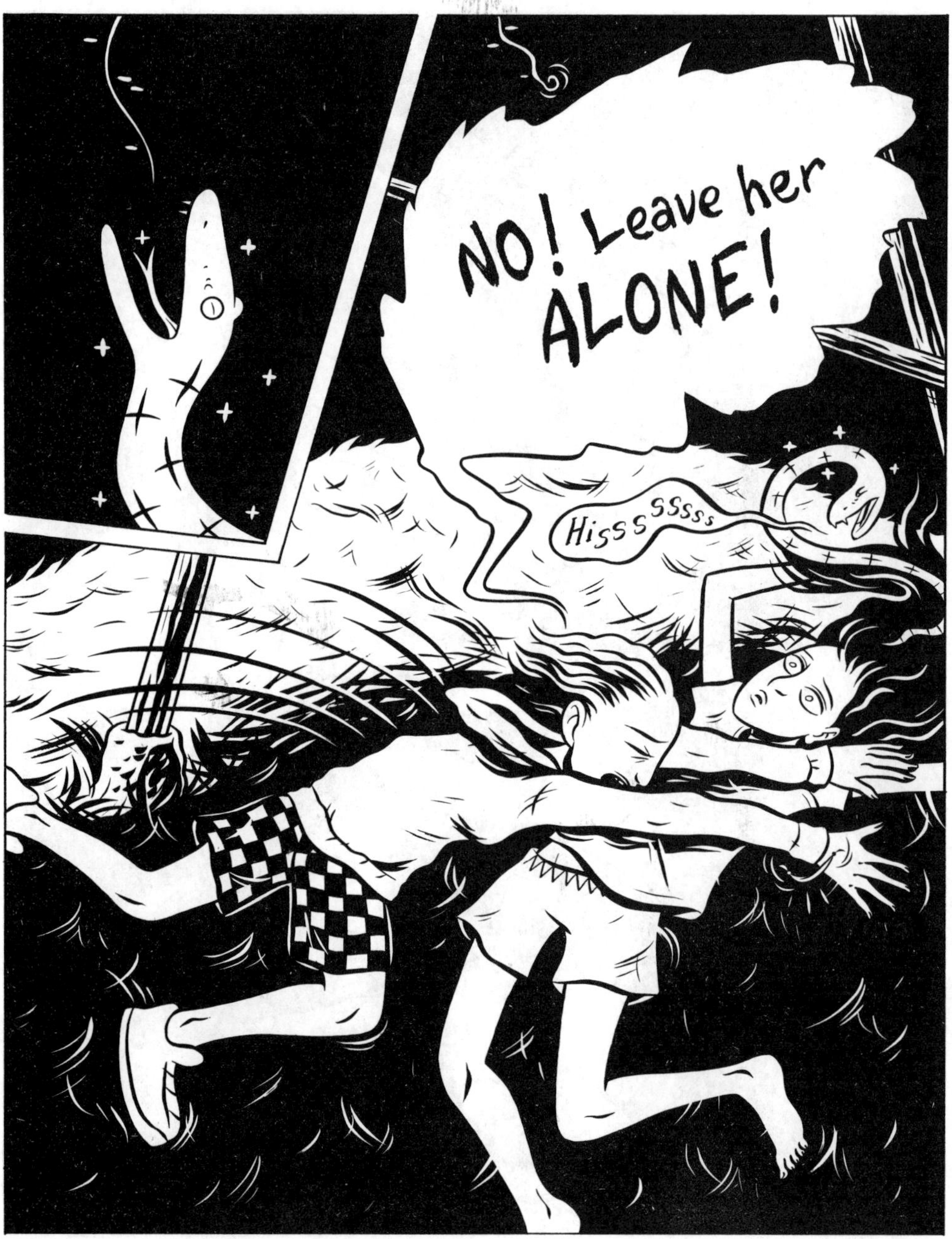
NO! Leave her ALONE!
HissssSSSSS

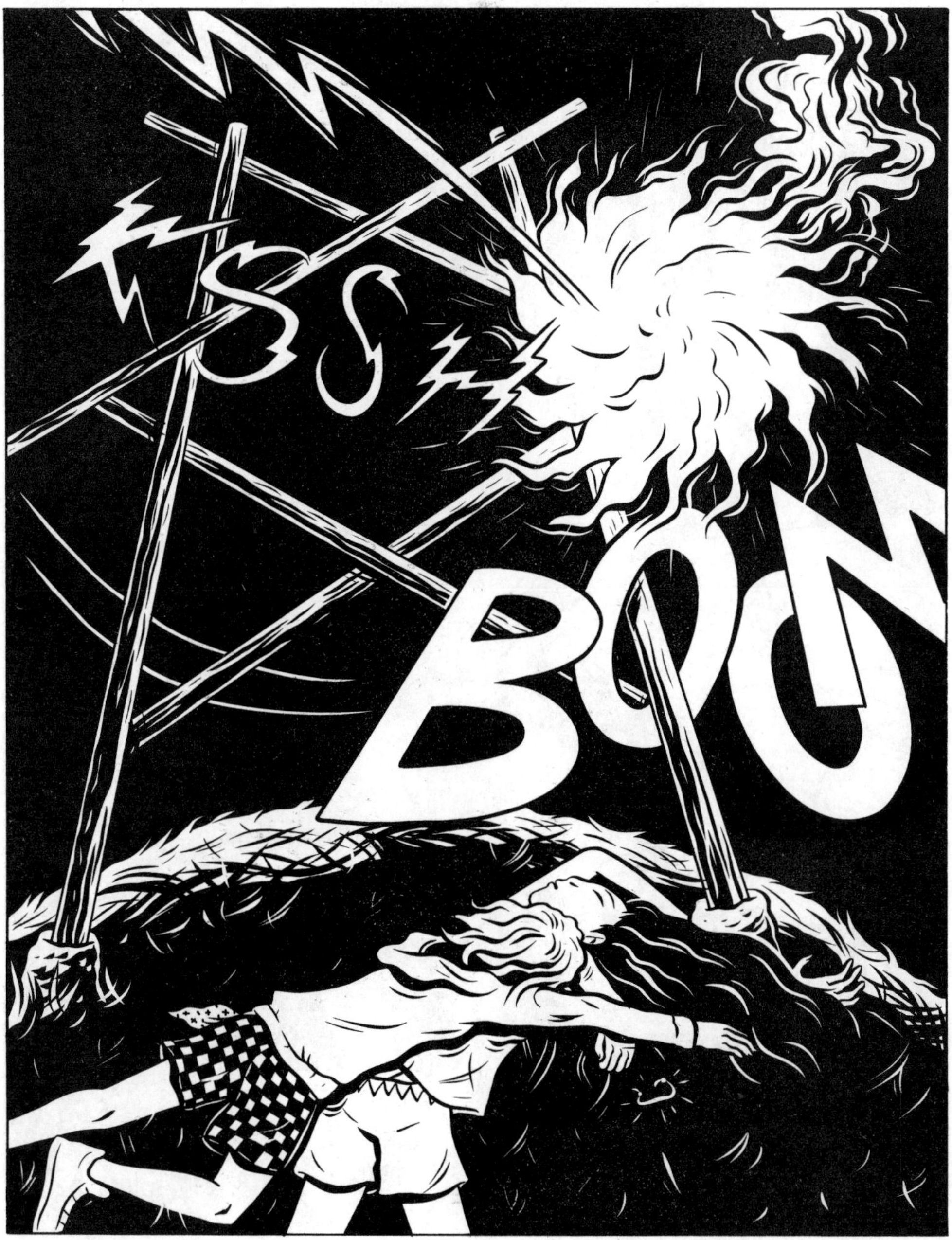
SS
BOOM

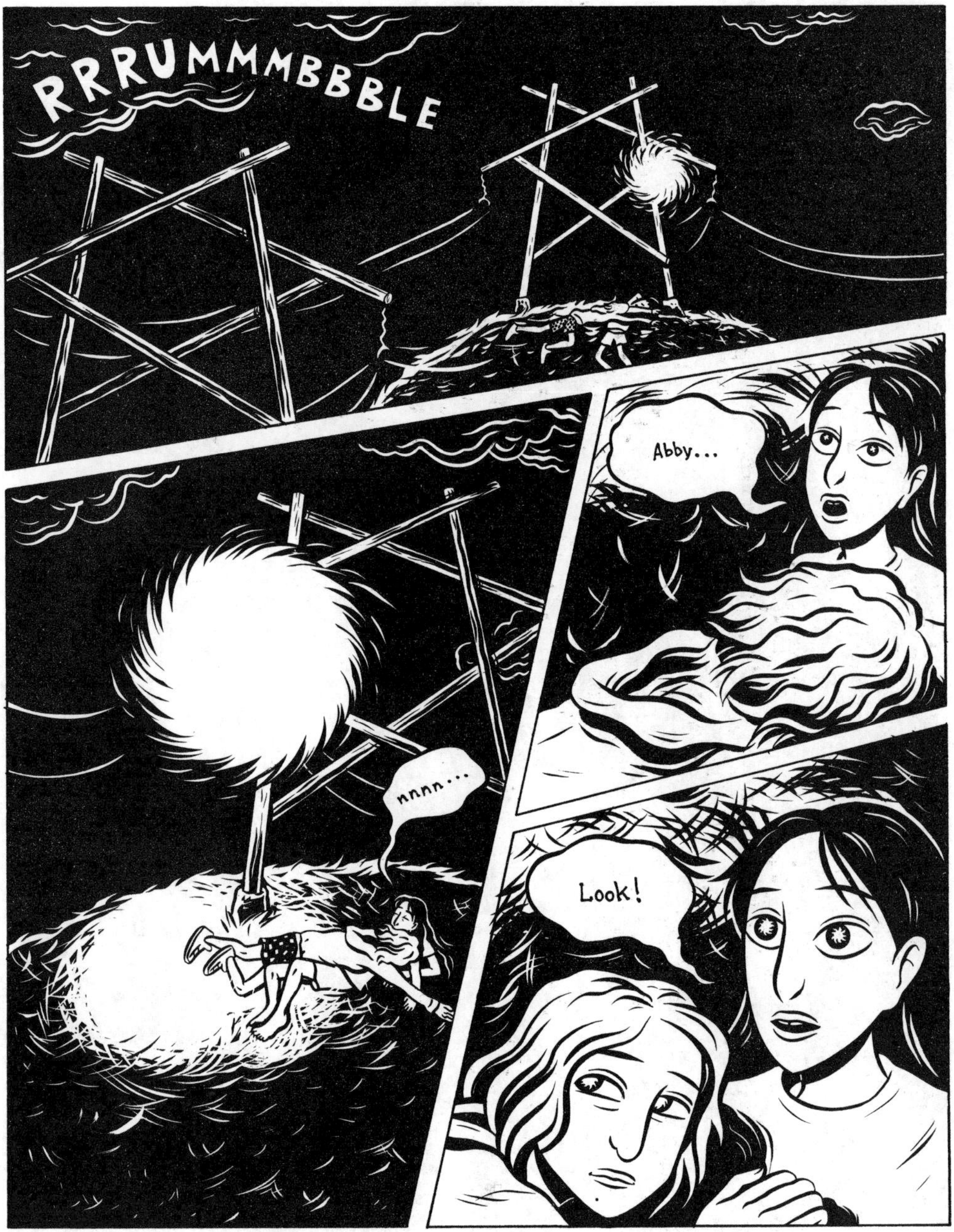
RRRUMMMMBBBBLE
nnnn...
Abby...
Look!

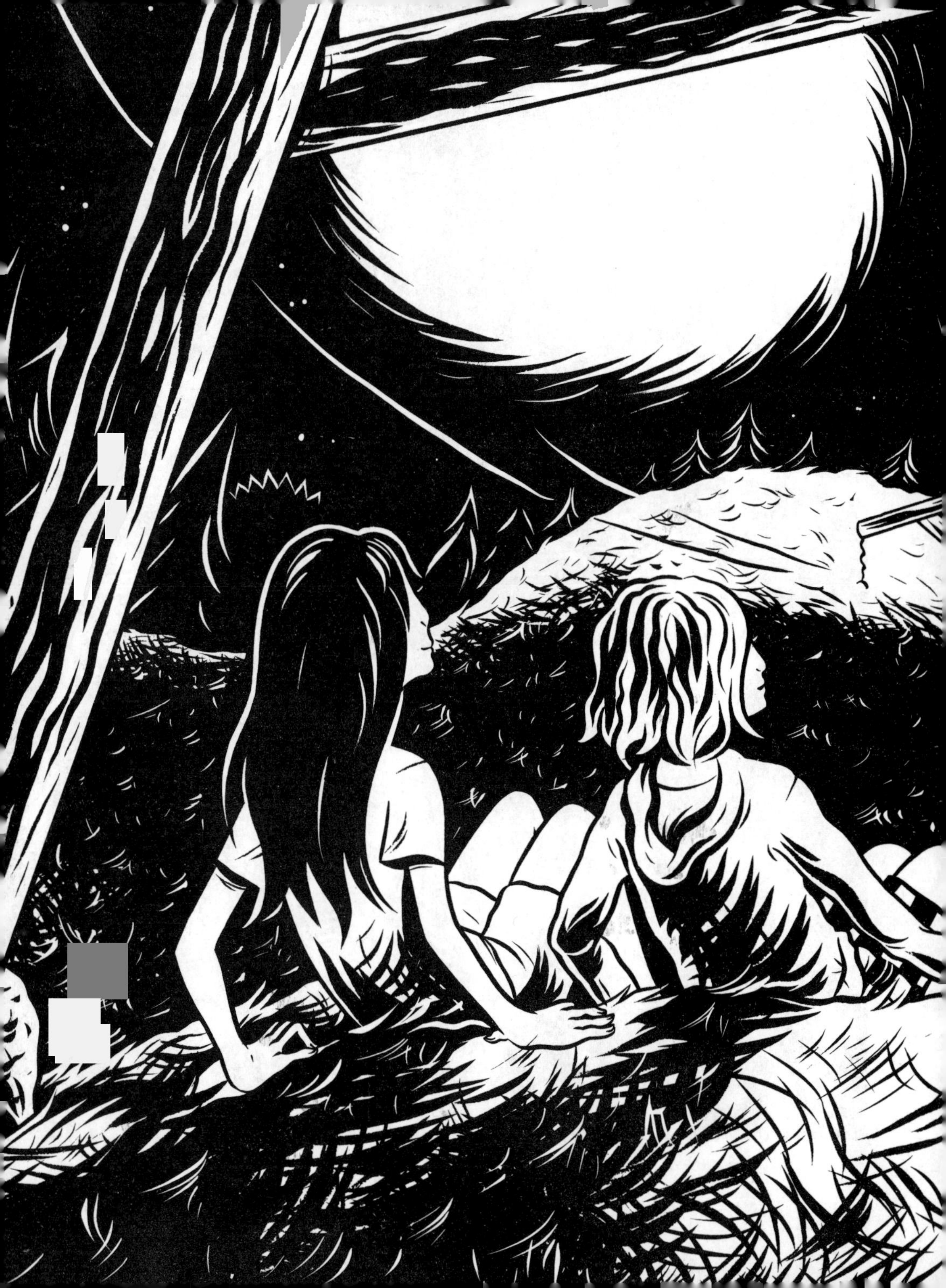

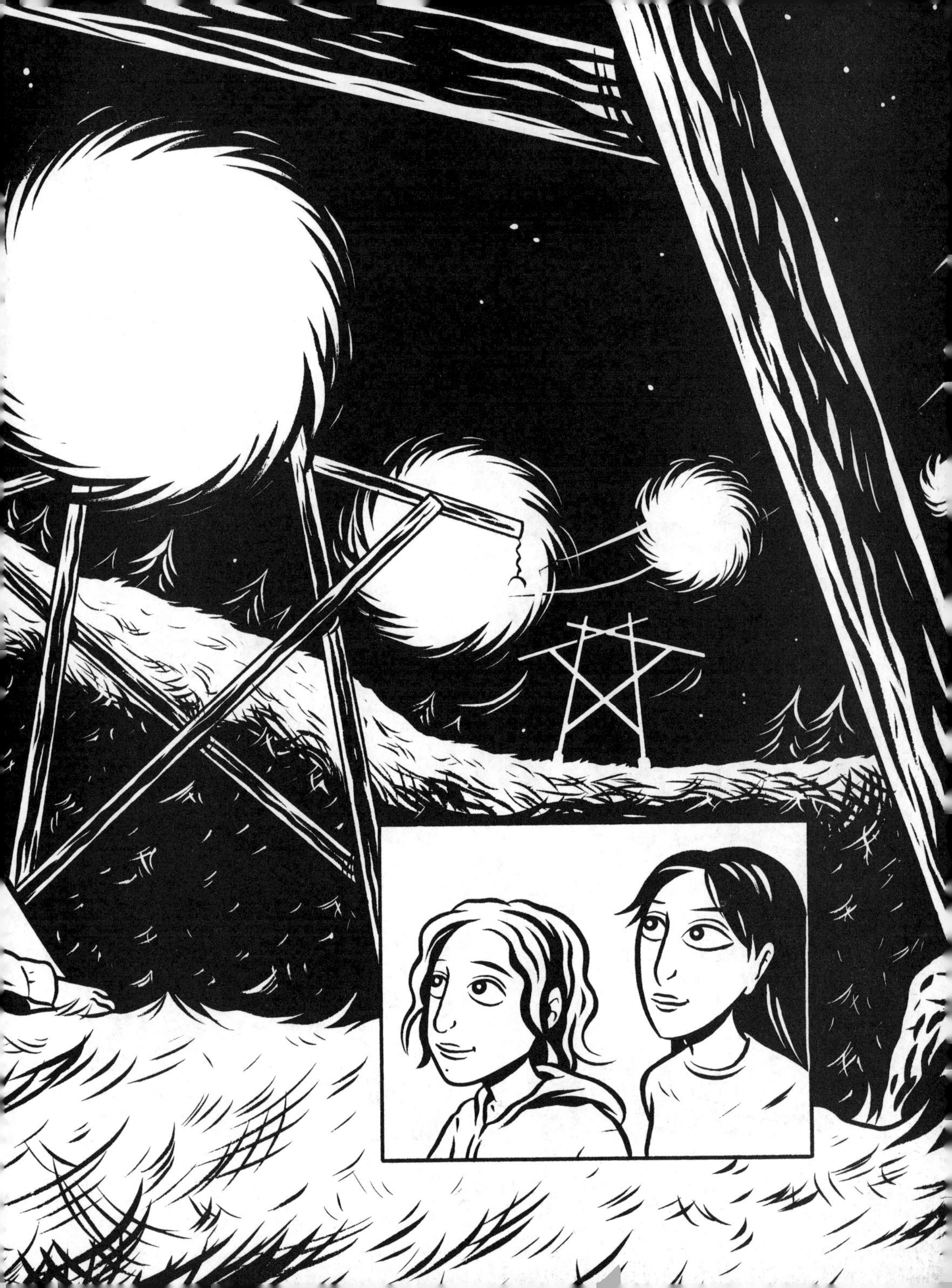

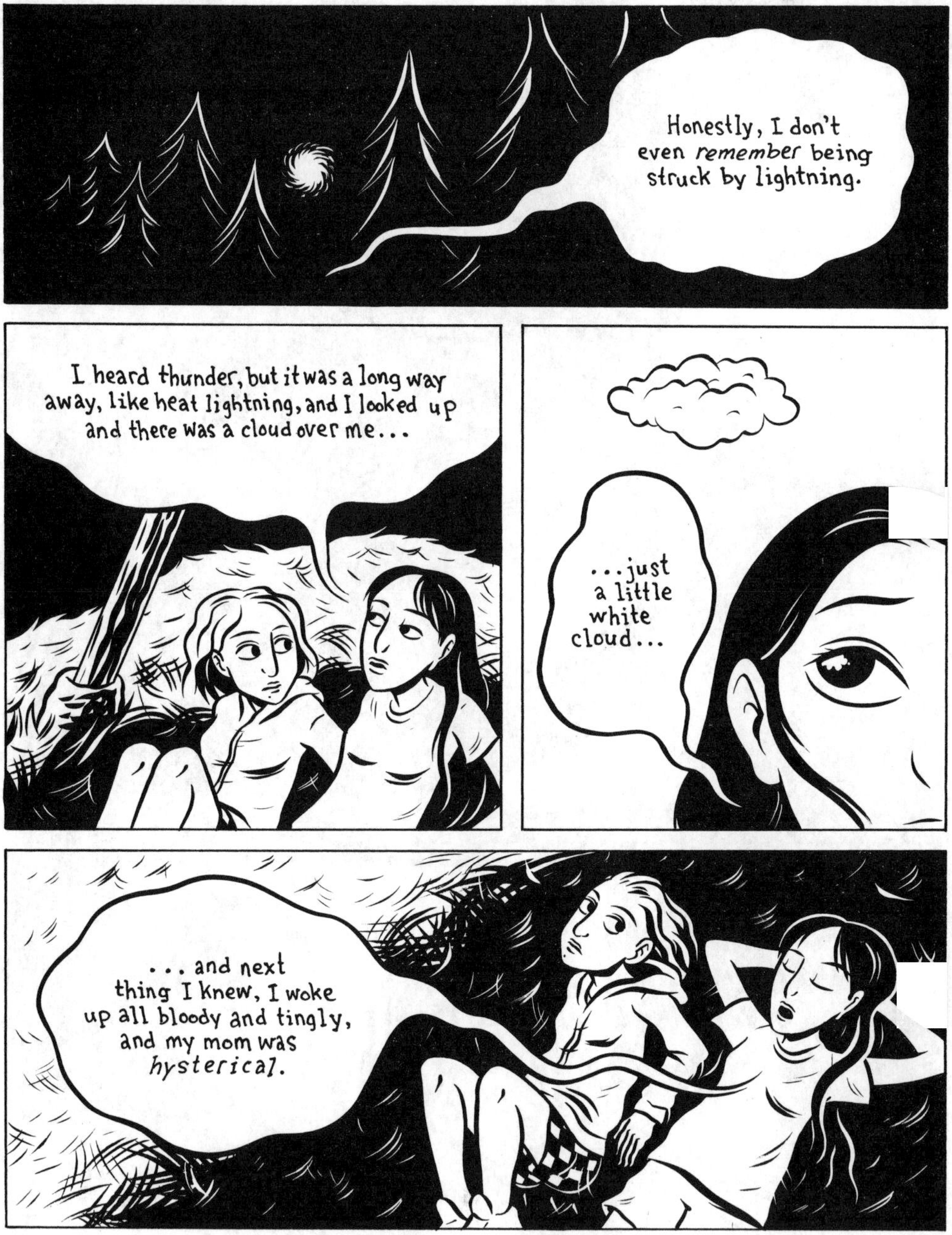
Honestly, I don't even *remember* being struck by lightning.
I heard thunder, but it was a long way away, like heat lightning, and I looked up and there was a cloud over me...
...just a little white cloud...
...and next thing I knew, I woke up all bloody and tingly, and my mom was *hysterical*.

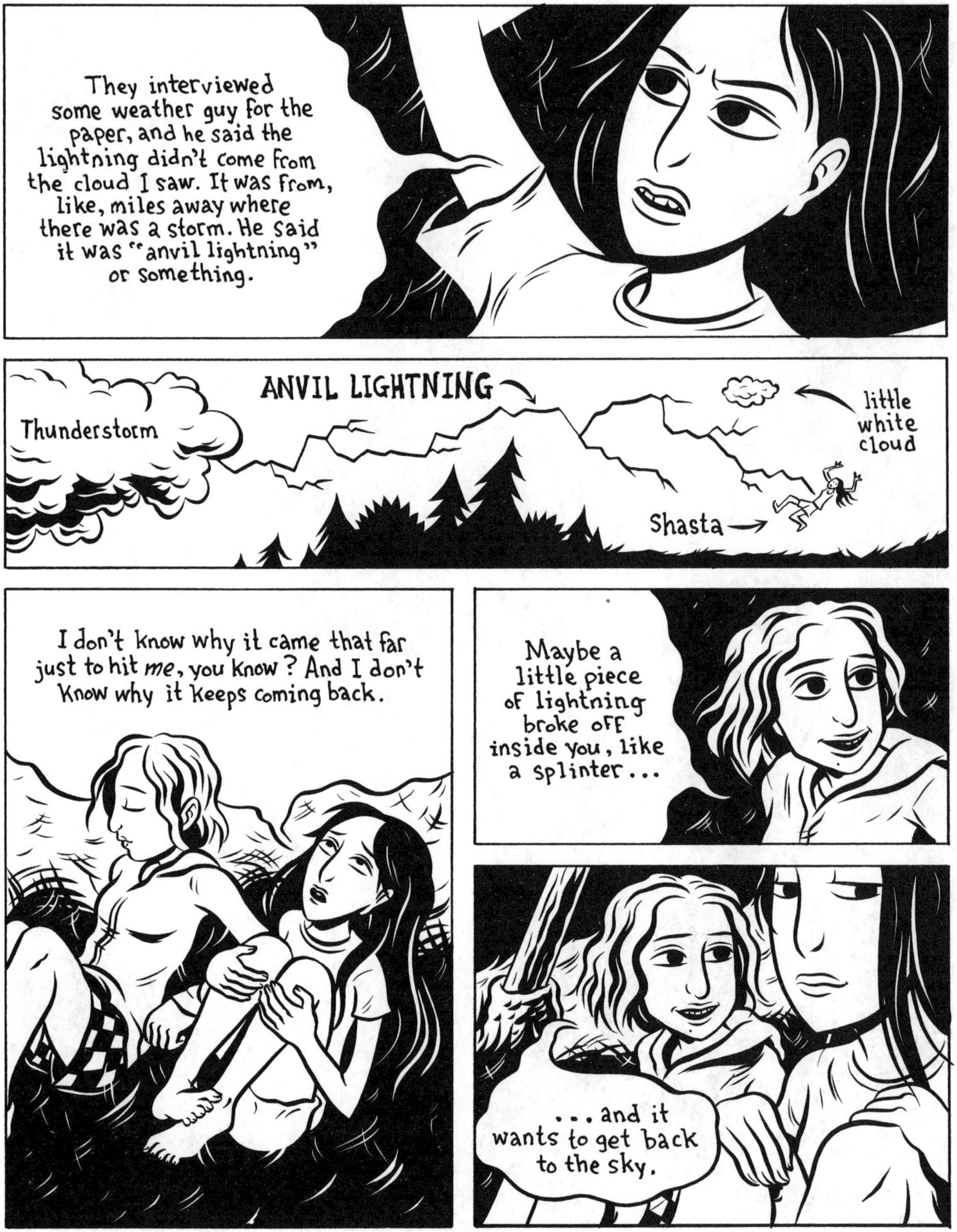
They interviewed some weather guy for the paper, and he said the lightning didn't come from the cloud I saw. It was from, like, miles away where there was a storm. He said it was "anvil lightning" or something.
ANVIL LIGHTNING
Thunderstorm
little white cloud
Shasta
I don't know why it came that far just to hit *me*, you know? And I don't know why it keeps coming back.
Maybe a little piece of lightning broke off inside you, like a splinter...
...and it wants to get back to the sky.

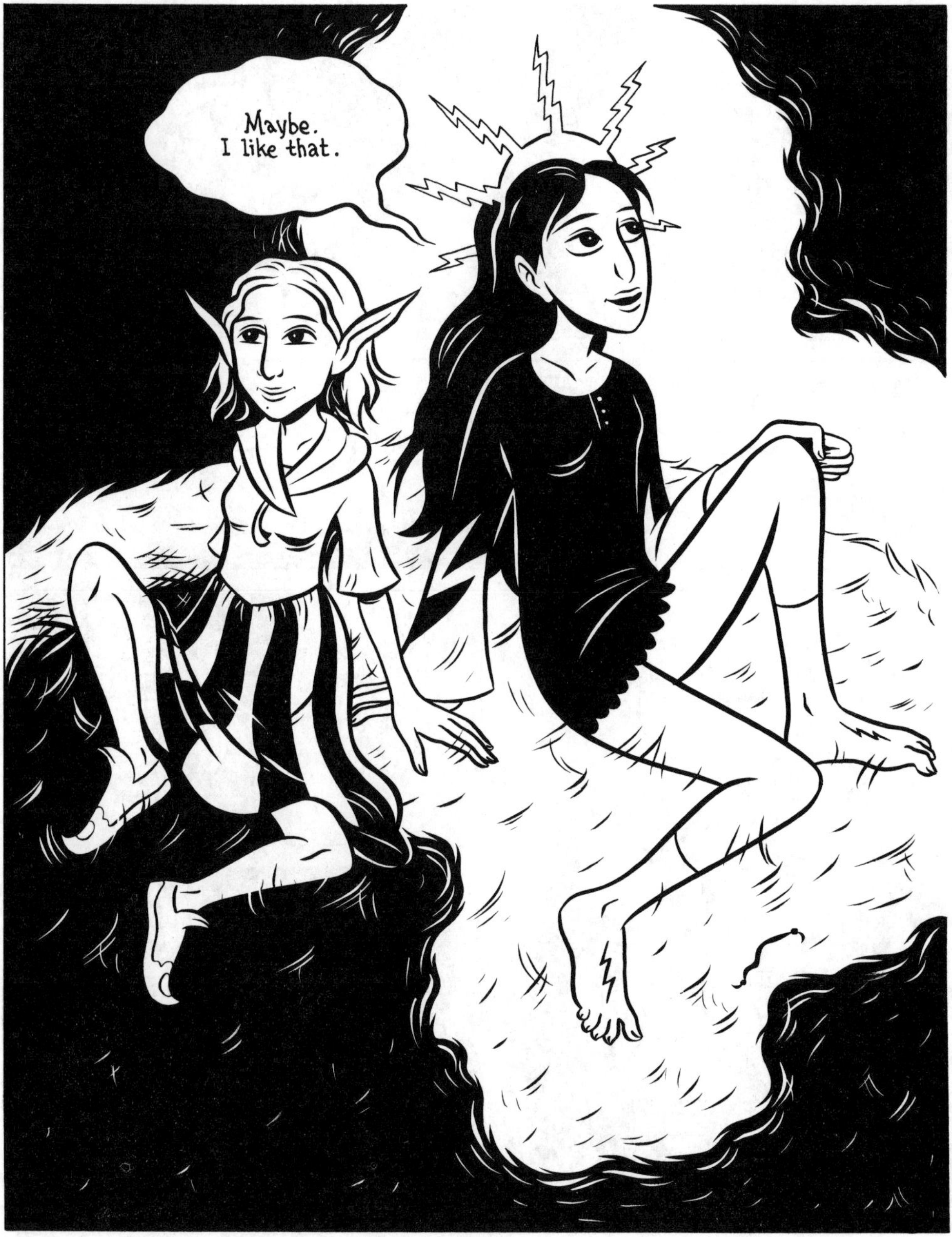
Maybe. I like that.

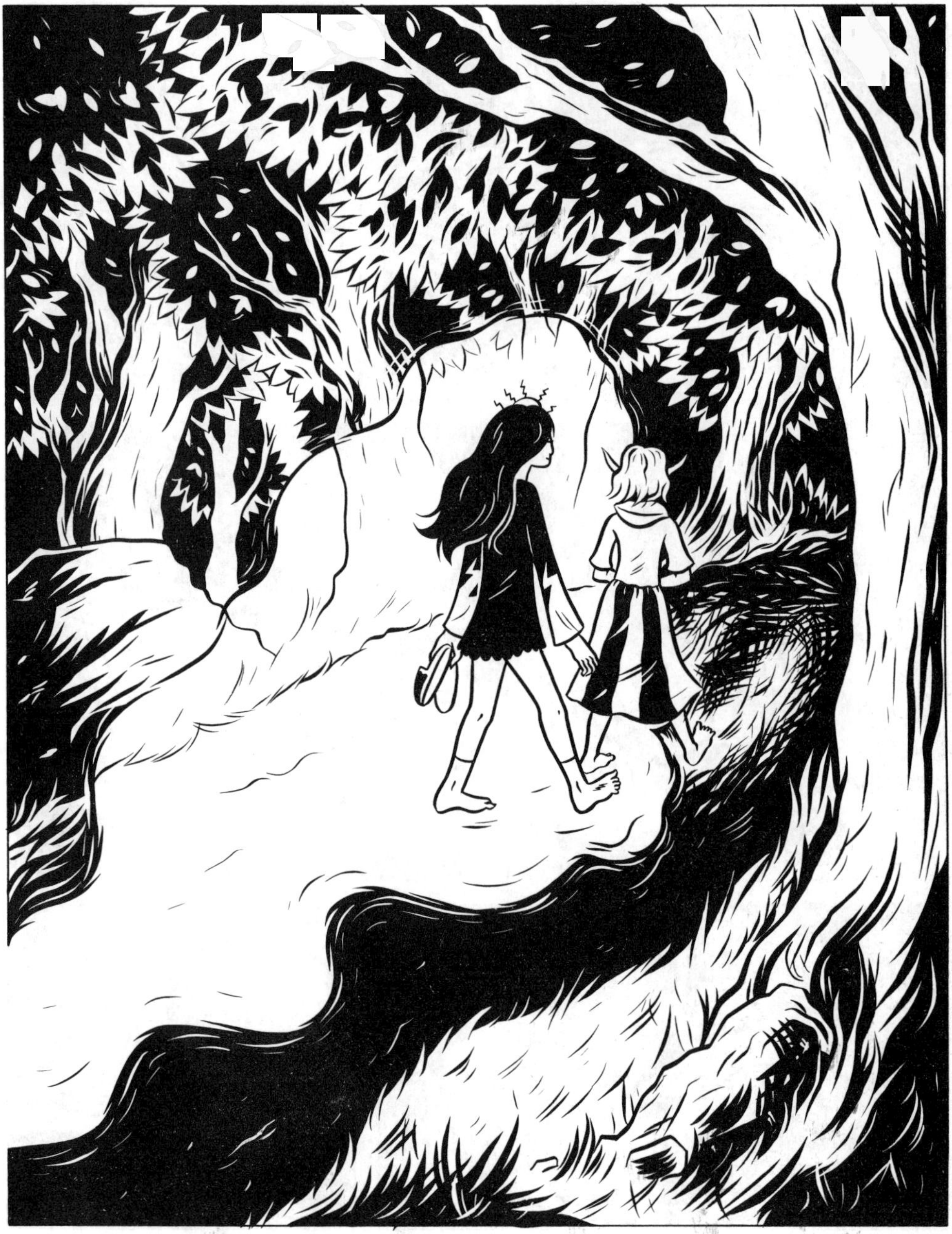

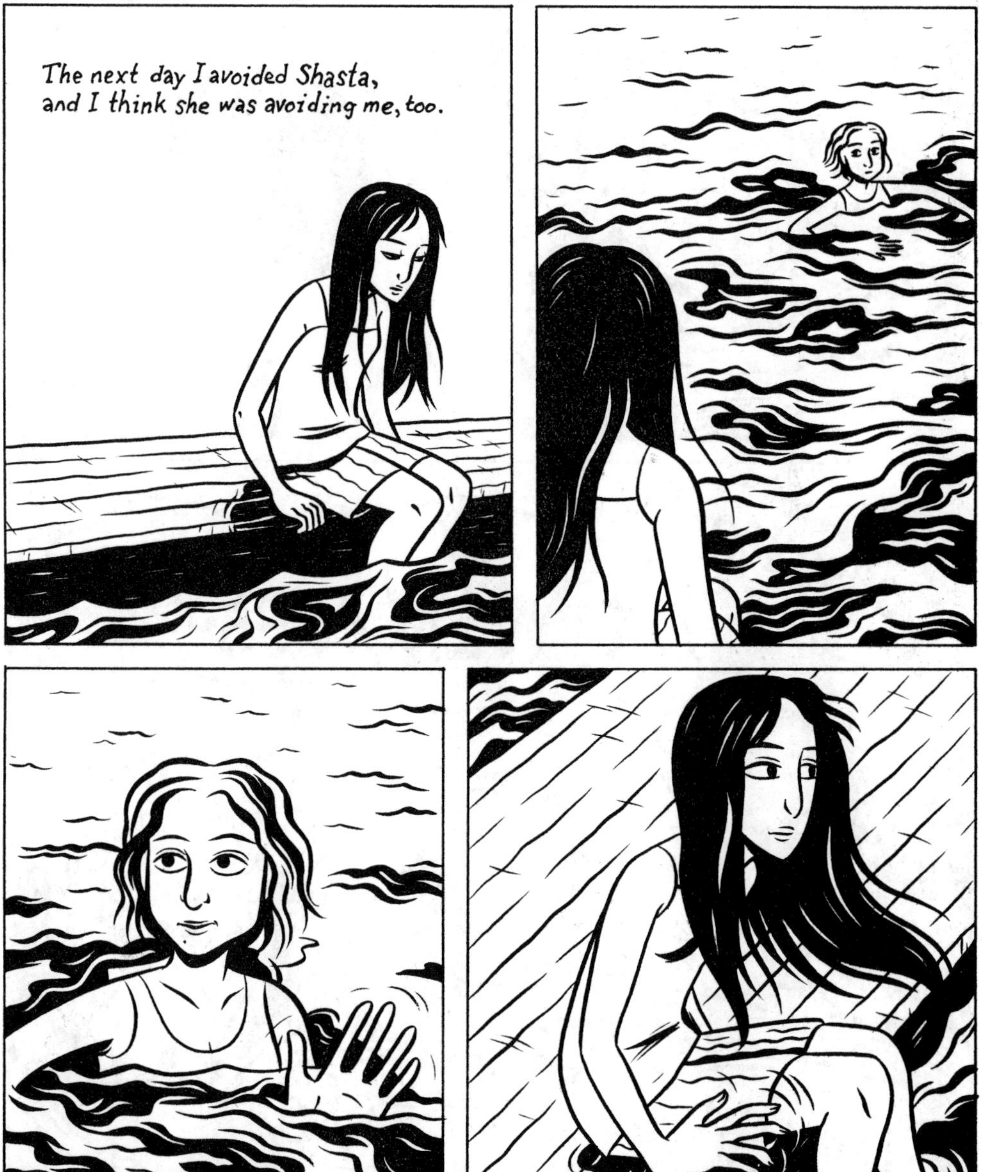
The next day I avoided Shasta,
and I think she was avoiding me, too.

GASSSSP!
I WIN!
GASSSSP!
SPLASH
SPLASH

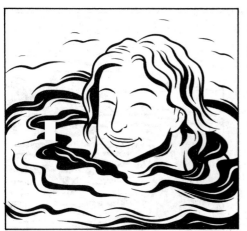

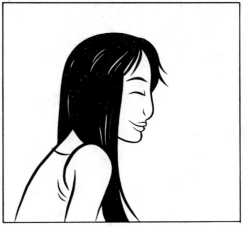

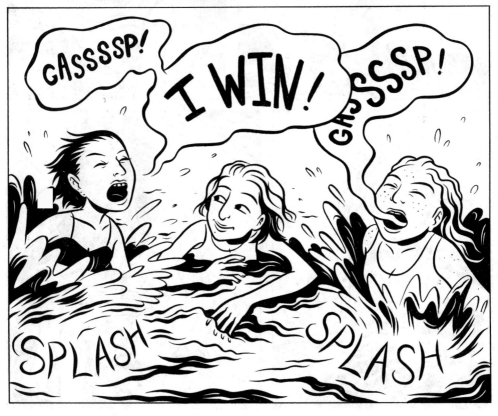

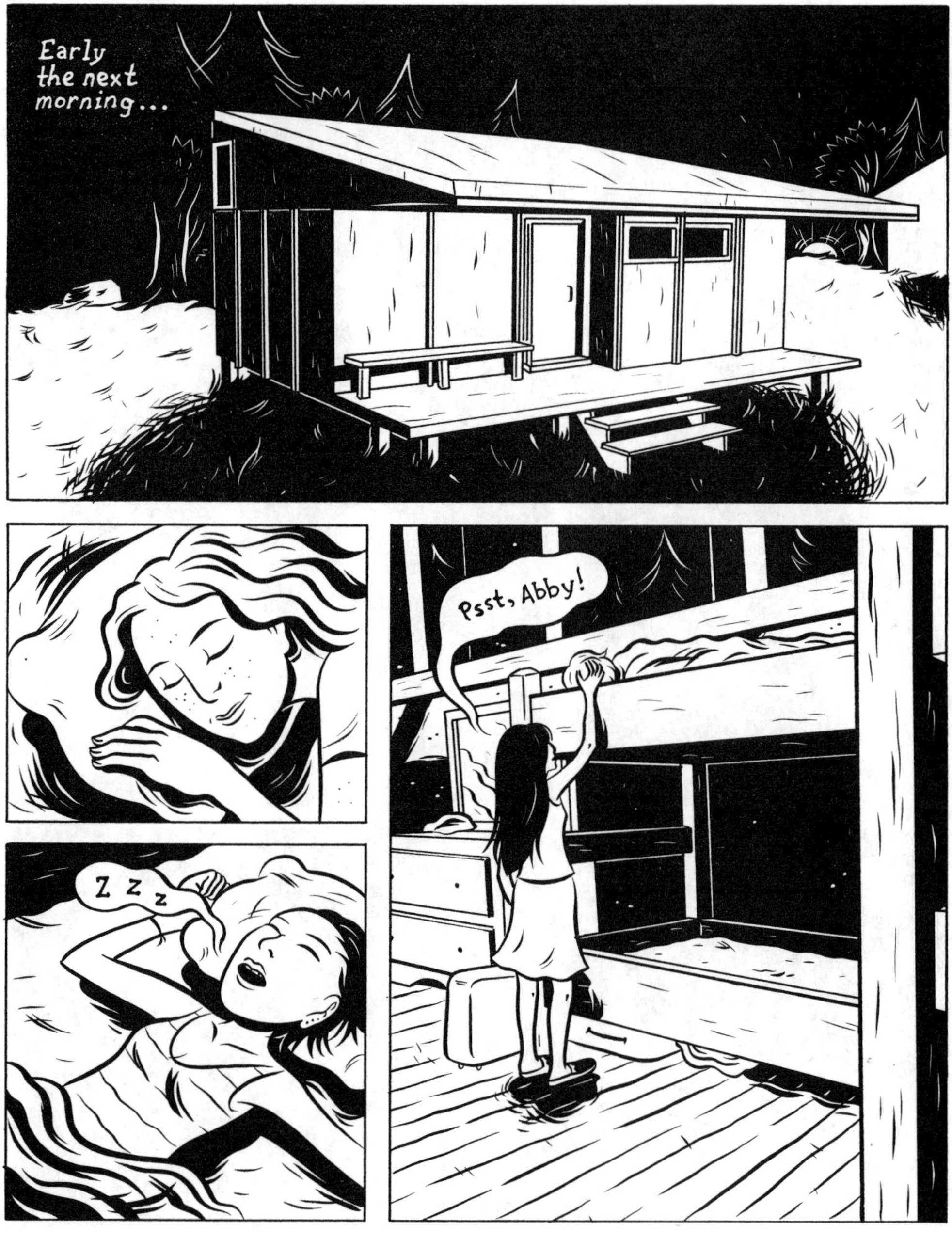
Early the next morning...
Z Z z
Psst, Abby!

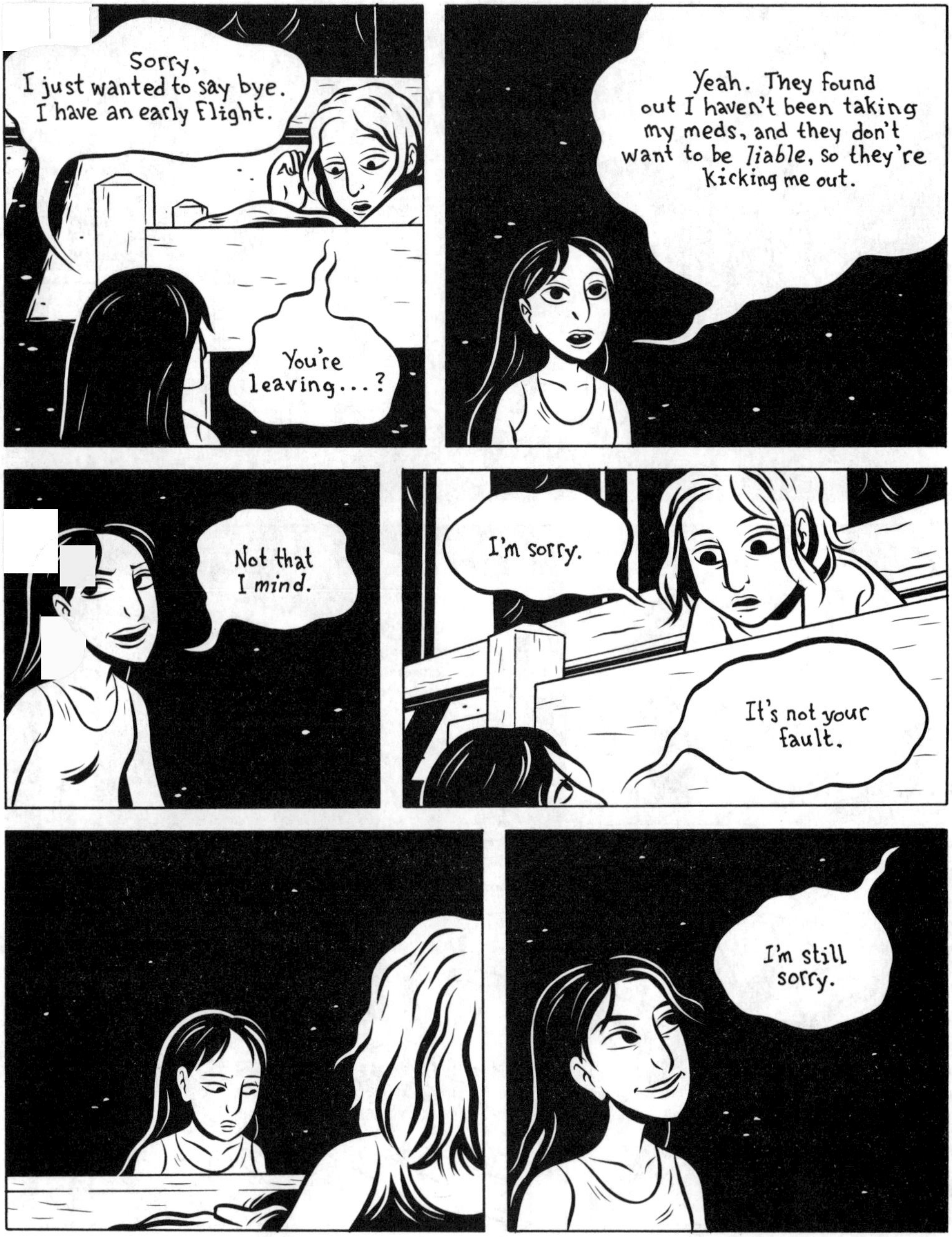
Sorry, I just wanted to say bye. I have an early Flight.
You're leaving...?
Yeah. They found out I haven't been taking my meds, and they don't want to be *liable*, so they're kicking me out.
Not that I *mind*.
I'm sorry.
It's not your fault.
I'm still sorry.

161

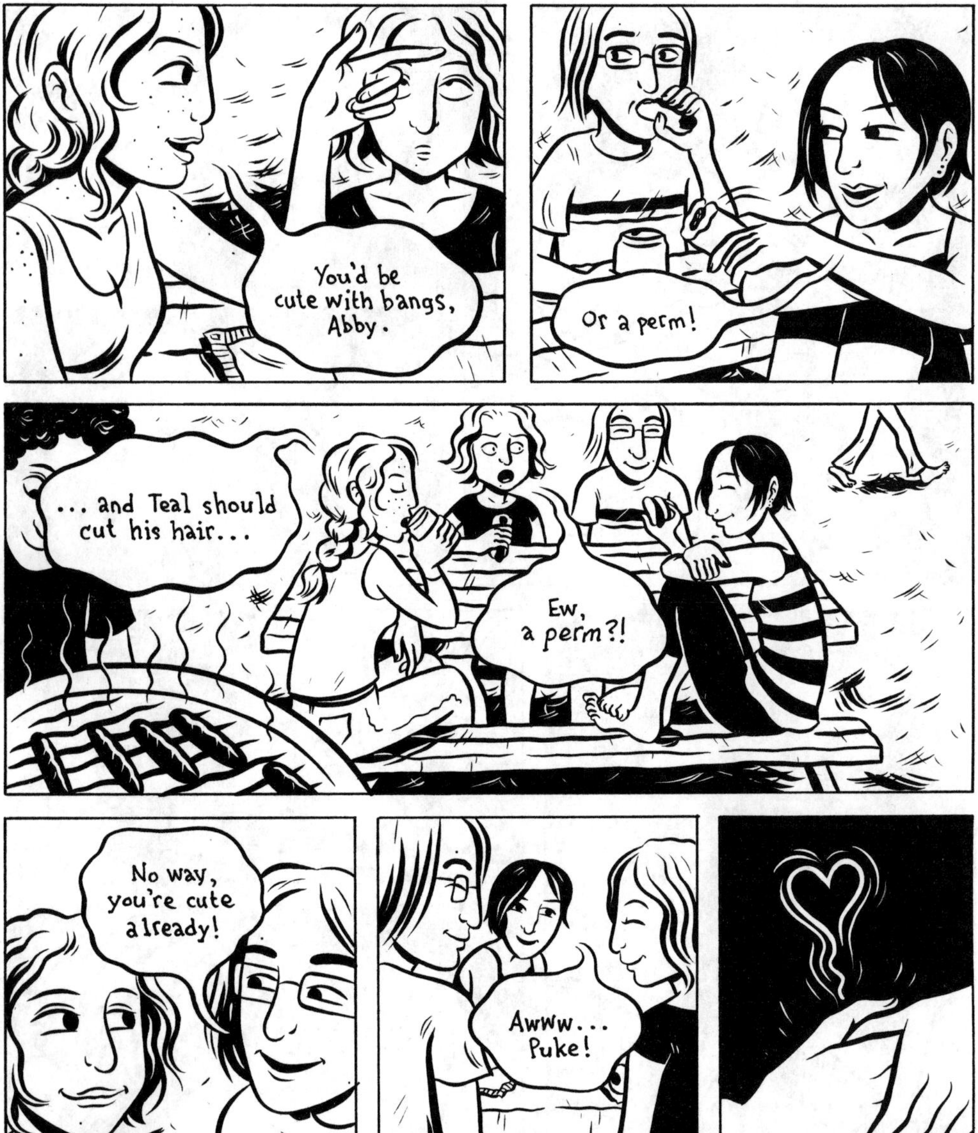
You'd be cute with bangs, Abby.
Or a perm!
... and Teal should cut his hair...
Ew, a perm?!
No way, you're cute already!
Awww... Puke!

164

What should I say? What should I say?
Ha ha ha
ha
ha
ha
ha
heh
Hee hee
Maybe she got chiggers.

Then camp ended.

The first car in line was my parents', of course, but it's better to leave early, before everyone gets sick of saying good-bye.

Honk!

Have a great summer! What's left of it.

Promise you'll write! And don't forget about the Three Musketeers.

I'll write you so many letters, Beth! Remember to send me a CD of your songs.

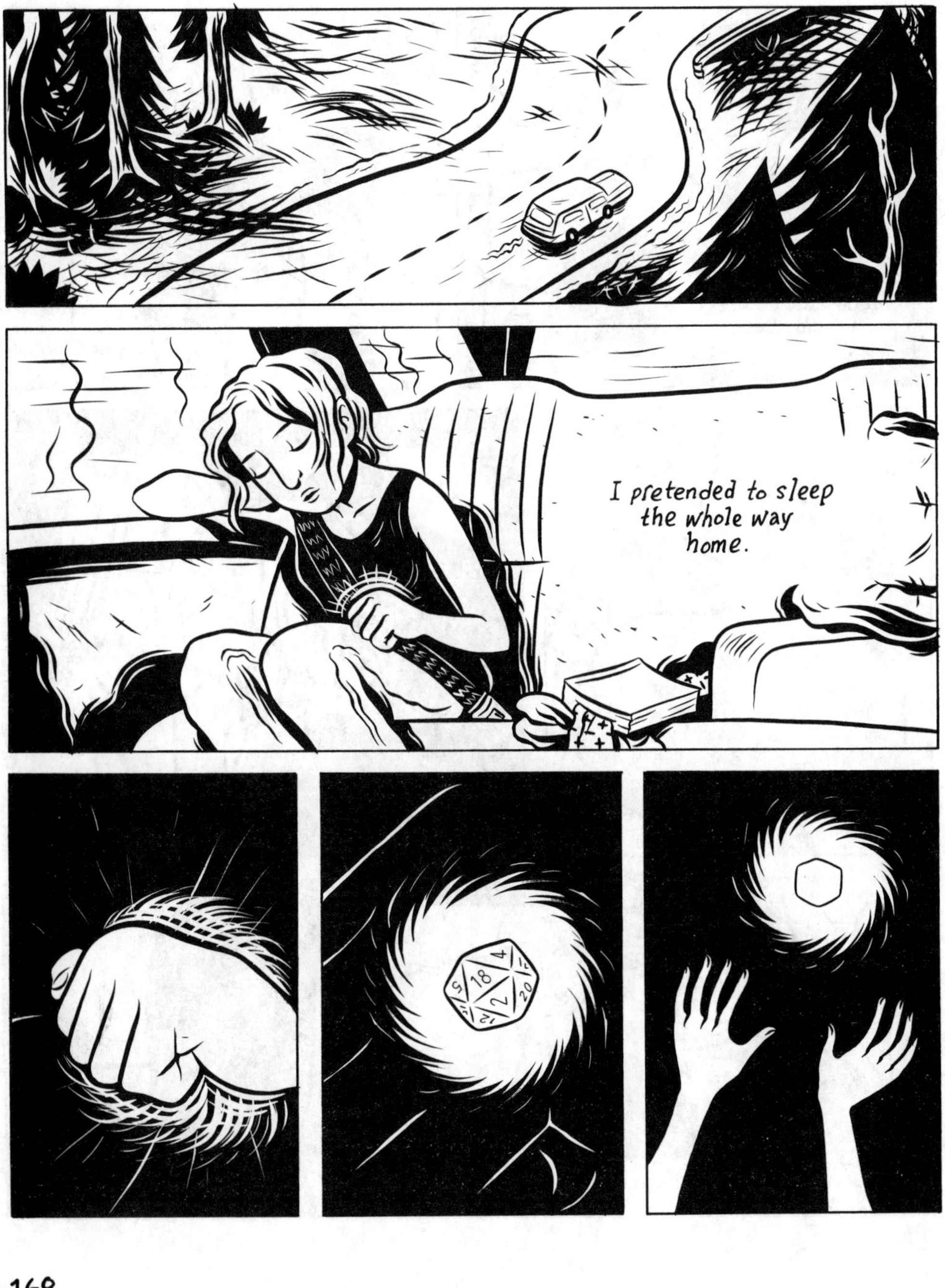
I pretended to sleep the whole way home.

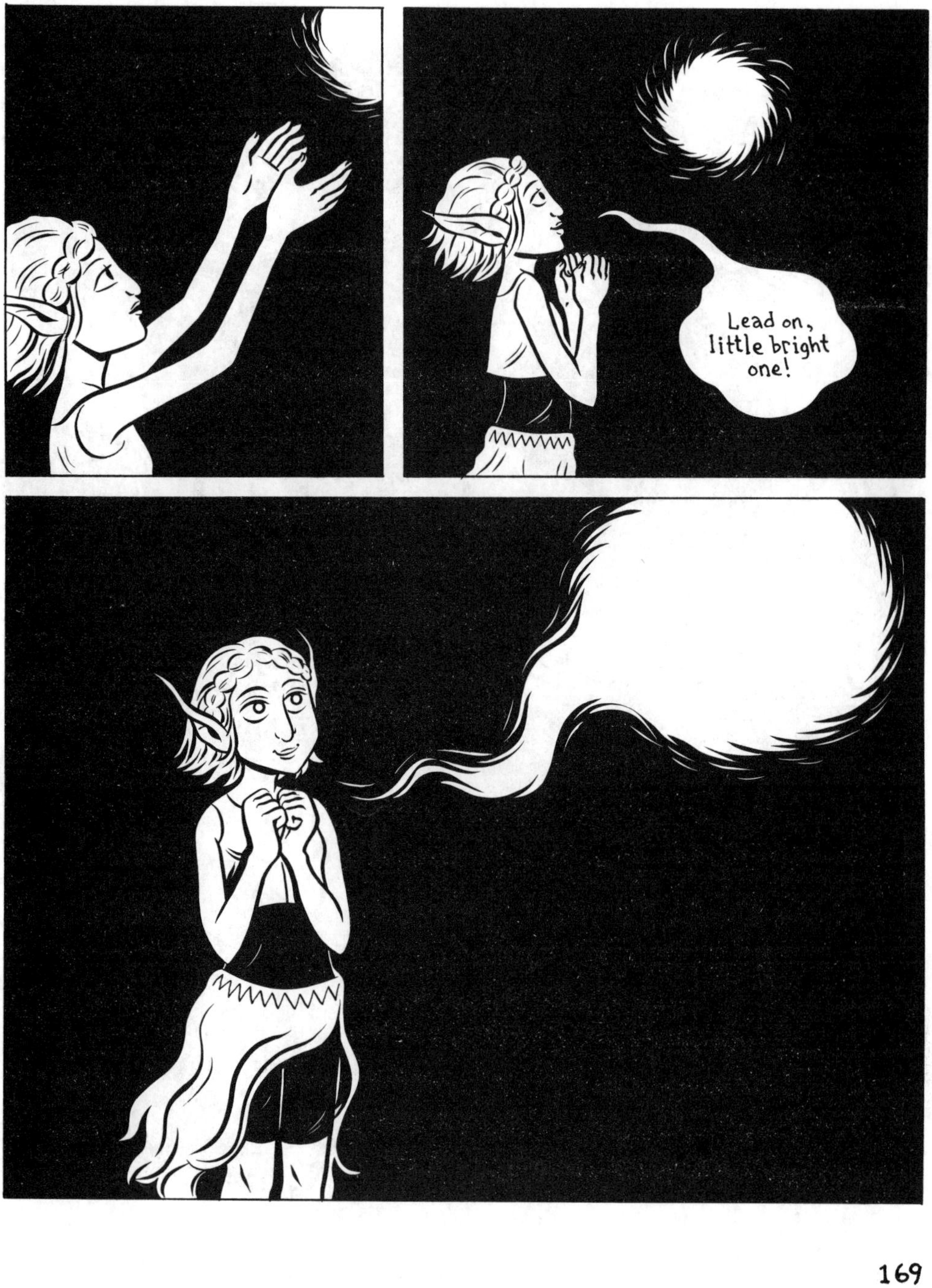
Lead on, little bright one!

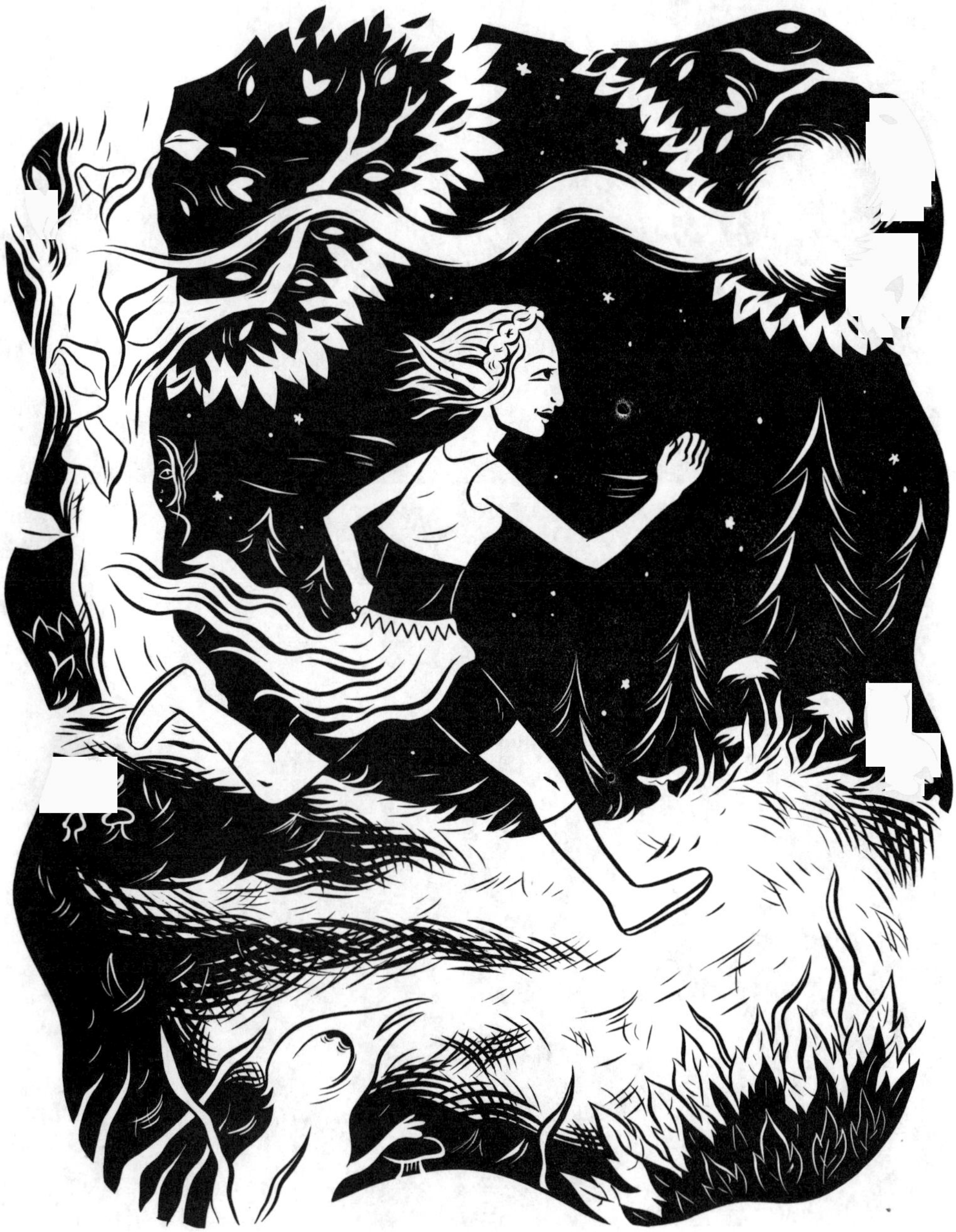

For a while I used Shasta's bandana
as a bookmark.

I don't know where it went
after that.

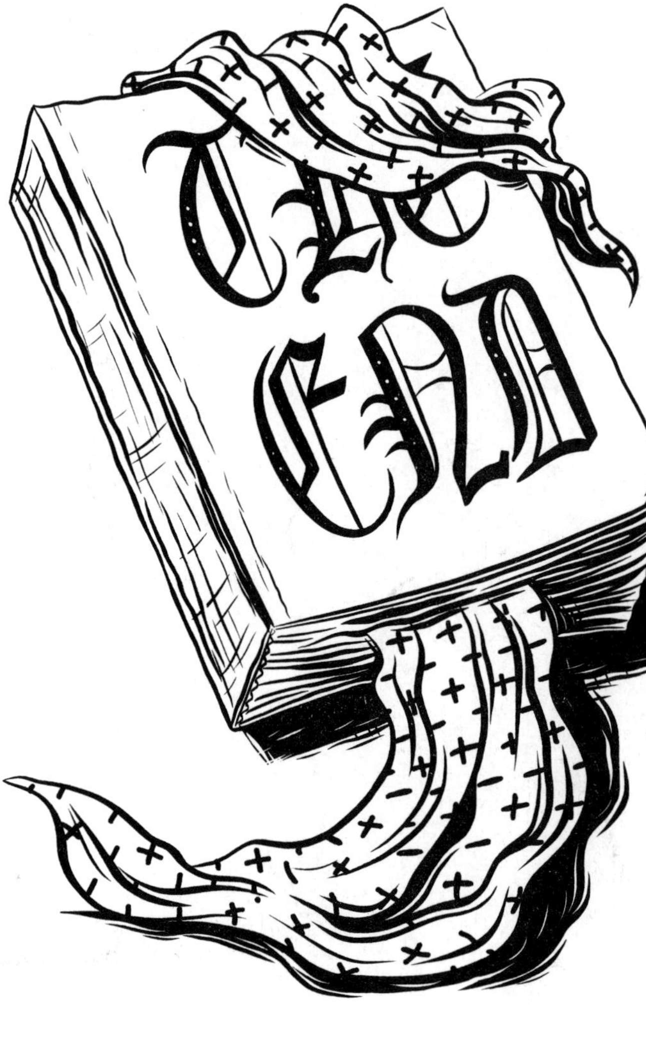
The End